The Bloody Spur

Black Curtain Press
PO Box 632
Floyd VA 24091

ISBN 13: 978-1627551151

First Edition
10 9 8 7 6 5 4 3 2 1

The Bloody Spur

Charles Einstein

There are no tricks in plain and simple faith:
But hollow men, like horses hot at hand,
Make gallant show and promise of their mettle;
But when they should endure the bloody spur,
They fall their crests and like deceitful jades
Sink in the trial.

—JULIUS CAESAR, IV, ii

ARNOLD LAMIN — Editor in chief, wire service (most important)
JON DAY GRIFFITH - Editor of Sentinel ←
HARRY KRITZER - picture service chief
MARK LOVING - chief, feature syndicate highest paid
↑
The (4) in line to succeed dead McGrady.

Chapter One

For the funeral of Cyrus McCrady, executive director of the Kyne publishing empire, appropriately it rained. This was fortunate for the high <u>Kyne</u> brass who attended McCrady to his final sleeping place in the Cemetery of the Heavenly Rest in Maspeth, Long Island, because it gave them something disarming to talk about. As it was, the great editors, managers, and directors of the Kyne chain rode together in large black automobiles to and from the funeral, because to ride with anyone but themselves would have invited the thought that they were conniving against one another. The bright blue eyes of <u>Walter Kyne, the publisher</u>, were attentive even when dimmed by tears for the lost McCrady, and when his men connived, those of them who made more than twenty thousand dollars annually, he preferred that they do so in concert. Individuals frightened Walter Kyne, and more for this reason than any other he mourned the loss of McCrady, who could handle men one at a time.

Especially to the Kyne distaste was the prospect that he himself would have to choose McCrady's successor. The Kyne enterprises consisted of a chain of newspapers only slightly smaller than Scripps-Howard and Hearst, bulwarked by KPS (Kyne Press Service, a national newswire network); KWF (Kyne World Features, a feature-story syndicate), and Kynpix (a national picture service), and within this hierarchy there existed no simple ladder, no mechanism for succession. Of four men Walter Kyne could have selected for McCrady's fifty-thousand-dollar-a-year post, one had the most important title, another was the highest paid, a third had been with Kyne the longest, and the fourth was the most influential. For a man like Walter Kyne, dedicated to impartiality as the easiest way out, this augured unwell. Even though he wept as the coffin descended, it did not escape him that the man on his left, whose name was Arnold Lamin and who clutched his arm in sympathy, was one of the candidates.

It was, in a way, to Kyne's personal advantage that the burying of McCrady was not the only current business for the Cemetery of the Heavenly Rest. Standing in a semi-circle that faced on the temporary brass fencing enclosing the open grave, Walter Kyne and his lieutenants could see, no more than thirty headstones away, another funeral in progress. They listened in magnificent grief as the minister did his seven-minute bit; and as the grave-diggers eased up on the straps which held the casket in suspension over the open grave, McCrady's pallbearers tossed their gray cotton gloves atop the now-descending coffin. They were, however, newspapermen all, and the funeral being conducted just down the pathway was one that interested them.

"That Felton girl," Arnold Lamin said to Kyne, indicating the other funeral with a small, nudging movement of his shoulder. "We've got a man there." This meant that Lamin, editor-in-chief of the Kyne news-wire service, had sent a reporter to cover the burial of Judith Felton, a young lady who had, only recently, been murdered. It was a good story, especially with the killer as yet uncaught: it had captured the imagination of newspaper readers not only in New York but out along the line, for in addition to such standardized ingredients as a knife, a rape and a nude body, the killer had added a grotesque touch. He had taken the dead girl's lipstick, and with it scrawled a plea for help on the bathroom wall.

Today's two funerals thus were not entirely unrelated, at least insofar as Walter Kyne, the publisher, was concerned, and it was a welcome distraction. It enabled him to examine his four trusted employees in action as they started bucking for McCrady's job. Lamin had a reporter there. Jon Day Griffith, Editor of the *Sentinel,* the key Kyne paper in New York, and advisory editor to the nine other papers in the chain, had a sob story already set in type back at the office ("They buried Judy Felton in the rain today. .. ."). Harry Kritzer, chief of the Kyne picture service, had his best cameraman on the story. And Mark Loving, who ran Kyne's feature syndicate, was ready to roll with a special series on notable killings of the recent past. The tentative title for the series was MURDER WILL OUT!

All of these modest achievements were brought to Walter Kyne's attention, each by its own protagonist, and Kyne could not help but admire the technique. It was a technique which served its purpose under the most difficult of circumstances—for one thing, the family of the late Cyrus McCrady was there on hand, and the ability to talk shop in these surroundings was a masterful thing to behold. It was done in quiet, tense voice. Lamin told Kyne about the reporter's being there. Then, in low but conversational tone, Loving asked Kritzer about his cameraman so Kritzer could ask Griffith about his front-page story so Griffith could ask Loving about his series.

As the rain fell, Walter Kyne wished to hell he had a board of directors to do his selecting for him. He wanted to suggest to his editors, here at the cemetery, that they shut up—that the race would not begin officially until they got back to the office. But to do so would have been to indicate that he, Walter Kyne, was not interested in the operation of his own company. Besides, the race was on already, and Walter Kyne knew it.

"Death is a bad business," Jon Day Griffith was saying now. They were walking toward the waiting automobiles, and the rain was falling steadily. "I wish I had a nickel for every murder I've covered. And I hate 'em."

"You can trade with me," Arnold Lamin said. "I once worked two electrocutions and a hanging all in the same year."

"The things that go on," Mark Loving said. "I was reading this series we're putting out. Terrible, some of the things."

Harry Kritzer, the photo man, did not say anything. Instead, he turned and walked away from them, along the path leading to the other burial. They waited at the cars for him to return. When he got back, he slapped his overcoat pocket.

"Plates," he said, referring to the exposed film his photographer already had shot at the burying of Judith Felton. "Just occurred to me we're going straight back to town. I can get these back to the office faster than my man can."

Walter Kyne's face betrayed nothing. He was not a simple person. Outside the trade, it was assumed generally that he controlled completely the vast Kyne organization. From within, however, he could be viewed more simply as the only son of the late Simon Kyne. The elder Kyne, regarding his son Walter as something of a mistake, early had vested operational control of the chain in McCrady, and, his place in history securely attained somewhat to the rear and the right of Joseph Pulitzer, he did not particularly care what happened afterward. He had, like anyone else, certainly including his son, infinite faith in McCrady.

But it involved a degree of danger to regard the younger Kyne too superficially. Only one man had got away with it, and that man now lay at peace in his family plot. It was not that Walter Kyne was not well known to his hired hands; his office was on the same floor as theirs in the New York City layout where the editorial rooms of the feature syndicate, the picture service, the news-wire service and the *Sentinel* were ranged the length of one long floor that ran through two adjacent buildings, the old Kyne building and the new Kyne building, known more briefly as the O.K. and the N.K.

And now, almost daily, Walter Kyne would stride through the various headquarters of his empire, inevitably stopping in the feature department to read the chattering teletype of the Kyne news-wire service; inevitably stopping in the picture department to read the same news coming in on another teletype; inevitably stopping in the great newsroom that served both the *Sentinel* and the wire service to read the battery of teletypes that all said the same thing. He addressed all of his men by their first names; many of them called him Walter.

"I don't like to call him Walter," Jon Day Griffith of the *Sentinel* had complained, on one occasion, to Arnold Lamin. "It makes it sound like he was a friend of mine."

"It's the business we're in," Lamin replied, in what was, for him, an uncommon burst of philosophy. "It's self-defense. Around here, a copy boy today is your boss tomorrow. That's why we all eat together and lie in gutters together and mess with each other's broads. You got to be democratic. It's in the rules."

In truth, the run of Kyne's top executives was a youthful one. The late McCrady had had a penchant for young men, something which Harry Kritzer, chief of Kynpix, the photo service, used to say deserved him a mention in the works of Krafft-Ebing. Walter Kyne himself was only forty-nine, and it was a source of gratification to old hands among his employees that he had no children to perpetuate the Kyne legend. In its way, too, this made the vacancy brought about by the death of McCrady even more desirable; for some day, Walter Kyne would retire, or die, or both.

Nonetheless, now that McCrady was gone, Kyne was no man to fool with. He had been showing an interest in the news of late: an interest that dated morbidly to the day McCrady entered the hospital for the last time. Burt Healey, City Editor of the *Sentinel,* swore that Kyne wanted McCrady's job for his own, hut this was generally disbelieved. Walter Kyne was not that dumb. More probably, he wanted it said of him that he knew what he was doing when he chose McCrady's successor.

Now the rain was falling, and they were on their way back from the funeral, and now Walter Kyne himself was talking about the news they handled. On the way out he had been quiet and sad. But he had helped carry McCrady's coffin and he had cried as much as anybody there, and the atmosphere in the car coming back was one of long live the king—whoever Kyne, in the uncertainty he masked at times so well, decided the king would be.

Arnold Lamin and Harry Kritzer were in the car up ahead. In the back seat of Walter Kyne's car were Jon Day Griffith, whose full title—Editor of the New York *Sentinel* and Advisory Director of the nine other Kyne papers—was the most important in the organization, short of Kyne's himself; and Mark Loving, of the feature syndicate, highest-paid of Kyne's men since the McCrady vacancy. Loving's surname was considered peculiarly appropriate: shop talk insisted that, despite a wife and a toupee, he was putting the blocks to Mildred Donner, the frequently red-haired women's feature writer for the Kyne papers.

Loving was blandly attentive; his face was large-jawed, with a dimple at the chin, and what it conveyed now was that whatever mood Walter Kyne wished to create coming back from the funeral was the mood that he, Mark Loving, most admired. But it was to Griffith, the lean, ulcerous figure on his left, that Kyne addressed himself. The proximity of the Judith Felton funeral was what was on his mind, but he was speaking, as well, of another unsolved murder, that of a forty-four year old woman who had been found strangled in her bed.

"You're not playing it up, Jon," Walter Kyne was saying. "There's a connection between the two. One murder's bad. Two are wonderful. Two murders can sell papers all day long."

"Connection?" Griffith said. "They happen three months apart. One's strangled, the other's stabbed. One's not a rape, one is. One's in the Bronx, the other's in Queens. There's one similarity. They're both unsolved. But this latest broad's only four days old. Give them a little time. Once in a while the New York cops come up with something."

"Oh," Kyne said, "and the lipstick."

"That's another thing," Griffith said. "This last murderer writes on the bathroom wall with lipstick. What the hell are you going to do?"

From the other side of Walter Kyne, Mark Loving leaned forward. "What was the story behind that rape?"

"You read it in the *Sentinel*," Griffith said, not completely without malice. Never forget, he told himself, we're both bucking for this job. He smiled now, but a smile did not help his looks. "No, Mark, all we know is what was in the paper, so help us. Apparently he gave her the business after she was already dead."

Walter Kyne shuddered. "Imagine," he said.

"I have," Jon Day Griffith said. The procession returning from the funeral had entered upon the Triboro Bridge; coming the other way, each car with its headlights on in the rainy light of late morning, was another string of cars, led by a hearse; headed, no doubt, for the same cemetery, though there were a dozen others to choose from.

Jon Day Griffith examined the rival hearse as it passed. "I wonder," he murmured aloud, "what one of those guys does if he gets a flat."

Ed MOBLEY - Sentinel Reporter
Judith Felton - murdered librarian

Chapter Two

Gerald Meedy - police reporter

The cliches within the newspaper profession had been, upon occasion, a source of entertainment to the men and women who worked for Kyne. Once at an office party there had been a sort of parlor game, to see who could come up with the deadliest lead sentence to a news story. Stories could be of any kind, but there was a ground rule that any story with a foreign dateline would have to include in its lead the word "Premier." The game had been won by a *Sentinel* reporter named Edward Mobley. His winning lead began, "Three people were killed today, two seriously, when .."

Stories written in the aftermath of crimes inevitably would begin, "Police were up against a stone wall today . . ." Now, sitting at his desk in the Kyne newsroom, Mobley felt strangely tempted to use this lead, with no alteration whatever, as the start of his story following up the death of Judith Felton, the murdered librarian. As far as his information went, police were up against a stone wall.

Mobley had not gone to the funeral of Cyrus McCrady. He had known McCrady mainly as the only executive he ever heard of who stuck his own pins in the map on his office wall. Once, in the Dell, the archly-named saloon in the basement of the O.K. building, McCrady had become drunk and asked Mobley to call him Cy. Two days later Mobley met him in the elevator and said, "Hello, Cy." McCrady looked at him through a set of rimless eyeglasses and said nothing. After that, they nodded to each other, and McCrady, Mobley noted, never went back to the Dell.

Someone had forgot to take down the notice from the bulletin board, the one that said Mr. McCrady was resting at the Wesson Memorial Chapel, and that staffers were invited to go there to pay their last respects. To Mobley's knowledge, the only working member of the *Sentinel* staff who went over to the chapel had been Gerald Meedy, the police reporter. Meedy was a heavy-faced, heavy-shouldered man with a great greasy sweep of brown hair. He had started his career with Kyne as a graduate of business school who took shorthand for Arnold

Lamin, the wire-service chief, and he became known as the only male whore Lamin ever had, although some of the office critics were not so restrictive. Now, graduated to the *Sentinel* as a full-fledged reporter—Meedy still took shorthand on his police beat—he went with Lamin to the chapel to say farewell to McCrady.

Then Lamin, regarded as the most influential of McCrady's lieutenants and viewed by some as a sure bet to succeed the deceased, went out in one of the black automobiles to the burial. According to his detractors, Lamin went to the grave so that, once it had been filled with earth, he could go over it with a roller.

For his part, Ed Mobley did not particularly care who won the McCrady Derby, even though Griffith had got him two raises. Mobley's money was, in fact, riding on the weathered nose of Arnold Lamin, who was up in the morning line at 7 to 5. Griffith was 3 to 1. Mark Loving was held at 9 to 1, despite his wealth, but still he was not the outsider. The longshot was Harry Kritzer, who had been with Kyne, man and boy, for twenty-three years. Harry Kritzer was regarded upon occasion as the only honest man working for Walter Kyne, including, most absolutely, Walter Kyne himself. Mainly for this reason he was up on the board at 25 to 1, though time was considered in his favor. Side bets were being taken on how long Walter Kyne would take to make up his mind; the estimates ran from two days to that of Archie Ginsberg, the telegraph editor on the *Sentinel,* who said twelve years.

Mobley had not know the elder Kyne, who had died before he came to work for the paper, but he was on a working basis with Walter Kyne, familiar enough with him so that he did not have to call him Mr. Kyne. He did not quite call him Walter, either, although Kyne called him Ed. Instead Mobley invariably phrased his conversations so as to avoid calling Kyne anything at all.

But what Kyne called his men had nothing to do with anything. Like others in the newsroom, Mobley had observed Kyne in action only recently, in the case of the Kyne All-America Football team; and it was an incident that pointed up too well the new interest that Kyne was taking in his enterprises, an interest that raised saddle sores on the men who wanted to become the new McCrady.

The All-America team had been chosen, and the list was about to be sent out in advance for that coming Sunday over the KPS news wires which served, in addition to the nine other Kyne papers throughout the country, some two hundred additional clients. Suddenly a phone call had come for Zipp Marshall, general sports editor for Kyne. The call was from Harrison, sports editor of the *Beacon*, the Kyne paper in Dallas. In many respects, the Kyne newspapers operated independently of one another, and Harrison was no more polite than necessary in informing Marshall that he thought a fullback named Wells, who played for Texas, should be on the team.

"He's not on the team," Marshall said.

"I'm sending up some stuff overhead on what he did this year," Harrison said. The word "overhead" meant via Western Union press message, and it always made Marshall shudder, because whenever a Kyne economy wave went into action it always started with the sport's department's Western Union budget.

"When," Harrison had inquired, "are you moving the team?"

"Tonight," Marshall said. "In advance for Sunday."

"Well, this is Tuesday. At least hold it up till you see what I'm sending about him."

"Listen," Marshall said, "you already sent up your recommendations for All-America. I didn't see Wells on it."

"I didn't have anything to do with that," Harrison said. "I was at the doctor's for my prostate. Some son of a bitch in here left him off."

"I still don't have room for him," Marshall said. But some base instinct, developed through working for Kyne, told him to hold off on the team. Sure enough, the next day the managing editor of the Dallas paper phoned Arnold Lamin, editor-in-chief of KPS. Lamin came out of his glass-enclosed office and walked over to Marshall's desk.

"Put a guy named Wells on that team of yours," he said.

"Yeah?" Marshall said. "Yeah," Lamin said.

"You know what it is, don't you?" Marshall said to him. "That son of a bitch Harrison has a piece of this Wells. He's got a movie or a comic strip or something. I can see what it's called: 'Buck Wells—All American!' So?"

"So put him on," Lamin said tiredly. "I talked to them down there. They won't take no for an answer."

It was a problem that arose from time to time. Each of the Kyne papers was successful in its own right, but unlike the other papers which took KPS, the Kyne papers did not pay the usual client fee for the wire service. They were assessed a large amount, and their money was, in good measure, what kept KPS going. It was more than a matter of bookkeeping, for, with two hundred non-Kyne clients receiving the service, the wire report was a matter of prestige and not a little influence.

All this the sports editor knew, but still, now, he said, "Always the same. They say bend over, you bend over."

"All right," Lamin said. "Now put him on the team."

"It's such a small thing," Marshall said. "The All-America's a phony to begin with. It always has been."

"Then why are you so unhappy? Just take some bastard off and put this bastard on."

"I'm unhappy," Marshall said, almost to himself. "I'm unhappy. You know why I'm unhappy? Because now Harrison's going to be going around saying, 'I put Buck Wells on the team. I made him All-America.' And next year instead of one editor calling up about their pet sons of bitches there'll be three. And the year after that ten."

"By that time we'll all have honest work," Lamin said. "Put this one on."

So Buck Wells made the All-America football team, a California player named Bergen being scratched from the list to make room, and the team line-up was sent out over the KPS wire network accompanied by an unsigned story, because Marshall indignantly refused to let his byline be used. Indeed, in his anger, he completely forgot that, the day before Harrison's phone call had precipitated the whole sorry affair, he had sent a copy of the original line-up in to the Kynpix offices so that pictures of the team members could be airmailed to all of the Kyne clients in time for publication along with the wire story on Sunday.

But Marshall did not forget for long. A reminder arrived the next morning in the form of a telegram from the *Express*, the Kyne paper in San Francisco, "PHOTOS FROM KYNPIX HAVE

BERGEN OF CALIFORNIA ALL-AMERICA BACK. UNFIND HIM ON KPS TEAM. HOW PLEASE?"

Marshall sent the telegram in to Lamin. Lamin read it, said, "Oh, Christ," and got Harry Kritzer, the Kynpix chief, on the phone. Kritzer listened to the story and said, "Do I have a picture of Wells? Is he any good?"

"I guess he's good," Lamin said. "Not good enough to be All-America, but all right."

"Well, you put him on the team, not me," Kritzer said. "All right. I'll put a mandatory on the machine and sub it."

"I didn't put him on the team," Lamin said, and hung up. He knew dismally that it was nobody's fault, and it worried him. It worried him because he knew the *Express* in San Francisco was equally as influential as the *Beacon* in Dallas, and that, once the *Express* discovered that its man Bergen of California was not on the team, some more hell would be raised.

It was. This time Whittier, the old publisher of the *Express* who had come in on the ground floor with old Simon Kyne before the first war, took it up as an issue. Whittier loved issues. It made him feel less removed from headquarters in New York, though paradoxically nothing could have made him leave San Francisco.

Thus it was that Walter Kyne came striding into the newsroom, and, without pausing to read the teletypes, over to Lamin's office. In the old days he would have turned something like this over to McCrady. Now he walked in, tall and not unhandsome, even though his facial features stopped short of what might be called the proper development—he looked like the result of a sculptor's effort to create a bust of a Roman hero after discovering that the block of marble was not quite big enough.

Arnold Lamin was dictating to his secretary. Lamin was a thin, nervous man in his early forties. His face was leathery and inevitably pale, and his eyes set close together. He always worked in a short-sleeved white shirt, and whenever he dictated a letter, as he was doing now, he looked directly at his secretary. Her name was Nancy Liggett; her figure was good, though she swore she meant to lose weight, and her face, topped by black hair that she wore in bangs, seemed somehow, without creases, lines, or a look of tiredness, to be older than she. She was twenty-five, and believed she was in love with Edward Mobley, the reporter. This did not disturb Lamin, even though he admired her looks and frequently found reason to bend over her shoulder as she worked at her typewriter. The not-overlarge office in which they worked, Lamin's private office, was ringed on three sides by glass, so that everyone could see in.

Walter Kyne waited, now, for no amenities. "We're in good shape with our All-America team," he said to Lamin. "Dandy." He almost threw the latest communication from San Francisco at the editor-in-chief of his wire service.

Lamin reached for a piece of copy paper, tore off a corner, and began to chew on it. He read Whittier's telegram at enough length to enable him to decide what sort of answer he would give. He, like Harry Kritzer, like Mark Loving of the feature service, like Jon Day Griffith of the *Sentinel,* had to be nice to the boss, because one of them would get McCrady's job. But being nice had its forms and byways. To crawl, to admit an error without offering a solution, to snap back at Kyne, to pretend ignorance, to offer a sound suggestion, a means of escape (an academic alternative, since he couldn't think of one)— all these could, each in its own way, have the effect of being nice. It was a question not of the right thing to say, but of what Kyne would expect. Then, if you knew what he expected, you also should possess knowledge of whether it would be of more value to give him a reply he did not expect. Then, too, there was the question of perspective: what this meant to the public, to Lamin, to Whittier in San Francisco, and what the sum total of these would mean to Walter Kyne.

In addition to all of this, one more point: would Kyne wonder why this had not been called to his attention earlier? While McCrady was active, this was not an issue, but with McCrady out of the office it always was a question of how much of McCrady's work Kyne had decided to assume, and it was not a question easy to answer, for it varied in degree from day to day.

All this Lamin had appraised. He set down the telegram and chewed his paper cud for a moment. Then he said, "Walter, it's something of a screw-up."

"What are we going to do?"

Don't jump, Lamin told himself. Don't think because he

asks that question that all is forgiven, or that he's helpless, or that he doesn't have any ideas of his own. All he's doing is throwing it back at you.

Aloud, he said, "I don't know. The team's already moved on the wire. We change it now, everybody'll know what's going on. And you can't very well make up a special team just for San Francisco."

Kyne looked at him briefly. It was a cold, blue-eyed look. "Why did Marshall take Bergen off the team?"

Lamin shrugged. Marshall, the sports editor, could not be thrown to the lions for this, for Marshall in this case was armed in righteousness, and was angry enough already. The obvious villain was Harrison in Dallas, but as equally obvious was the fact that Harrison could not be blamed. It was he, Arnold Lamin, who had ordered the change, even though specifically he had not ordered that Bergen be taken off the team. He had insisted only that Wells be put on.

Now he said, "Bergen's a fullback. Wells is a fullback. What are you going to do?"

"Why do you have to name your backs by position? Why not just four backs?"

"Why not five?" Lamin inquired. He saw, almost literally saw, the germ of the idea leap across his desk to Walter Kyne. Intrinsically, he could not claim credit for it, since he had said it before realizing that this was, in fact, a way out. Besides, it would not be wise to let Walter Kyne think that Lamin had plotted this out in advance as a solution.

Kyne thought for a moment. Then he said, "All right. It's the only way out." He was saying that he credited Lamin for the idea but that he didn't think much of it. "Put Bergen back on the team. What's today? Friday. You can still do it for Sunday release. Change the back-field positions just to read 'back.' Cut out that quarterback, halfback business. Stick a paragraph in the story explaining the different performances made it impossible to pick four backs this year, so that out of fairness we picked five."

Lamin thought for a moment. "You don't think it's going to look a little funny?"

Walter Kyne gave him the answer he wanted. "No. Clients already realize something's wrong, because we've already named five men—one we had a picture of wasn't on the team. Maybe we can shape a note to editors with it pointing that out and explaining we intended to name five all along and that an inadvertent error in preparation made us leave Bergen off the team and Wells out of the pictures."

Arnold Lamin had to admire him. He had wanted an answer like that from Walter Kyne, but he had not expected it; not expected it, hell, he hadn't even thought of it himself. He said cheerfully, "Good, that'll do it," and saw that Kyne already was headed out the door.

Kyne closed the door behind him; then, his hand still on the doorknob, he opened it again and leaned in. "Next time," he said, "bring something like that to me right away. Don't wait to mess it up."

So it's my fault, Lamin said to himself. I should have known. And he doesn't really expect me to bring stuff like that to him. But under the circumstances, Lamin said the only thing he could say. "I certainly will, Walter."

The details of this episode had filtered with remarkable speed through the worldwide corridors of the Kyne empire. Edward Mobley had heard it from Nancy Liggett, Lamin's secretary. Now, thinking of the story he had to write for the next morning's *Sentinel*, the follow-up story on the murdered librarian, Mobley tore off a corner from the top sheet of copy paper on his desk—a habit he had got from Arnold Lamin—and began to chew on it. Nancy had told him once that copy paper contained arsenic, but he was only thirty-four years of age, and he felt all right.

He could see Nancy, working alone at her typewriter, through the glass wall of Lamin's office across the room. He picked up his phone and asked for Lamin's extension, and when Nancy answered, he said, "I wasn't sure. I thought maybe you went with Lamin to the burying place. To hold his hand or something."

"Oh," she said, "he never asks me to hold his hand."

"Does he ..."

"Shut your obscene face," Nancy said over the phone. "Everything with you is always sex. It's naked."

"It is?" Mobley asked. "I didn't say anything. All I wanted to know was did you want a drink later."

"Where?"

"Your place."

"That's what you said the last time."

"And that's where we went the last time. Where do you want to go? Madison Square Garden?"

"Yes," Nancy said, "but you said a drink."

"So I had a drink."

"That wasn't all you had."

"Well," Mobley said, "I can't help it if you bring out the beast in me. You've got beautiful black hair and nice brown eyes and wicked legs and a belly like that one in the Bible. You want to hear more?"

Nancy said, "I don't like that word."

"What word?"—"You know what word."

"Belly?"

"I'll have one drink with you," Nancy said. "Downstairs."

"What about my supper?"

"The hell with your supper."

"I'm no good on an empty stomach."

"That's what I'm counting on," she said, and hung up the phone. He gazed at her through the window from across the room, but she had turned back to her typing.

Ed Mobley conjured up a mental image of Nancy as she had looked the last time in her apartment on West Twelfth Street in lower Manhattan. He himself had lived not far from there when he was a kid, had played stoop ball against the side wall of the Greenwich Theater on the wide sidewalk across the street, had fought Italians daily outside Public School 95 on Clarkson Street, had refused a five cent tip for running chile con carne to the firemen at Engine Company 18 on West Tenth Street off Greenwich Avenue. He had even known a kid who lived in the apartment house where Nancy lived now. The first time he had taken Nancy out, he had astonished her with his knowledge of how the self-service elevator in the building worked. She had not let him come past the door of her apartment that first night: and he remembered feeling the button-lock in the door with his finger as he stood there saying good night, and thinking how easy it would be to push it to the open position, and to come back later.

I could have, he said to himself now, I could have. He

shrugged to himself, sitting there and thinking. How nuts, after all, could you get?

And he thought, now with new meaning that made him put his chin in his hand and read with intensity the copy before him, about the murdered girl, the librarian Judith Felton. She, too, had lived alone.

Mobley picked up his phone and got Gerald Meedy on the *Sentinel's* direct line to the press room at police headquarters. He said, "Gerry, this Felton girl. What kind of a lock did she have on her door?"

"Come on," Meedy said from the other end. "The guy come in through the window."

"What about the other one?"

"What other one?"

"That woman that was strangled."

"When?"

"Couple of months ago."

"What about her?"

"Did she have a button-lock on her door?"

"What's a button-lock?"

"You know," Mobley said, "the two buttons right over where the little thing comes out, the latch. You push one in, it's locked. You push the other one in, it's open."

"What do you want to do?" Meedy asked. "You want to sign a full confession?"

"I'm trying to write a piece, is all."

"So leave me alone," Meedy said. He hung up the phone.

Burt Healey, the fat city editor of the *Sentinel*, came over and said, "Take your time, lover. I'm putting out a monthly."

"All right," Mobley said. "I'm going to write it now. What do you want? Three hundred?"

"Three hundred."

"All I got is police are up against a stone wall."

"So write it three hundred times. What did Greaselips tell you?"

"I just talked to him. Greaselips was nasty to me over the telephone." Healey took the cigar out of his mouth and examined it. "I don't like Greaselips and Greaselips doesn't like me."

"Nobody likes Greaselips," Mobley said. "He's like cancer. Everybody's against him."

"You think Meedy's his right name?"

"Sure. Must be. Who would invent a name like Meedy?"

"I don't know," Healey said. He looked briefly around the newsroom. "Boys ain't back from the burying yet?"

"They're doing the gravedigger scene," Mobley said. "Or maybe Kyne has got them lined up against the cemetery wall, playing eeny-meeny-miney-mo."

Healey stuck the cigar back in his mouth. "Who you betting on?"

"The guy in the cage."

"Lamin?"

Mobley nodded and put a fresh corner of copy paper into his mouth.

Healey smiled down at him. "Sucker."

"Why? Who you got?"

"Lover boy."

"Loving?"

"Yep."

"Why?"

"He's a Republican," Healey said. "Will you please write this piece you're doing? I'm holding the presses." He paused momentarily. "Both of them."

Chapter Three

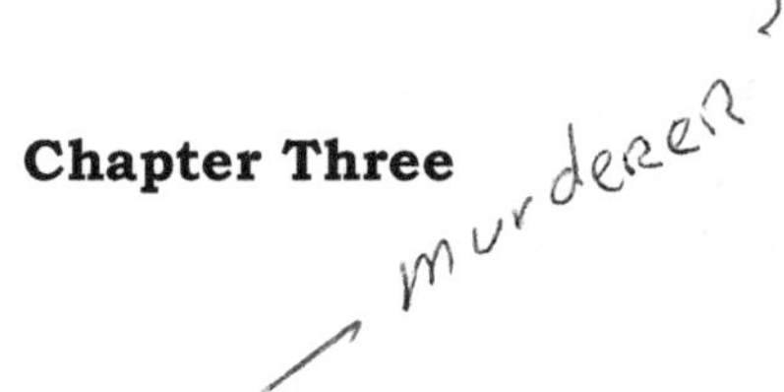

The things that Robert Manners would think of, at the age of twenty, were things men think of only separately. Ambitions that he had, and lusts, he outlined in his mind beforehand in uncanny coupling, almost in scenario form, so that he knew what he would say, and what she would say, and what her room would look like, and what she would be wearing, and how she would look to him, and what he would say to make the whole thing reasonable, so that it would be a fair act—though never a proper one. Some day it would be something that went right. Some day a woman would submit, even beyond the curtain of his own fancy and planning, willingly and wantingly, and the mere fact of it—a consummation that eclipsed even his own schedule of desire—that would be the new height, the end all, the be all.

He did not want to know her name, whoever she might be. He wanted to know nothing about her, for when he was through he would know about her things that no one else had ever known.

Only two things beset him, and made him worry and puzzle and re-examine the mindful details of his plans. It was not that he lacked the boldness; certainly not that he lacked the will. It was, first, that things had not gone right so far; and second, that if they ever did go right, if the climax did come, if he could walk into a strange woman's bedroom and make his loving self known to the point even of incandescence—then what would he do thereafter? What would be left?

He was twenty, Robert Manners, and if he had walked into a New York City police station and said, "I am the most terrible criminal of all," he might have been disbelieved. He was a college man. He attended the University in the Bronx, and he told himself that he knew things beyond the years he had lived. He told himself that the thing society called crime was a question, merely, of consent. The difference of degree in the way a man gave something up was difference between philanthropy on one man's part and robbery on another's. So, if a woman consented to his will, he would not be committing a crime. But in so consenting, the woman would become therefore part of the action that should be his, Robert Manners', alone.

Thus what he wanted, he did not want. To solve the contradiction, he proposed to himself two alternatives: one, that his victim—that was the word, a thrilling word, a word no language but English could boast: the incisive, knife thrust of the first syllable, the lingering, aromatic sensuality of the second—that his victim, having consented, should be subjected to violence of a kind she never envisioned; of, two, that his victim would submit to him not through a process of conscious consent, but through innocence itself.

Those were the words: victim, and innocence, and submit, and unclothed, and remove, and garment, and handkerchief, and underthings.

Now ten times in the night he had planned and watched and entered: there was the open window, the open door, the woman asleep. Ten times, and the first nine he had found what he wanted, the soiled handkerchief (twice it had been unsoiled, and it maddened him), and he had left the way he had come, out into the night, pausing each time to commit the one compulsive act of selfness—and breathing the night air of freedom afterwards and promising the black skies above he would never do it again.

But the tenth time he knew it would be different, for reason so insisted. To compensate for the risk he took, the delight, the gratification that preceded the ultimate lone act of perversion must be added to. There must be something more, and he knew what he desired it to be.

It wasn't a thing he had planned in advance. Working part-time for a drug store just off the campus of the University, delivering prescriptions, he had watched the druggist wrap a bottle of sleeping pills. He delivered them—it was eleven o'clock at night—to the apartment of a woman. Her name was Mrs. Lena Tally, but he knew from seeing the apartment as she opened the door that she lived alone. It was a single room, with one of those beds that come out of the closet, and the bed was already down for the night. She was, he told himself, in her early forties. Her body, clad in a frayed green robe that reached about halfway down from her knees, seemed worn, and there were the marks of the veins on her legs. Her black hair was done up for the night, and she had cream on her face and forehead. She was a slight woman, not scarcely so tall as Robert Manners, but her face, devoid of makeup, was not unpleasing to him; nor was her walk, as she went away from him to get the money.

As he stood there in the doorway his hand moved quickly to the button-lock in the door; and he found it was already open. His heart began to beat as if come back from the dead within him. He thought of saying something to her as she returned—something about the pills: "I hope these make you sleep, Mrs. Tally"—something that would make her reply in words that would tell him whether she would take the pills that night, perhaps how many. But people knew he was here. The drug store had sent him, the elevator man had taken him up. The wave of defeat that came upon him was accompanied with a rash of boldness, and when she came back he said—and diabolic was the word he would have used to describe it—he said, "Careful of those, Mrs. Tally. There's enough there for a week."

It was almost tenderness that he felt for her because of what she said. Of all the things she could have said, she only smiled and said earnestly, "It's just while I'm getting over this cold." How simple she was I She closed the door, and he knew that the button-lock had remained unchanged, that merely by turning the knob, the door would open.

So he would return tomorrow night, this time with no one knowing he was there, not the drug store, not the elevator man, not Mrs. Tally. He would walk the street slowly, late at night, until some one went into the apartment house. That someone would go up in the elevator, and he, Robert Manners, would walk through the empty lobby while the elevator was gone, and through the door marked "Exit" past the elevator, and quietly up the stairwell to the fourth floor where she lived, and he would turn the knob, and it would turn freely.

She would be asleep, the woman, and he would get into the bed beside her as she lay drugged with the pills he had brought her the night before.

And indeed, everything he had foreseen—even to the point of, when he left, walking down the stairs to the second floor, then ringing for the elevator, then darting down the final flight of stairs and out of the building while the elevator man was answering the phantom summons—everything went as he had planned it.

What did not go right was what he had not foreseen. Two things, and which of them enraged him more he would never be able to say. For the first thing was that when he got into the bed, he fully clothed, even to his shoes, and she lying on her side, her mouth open, sleeping heavily; and when, there in the dark, he put his hand upon her, there came on him a wave of something he might have described as disgust. It was not disgust, not in actuality. It was something far more subtle. It was, in fact, a punishment, a negation: what kept him from doing this now, even though he had robbed and would rob again, would in his rage slash, rape, and kill, was the thing that would make a psychiatrist find him, Robert Manners, to be legally sane. According to every test known to psychiatric medicine, it would have to be said he knew what he was doing.

Still the woman, Lena Tally, lay there sleeping; she moved slightly, and he pushed himself quietly away from her, put his feet on the floor and sat there for a moment, looking at her. The vicious factor, to him, was that he could not now physically justify the risk he was taking, nor live up to the glory of what he had planned. He stood up and walked toward the door, slowly and quietly, trying to make the desire come back to him. Perhaps it would have come. This he would never know, for now the second thing went wrong.

Lena Tally woke up.

She woke up abruptly and sat up in her bed and looked at him, and now for Robert Manners there was the question simply of his own safe-being. He stood there, where he was, for a moment in time. Then in three strides he was at the bedside, looking down at her. Lena Tally said one word. She said, "No," loud and clear. Then his hands came up convulsively from his sides. His thumbs met at the great vein in her throat. Her fingernails raked at his arms where the muscles of his forearms stood out just below the elbow. Her body from the neck down danced like a snake's. Her knees drew up convulsively, and then went flat again.

They did not find her for two days. He met Evelyn on campus after his ten o'clock class in social science and they had coffee together, and read the first edition of the afternoon paper, where the headline said:

HUNT WOMAN'S SLAYER

Evelyn was a thin girl, too leggy, and she did not dress well. Her face was too up-and-down, and her chin was pointed. She sat while Robert read the paper, saying:

"When was she killed?"

Robert Manners scanned the story in an effort to find out. "She was," he said at last, "dead at least thirty hours. Funny thing. This guy didn't do anything to her. I mean, rape or steal something. He just killed her."

Evelyn said, "Do they know it was a man?"

Robert looked at the story again. "Well, it sounds that way. It must have been a strong person, and it says here they've got a line on her estranged (he pronounced the word with a hard g, but Evelyn did not say anything) husband. He lives in Indianapolis."

"Maybe she wouldn't let him. .." She left the sentence there, neither complete nor incomplete, as befitted a girl in her first year at college.

"I guess that must have been it," Robert Manners said, and smiled at her over the newspaper. "Let that be a lesson to you when you're out with me."

The night before, they had gone to a dance in the gymnasium, he and Evelyn. They had left early and had walked back to her dormitory, holding hands. The dormitory had once been a large church. Indeed, services still were held in the church proper, but its annex now housed the girls who came from out of the city, or who did not like commuting to the Bronx from Brooklyn or Queens. Robert Manners himself had a home in Brooklyn, in the distant Canarsie section, but he too lived at the University. It was the way he wanted it.

His home was not unpleasant, but he was an adopted child, and it was something that was never far from his mind, even though he had been taken from an orphanage at an early age, had taken the name of the man and woman who adopted him to ease their lonesomeness, addressed them and even regarded them always as mother and father. Still, there was something to be said for being away from home.

In front of the girls' dorm was a wide sidewalk. Someone had planted an apologetic row of trees along the curb, each slender tree set in a square of dirt and ringed by an iron guard-fence reaching some five feet up the trunk. It was dark in front of the dormitory, except where the light from the doorway sent a brief double-squared patch of yellow onto the sidewalk. To either side, there would always be two or three couples, kissing goodnight. It was not yet eleven o'clock, and Robert had never kissed Evelyn before, but it did not seem unnatural that they should step away from the light of the dormitory doorway.

Evelyn leaned back against the tree and looked up at him. He was a big-shouldered boy, and his light hair was curly in an undisciplined fashion that made her want to touch it. His nose and mouth were overlarge, his lower lip pronounced, and his eyes were set close together: they were black, and seemed too small.

She said to him, "I like nights like tonight."

He looked up at the sky, where dark clouds moved at varying heights and speeds underneath a small overhead moon. He said, "So do I."

"I mean what we did. It was ..." She cast about for the correct description. "Well, it was normal."

"Maybe we're normal people," Robert Manners said to her.

"I think so," she said vehemently. "That's the trouble with this university. You get so excited when you meet somebody who's normal you don't know how to act. Seems like everybody you meet has something wrong with them."

"Well," Robert said, "we're all a little nuts, in one direction or another."

"Ah," she said, "you want to be a doctor so you talk that way. But I mean, really, the craziest people go to college."

He put his hands suddenly, almost roughly, on her shoulders. "Evvy," he said, "lets always be normal."

"Bob," she said, and put her mouth up to be kissed. It was not, in itself, a particularly satisfying action, and both of them realized it. Robert Manners thought to himself, kissing is no damned fun at all. You're supposed to do it. If you don't do it, you're not normal. So you do it. Big prelude, big build-up, for what?

They moved back into the lighted doorway of the dormitory, and Evelyn, looking for something to say, to do, reached into the pocket of the light autumn coat she wore and said, "Here. You're all lipstick. Let me use my handkerchief on you."

"No."

Her hand stopped, inches away from his mouth.

He said quickly, "Let me have your handkerchief."

"Oh," she said lightly, "don't be silly. Here, I'll do it."

His hand closed on her wrist with a strength that startled her. "I mean, I want it. To keep."

"Why, it isn't even clean," she said. "It's the silliest thing I ever heard of."

He let go of her wrist. "I just wanted something to remember you by."

"Well, next time you can have one. A clean one." Looking at him in the light, she saw the face of a stranger. "Good night. Good night, Bob. Thank you. I had a wonderful time." She turned from him quickly and went in.

He stood there outside for a moment, then wheeled and began walking down the street to the dormitory where he lived. Remember, he told himself, remember, remember, if you're crazy, then what seems crazy to you won't seem crazy to other people. Don't think the world is coming down around your ears because you use the word handkerchief in conversation. Other people don't think anything of it. *They don't know.*

And truly, the next morning when he met her for coffee and they read in the paper about the murder of Lena Tally, she had not brought up the question of the handkerchief. Somehow, this to him represented a new and major triumph, for he had exposed an inner part of himself and had got away with it. Suddenly, leaving her now as he went to attend a lecture in biological science, the violence came back upon him.

He had killed, and he was free. What could he not do now?

He would wait. He would ride the subways to far parts of the city and Walk streets and plan as he had never planned before. It would take time, but the wait would be worth it. It would have to be.

His journeys at night took him to Brooklyn and to Queens; in Queens, his walking along the streets, through block after block of new garden-type apartment houses, each with its row of garages and play areas in back, told him, for one thing, that the influx of population to this part of the city had outstripped the manpower of the local police precinct. There were no foot patrolmen here; none that he saw. He saw no patrol cars on the side streets. He knew that this way safety lay.

The windows of the apartment houses were of the casement type. At night, walking quietly in the areas behind the houses, he saw her, in the lone bedroom of what he assumed was a three-room apartment. Her window was open, open wide enough for him to move through it; but the blinds were down. They were down, but not drawn closed, so that he could see her. She wore a white slip, and he saw that she was a small woman, but with a good figure. Was she, he wondered, really alone? She went out of the room, and the next window, the small frosted pane of the bathroom, became yellow with light. It remained that way for maybe ten minutes; then it went out, and when she re-, entered the bedroom she was naked. Standing there, ten feet from her window, leaning within the protection of the shadows against the row of garages in back, he went weak with looking at her. She came without hesitation to the window, then flicked the cord on the left side of the blind so that the slats turned downward, closing off Robert Manners' view.

He had his job at the drug store; it was not wise to give it up. He had his classes at the University; it was not wise to stay away from them. In three days he returned, in the afternoon, going in the front door this time, checking the apartment numbers on the doors inside, then looking at the name-plates over the mail boxes. Hers told him what he wanted to know: *JUDITH FELTON.* So indeed she lived alone.

Then by night he returned, three and four times, each time carrying the pocket knife with the blade newly honed. Each time the blinds were down and closed.

It became late autumn, and he returned again. The night was dark but not cold. It was dark in her bedroom. Her window was wide open. The blinds were up. The light was on in her bathroom, and he could see the vague silhouette moving against the frosted glass.

In the darkness, he leaped, cat-like, to the level of the bedroom window. His strong arms supported him on the sill, and he upped his way through the window. He could hear her closing the medicine chest. Then the water ran in the bathroom sink. He stood there, holding his breath, waiting for his heartbeats to subside. Then he heard the opening of the bathroom door, saw the sudden oblong spread of light against the wall of the foyer beyond the bedroom door.

He met her there in the hallway, put his large left hand against her face, and drove the knife, held in the other hand, into her throat. The knife stuck and he left it there. The last thing he did, when he had done everything else, when she lay dead across the rim of the bathtub, head down in her own blood on the floor of the tub, was done in a sickening wave of sanity and realization. The opened lipstick was on the wash basin next to one of the faucets. He took it and wrote on the tiled wall above the bathtub:

HELP ME FOR GOD'S SAKE

Chapter Four

Impartiality was a creed with Walter Kyne. Once a year he invited everyone, even the copy boys who got drunker than anyone else, to a Christmas party in his office. Once every summer he had the secretaries and stenographers out to a steak fry at his summer home on Long Island. Once each year he played golf with Arnold Lamin, went to a football game with Mark Loving, and got drunk with Jon Day Griffith in the Dell, the saloon in the basement of the O.K. building. He lunched occasionally with his top editors, met them at night in restaurants or at cocktail parties of the various newspaper and publishing meetings and conventions.

And he could state that he was not violating his premise of impartiality by having a quiet dinner at his home from time to time with Harry Kritzer, chief of Kynpix and an honorable man. Harry Kritzer had been with Kyne longer than any of the other candidates for McCrady's job. He was not a tall man, and he inclined now to overweight. His age was the same as that of Walter Kyne, forty-nine. He dressed immaculately at all times, and the most noteworthy thing about him was the way he walked: he had the slow, measured step of a retired five-star general.

Harry Kritzer was not without sex appeal. He had been married for six years to a former showgirl who, he discovered toward the end of their union, was improving her technique in bed by practicing with other men while he was away. His close friends got the impression that this was not the basic cause for the breakup of Harry Kritzer's marriage. He took an encouraging view of sex, supported by a collection of rather vulgar stories, the latest of which he was recounting tonight in the living room of Walter and Dorothy Kyne.

The story dealt with an American who had visited Mars and observed how everything on that planet, complete down to having a baby, was accomplished by pushing buttons. His Martian guide then accompanied the American back to earth. The American took the man from Mars to his home, introduced him to his wife, then hid the planetary visitor behind a curtain in his bedroom and proceeded to demonstrate how earthlings reproduce.

The demonstration over, the American, justifiably proud of himself, swung back the curtain.

"See?" he said.

The Martian was puzzled. "Where's the baby?"

"Oh," the American said, "that takes nine months."

"Nine months?" the Martian said. "So what was the rush at the end?"

Kritzer told his stories well, and the reaction from the publisher and his wife was gratifying. An outsider might have thought, from all such evidence, that here was the man closest to Walter Kyne and likeliest to succeed the late Cyrus McCrady as executive director of the empire. But two men, at least, knew that, stacked against the importance of Griffith, the influence of Lamin, and the salary of Loving, Harry Kritzer's credentials were somewhat suspect. The two men were Harry Kritzer and Walter Kyne. The fact that Kyne was on closer social terms with Kritzer than with any of the others could be balanced, in addition, by the fact that as a photo man, Harry Kritzer was farthest removed from the kind of job McCrady's successor would perform. Griffith with his paper, Lamin with his wire service, and Loving with his syndicate all moved in orbits closer to the goal.

But if Harry Kritzer had his drawbacks, here, nevertheless, he stood this calm early December evening, two days after the McCrady funeral, sipping bénédictine with the multi-millionaire he called his friend. The drinks were served in the elegant living room of the four-story residence Kyne had on Sutton Place; they were served by a butler named Steven, so trained to perfection in his job that he could move among a swarm of people at the frequent Kyne cocktail parties, balancing a large tray of drinks of all varieties, so that a guest could select the one he wanted without having had to order it first, and yet never knock over one of the dozen or more photographs Kyne had situated precariously on all the tables in the room. Walter Kyne himself had observed this fact. A little drunkenly, he told Steven once, after a party, "You came within an eighth of an inch of knocking Truman on the floor six different times. How come you missed?"

"It was autographed, sir," Steven replied woodenly.

At the moment now, Walter Kyne, his wife Dorothy, and Harry Kritzer were discussing politics. Kyne called many Republicans friend, and they in turn called him fearless. Excerpts from Kyne publications dotted the lineage of the Congressional Record. Harry Kritzer, on the other hand, was a man who saw something good in everyone except the extremists on either side. He was a middle-of-the-roader, a man whose Opinions it was Worth While Knowing, the personification of the unswayed mind and the independent vote. For this, he was complimented frequently on every side, and it boosted his stock as an honest man. If he had gone on the television program "I've Got a Secret," his secret would have been that he had voted straight Democratic ever since 1924.

If Walter Kyne suspected this, however, he did not let on. "The essential makeup of the basic differences between the two parties," he was saying now, "lies in the tariff. You know, Harry?"

"I know," Harry said. "It dates back to Smoot."

"Well, all right," Kyne said uncomfortably, "but I think you ought to look at it in a more present-day light. Do you realize how much of our money (he used the word our in its inalienable Grand Old Party connotation) went into vaults, because we were scared of letting them (the *them* was equally apparent) tax it?"

"I suppose it was a good chunk," Kritzer said, and smiled wanly at Dorothy Kyne, who sat on the couch, her pretty brow furrowed, listening to the conversation. Walter Kyne had found her in Las Vegas seven years ago. He was forty-two then, and she was twenty-six, without money of her own but with the distinction of having been married briefly to a sculptor. She exhibited an artfully goldened sweep of yellow hair and an excellent figure that seemed tailored for the bedroom. Kyne had propositioned her while swimming at three o'clock one afternoon, and he would never forget her answer. He was in the pool, looking up at her legs, and she was sitting on the side of the pool, looking amusedly down at him. What she had said was one word:

"Here?"

Walter Kyne thereupon had broken the indoor record for dressing after a swim, and twenty minutes later he was breaking the indoor record for undressing after dressing. They were married three nights later.

If she tired of her husband, if she disliked his occasional spurts of interest in his work—an interest that had accelerated in manifold degree since the death of McCrady—Dorothy Kyne kept it to herself. She kept a lot of things to herself, including what she thought about that honest man, Harry Kritzer.

From another part of the house now, the telephone rang, and after a bit, Steven, the butler, came to the archway at the entrance to the living room and said, "Mr. Kyne, sir. Mr. Griffith is calling from the *Sentinel*."

Kyne took his glass with him and followed Steven with the look of a man who was not quite sure where the telephone was in his own house.

Dorothy Kyne watched him go. Then she said, "Sit next to me, Hairy."

"No," Kritzer said, and looked at the drink in his hand. "I don't like the walls in this room. They look like they've got sliding panels. All I have to do is get my hand inside your dress and the wall will open and Walter'll walk in."

"I didn't tell you to put your hand inside my dress."

"It's a thought, though," Kritzer said.

"I know it is," she said, looking directly at him.

Kritzer sipped at his drink again and made a face as he swallowed. He said, "He's probably got microphones behind those pictures, too."

"You don't know," Dorothy said. "He told me that before I married him he lived for a while with a woman and he used to rig a camera with a flash attachment and point it at them when they went to bed. Then at the big moment he'd push the cable thing and get a picture of it. He loved to see himself in action."

"Well," Kritzer said, "the Greeks used mirrors. Did you ever see any of the pictures?"

"A hundred times," Dorothy said. "He's proud of them."

"Well," Kritzer said, "I've been in his photo department for twenty-three years. The least the son of a bitch could have done would have been to give them to me to develop. What I'd give to be able to blackmail him." He turned so that he faced her, and his eyes were bright. "Especially now."

"Don't you think you have something to blackmail him with?" Her body moved slightly as she spoke.

"No," Harry Kritzer said. "I wouldn't want to involve you. You know that."

"My hero," she said, but she did not say it in an unfriendly tone of voice.

"Besides," he said, "the best thing you can have going for you is a friend in court. I'm assuming you're telling him in the privacy of your boudoir what a hell of a man I am."

"Every night," Dorothy said. "But I like your boudoir better."

"So do I," Harry Kritzer said. "When's the next time you can visit your mother?"

"Thursday night," Dorothy Kyne said. "And I don't like keeping up this mother business."

"Listen," Kritzer said, "that's the excuse my wife gave me."

"But you found out about it."

"Not for a while," Kritzer said. It crossed his mind that there was an elementary form of justice here, in that he now was playing the role with another man's wife that another man had played with his wife. This, he suspected, was the reason that originally had led him on with Dorothy Kyne. What had led her on with him was more subtle. Probably it consisted in the main of not a physical, but a mental, reaction that she had to Harry Kritzer when she saw him together with her husband. Harry Kritzer was more of a man than Walter Kyne—he knew more things. Perhaps Dorothy Kyne was justifying what seemed to her an unfair situation in giving one of her husband's possessions—in this case, herself—to such a richly deserving underling.

"Careful," she said now, and Harry Kritzer turned away from her as Walter Kyne came back in the room.

Kyne was excited. "I kept telling the son of a bitch," he said. "I told him coming back from the funeral the other day. If I told him once, I told him ten times. Well, by God I was right."

"What was it, Walter?"

"Harry," Kyne said, "those two murders. The old gal three months ago and the library girl the other day. I told Griffith the same one did it. Damn it, I was right."

"They caught the killer?"

Kyne said to his wife, "Tell that goddam Steven to bring us some whisky. The hell with this after-dinner crap. I want Old Granddad in a water glass and water in another water glass so

I can drink like a human being. Hell, no." He was talking again now to Harry Kritzer. "They didn't find him. But they know the same man did it. You know why? The damnedest thing I ever heard of. This guy, see, he's a pervert. Both times, you know what he did?" Something told him the presence of a woman in the room, even his wife, called for moderation of expression. He lowered his voice. "He moved his bowels on the floor."

Dorothy put her hand to her throat and said, "Oh."

Harry Kritzer said, "I'll be a dirty slob."

"We're going with it in the morning editions," Kyne said. "All papers. We've got it sewn up."

"How are you going to phrase it?"

"That's what took me so long on the phone with Griffith," Kyne said. "We're going to lead with the bare fact that police know these murders were committed by the same man. Then a good ways down in the story, all we say is that the killer is known to have committed a certain additional action linking him to both crimes."

"One thing," Harry Kritzer said. "If that's what the guy did, why did it take the police so long to figure out it was the same one? Seems to me if I walked in on the scene of a crime, that would be one of the first things I'd notice."

Dorothy said, "Harry!"

He looked at her and spread his palms upward. "What'd I say?"

"I know," she said, "but the way you said it."

"Oh, use your head," Kyne said to him. "The cops knew about it but they weren't letting it out. One of our boys found out about it today." —

"Which one?"

"Ed Mobley," Kyne said, and said it in a tone of voice that expressed great admiration for Mobley: an admiration greater, and one that made Walter Kyne the more secure, for the fact that Mobley had no stature with the company above that of reporter-rewrite. It would have been a more difficult thing to deal with if one of his top editors had come up suddenly with a beat of this kind, even though it was Jon Day Griffith to whom Mobley had relayed his discovery.

Kritzer said, "Do the police know we know?"

"Not officially," Walter Kyne said. "I want to protect Mobley on this, too, because he's got a friend down at headquarters, somebody he used to know on the west side, and there may be some more tips coming."

This last, Kritzer was sagely convinced, was not Kyne's idea. The idea of protecting Mobley would be Jon Day Griffith's, for reasons both many and obvious.

"So," Kyne went on, "we're using Gerald Meedy's byline on the story. Damn it, Harry, it's a good story."

Something in the way he said it made Kritzer say quickly, "Walter, you'd better show me where the downstairs phone is. I want to call my desk. We'll want to use some new art with this."

Walter Kyne said, "I told Griffith to do that." The look in his eyes as he said this told Kritzer many things at once. Maybe I told Griffith, Kyne was saying to him, or maybe it was Griffith's idea, or maybe the question of pictures didn't come up at all, but you're not going to jump into this thing while you're using my house as a base of operations. I'm a little frightened of you all, the look in Kyne's eye said, and this is the way I make up for it. I am, the look in Kyne's eye said, as good a newspaperman as any of you, even if, the look in Kyne's eye said, my raying that I'm as good a newspaperman as any of you is a lie.

Out loud, Harry Kritzer said, "I'm glad you thought of that, Walter."

Chapter Five

On important stories, the man on Jon Day Griffith's *Sentinel* worked interchangeably with Arnold Lamin's Kyne Press Service, the news-wire network, for both operations were carried on in the Kyne newsroom, a big barn of a place which to the uninitiated seemed to spill endlessly upon the eye. On one side of this room were the cubicles and desks of KPS; the opposite side was the *Sentinel's* domain, and separating them was a battery of desks used by reporters for both the newspaper and the wire service.

Even though each was a separate organization, it saved manpower to have KPS use carbon copies of local news stories written by *Sentinel* staffers. When an important story was breaking, unless it happened to be right on the *Sentinel* deadline, the copy was turned over immediately to KPS to be transmitted over its wires not only to the banks of teletype machines scattered about the newsroom itself but to similar machines in newsrooms of more than two hundred other dailies from coast to coast.

Under this reciprocal arrangement, it was now KPS that was carrying the fresh early-afternoon bulletins on the *Sentinel's* newest story. Cyrus McCrady was now dead two weeks. The murders that Walter Kyne was interested in were still unsolved. But what was breaking now over the chattering teletypes might have something to do with them:

BULLETIN (KIDNAP)
NEW YORK—(KPS)—POLICE SAID TODAY THEY BELIEVE AN EIGHT-YEAR-OLD GIRL WHO DISAPPEARED FROM HER BRONX HOME THIS MORNING WAS KIDNAPED.
(more)

Copy boys tore the paper off the machines and distributed copies of the bulletin around the newsroom. One of the copies reached Arnold Lamin in his glass-enclosed office. Lamin read it, said, "Ah, sons of bitches," and got up and walked out of his office and over to Joe Levine, head desk man for KPS. He said, "Hell, Joe, we already know they found a ladder leading to her window, and all of a sudden you put out a bulletin saying she was kidnaped. What'd you think before? She eloped?"

Levine peered at his superior over rimless eyeglasses. He had a large adam's apple, and whenever Lamin shouted at him it moved up and down in rapid sequence. He said, "Well, Arn, number one, this is the first time the cops actually came out and said she was kidnaped. Number two, the night wire's open now, so we had to go with it this way."

The night wire was the name for the service which began at two o'clock each afternoon and went to morning newspapers. For their benefit, earlier stories frequently were repeated. Still, now, Arnold Lamin had a point to make. "I know the night wire's open. But instead of laying down a complete story, all you give them is this one little bulletin like you just found out Jesus Christ returned to earth. You've been talking about she was kidnaped all day."

"Yes," Levine said. His adam's apple worked. "But this is the first time we hung it on the cops."

"Well, get the add out," Lamin said. "What's AP saying?"

"I haven't seen AP," Levine said. "The add's already moving."

Lamin turned to the teletype machine and read:

BULLETIN FIRST ADD KIDNAP XXX KIDNAPED.
A LADDER WAS FOUND PROPPED AGAINST THE OPEN WINDOW OF THE SECOND-FLOOR BEDROOM OF LAURA GRABOWSKI, DAUGHTER OF PHILIP AND MARIE GRABOWSKI (OF 23045 PARK AVENUE). IT WAS BELIEVED THE YOUNGSTER DISAPPEARED

Lamin did not read further. He turned to Levine and said, "Joe, did you read this before it went out?"

"No," Levine said. "I was on the phone. Max said the cops had sent out a kidnap alarm, so it sounded all right to me."

"Where did Max get the story?"

"Meedy dictated it to him from police headquarters."

"Don't you know enough not to let Meedy ever dictate or write a story? Here, get me the dupes on the new stuff." Lamin moved a chair up to the desk that sat at right angles to Levine's desk, wheeled a typewriter in front of him, and looked quickly at the smeared carbons that a copy boy stuck in his hand. Then, using only two fingers but typing with remarkable speed, he started to write. The new lead was on the wire four minutes later:

BULLETIN NEW LEAD (KIDNAP)

NEW YORK—(KPS)—AN EIGHT-YEAR-OLD GIRL WAS KIDNAPED FROM HER BRONX HOME EARLY THIS MORNING IN WHAT POLICE FEARED WAS ANOTHER CRIME BY THE UNKNOWN MURDERER OF TWO NEW YORK WOMEN.

(MORE)

BULLETIN FIRST ADD NEW LEAD KIDNAP XXX WOMEN.

A LADDER LEADING FROM THE REAR COURTYARD TO THE SECOND-FLOOR BEDROOM OF LAURA GRABOWSKI WAS THE ONLY IMMEDIATE CLUE FOR FBI MEN, WHO JOINED POLICE IN A CITY-WIDE SEARCH.

FEARS OF VIOLENCE WERE HEIGHTENED BY THE FACTS THAT NO NOTE WAS LEFT AND THAT THE DISTRAUGHT PARENTS OF THE MISSING GIRL, PHILIP AND MARIE GRABOWSKI, ARE NOT WEALTHY. (MORE)

"Here," Arnold Lamin said, and got up from his typewriter. "Have Max rewrite it from here, and have him write down another six or eight paragraphs before he picks up into the early. Tell him to point out that the part of Park Avenue where the house is isn't the ritzy part."

Levine said, "What about justifying that lead paragraph?"

"The hell with justifying it," Lamin said. "Mention the two other broads someplace down in the story and let it go at that."

"Won't it look funny?"

"Not to Walter Kyne," Lamin said. "Damn that Meedy anyway." He went back to his office, where Nancy Liggett sat typing letters. When he was fresh from participating actively in a story, as he just had done, Lamin carried with him a male scent of excitement. It had unnerved women in the past, and something told him, from the way she looked up when he came back in the office, that Nancy sensed it now. He smiled at her. "Whatever you do," he said to her, "don't fall in love with Gerald Meedy." It was a very oblique way of telling her he knew he, Arnold Lamin, was not unattractive to her, and she knew it. She was aware of the way her breasts pushed at the green sweater she wore, and she knew he was looking. She said now, "I didn't really plan on it."

"Sometimes," Lamin said, "I wish these walls weren't made of glass."

Nancy smiled and said nothing. Lamin knew how it was with her and Mobley. If she turned around, she would be able to see Mobley at his desk on the *Sentinel* side of the newsroom. It afforded her a feeling of protection, and that was what heightened her enjoyment of Arnold Lamin's desire.

Lamin knew how it was with her and Mobley, but how was it, really? Nancy wished she knew. She told herself she loved him, but he was a strange, and sometimes difficult man, and their affair together was one whose future was a clouded one, at best. At times, Nancy told herself that her thinking of Mobley as a complicated person was no more than a way of explaining the things she wished could be explained; or, perhaps, merely that she preferred not to think of herself as one who would fall in love with a simple man.

But there was abundant evidence to demonstrate that Mobley was, indeed, complicated in himself, no matter who dealt with him. His face was sad, his tongue frequently acerb. He was tall. His black hair was beginning to whiten surreptitiously at the temples. He never wore a hat. His eyes were a deep, deep brown, eyes that invariably looked directly at the person he was speaking to.

She had known him for a year, and had come to feel there was a great kindness in Edward Mobley, the sort of kindness that dampens the ambition, sometimes even the pride of a man. He had put his hands honestly upon her hips the first time he kissed her, and later that night, when she dreamed of him, she knew they would not stop at that. In the dream, he was walking toward her steadily along an endless street. Like a camera dolly, she moved away from him as he came, yet she was not afraid. In her dream, she said to him, "If I told you I wanted to know more about you, would you tell me there was nothing to know?" Then she said, "Answer me, Ed, answer me." But he only kept coming toward her, without speaking.

He had had many women before her, this she knew, and she wondered if each in her turn had felt as secure as she felt now—even though there was nothing in particular to feel secure about. Strangely, after the first few months, she questioned his faithfulness no more than she questioned her own, and the subject had never come up between them. Neither had the subject of marriage, except once or twice, when he had been drinking. Once in the ladies' room she had heard two stenographers talking about him. "He asked me," one of them said, "if I wanted to meet him at the Park Sheraton for a French kiss." The other one giggled and said, "Why the Park Sheraton? Is that all he asked you?" The first one said, "He didn't propose marriage, if that's what you mean." The second one said, "He wouldn't."

Nancy went back to her typing, now, sitting at her desk while outside the early December night closed in with the inevitable rush that left New York, its skyscraper offices still humming in their day's work, a sight of electric splendor. There were letters to be typed: letters from Lamin to Groveland, the Kyne chief in Chicago; to McFaddin in Cleveland, Faust in Hollywood and Sturm in Washington. The influence of Arnold Lamin reached far and high; it was not for nothing that people like Edward Mobley had bet their money on him to succeed McCrady. For every letter Lamin sent out in the day's routine, there could be expected a letter in return, and each would contain a paragraph that would tell Arnold Lamin, though not, perhaps, in so many words, that the writer knew all about the McCrady Derby—and that he was on Lamin's side. Such allegiance, now stated, was in the form of calculated risk. One could not be vague in writing to Arnold Lamin; one could only assume he stood the best chance of getting the job. And every such letter Lamin received improved his chances.

When she got up to put the letters on Lamin's desk for his signature, Nancy could see Mobley at his desk across the room. He was talking to a thin copy boy, the kind she knew Mobley would swear had pimples on his back even though his face looked okay.

The look of resignation and attention, in combination, upon Edward Mobley's face could be misleading. He almost always looked that way, even, Nancy would swear, when they were together and the lights were out.

What the copy boy had said to Mobley was hardly a masterwork of English prose. He had said, "Did you hear them bells?"

"What bells?"

"On the machine," the copy boy said, and waved across the room to where the teletypes were. "Mr. Levine said to tell you."

"All right," Mobley said. "Now go ask Mr. Levine why he wants me to listen to bells."

"All right," the copy boy said, and went across the room. He was back almost immediately with a jaggedly torn piece of teletype paper in his hand. He gave it to Mobley, and Mobley read:

BULLETIN
NEW YORK—(EPS)—A BLOODY AXE WAS FOUND LATE TODAY IN THE BASEMENT OF THE HOME WHERE EIGHT-YEAR-OLD LAURA GRABOWSKI DISAPPEARED THIS MORNING.

Mobley looked across the room and saw Levine, the KPS desk man, standing over one of his rewrite men as the man, telephone headset in place, worked at his typewriter.

Then Levine tore the page out and handed it across the desk to the wire filer, who instantly thrust it across a narrow table to the man who was punching the keyboard of the teletype transmitter.

Burt Healey, from his desk on the *Sentinel* side of the room, called over, "We're getting it here now, Ed."

"What?" Mobley said. "The axe?"

"Yeah. Downstairs. Blood to hell and gone all over the place."

"What about a body?"

"Who knows from bodies? I only hope that son of a bitch Kritzer got the camera out of hock."

Mobley said, "Some day you'll go to work for a paper that's got two cameras."

"It's academic," Healey said. "We only got one roll of film."

The copy boy came over from the KPS side of the room with another take:

FIRST ADD GIRL XXX MORNING.

THE AXE WAS FOUND BENEATH A PILE OF RAGS IN a WASHTUB. THE RAGS AND THE TUBS WERE BLOOD-STAINED.

EARLIER A LADDER WAS FOUND LEADING TO THE OPEN WINDOW OF THE MISSING GIRL'S SECOND-FLOOR ROOM.

Levine came over across the room to Mobley's desk and said, "I'm getting more, Ed. Do me a favor, I'm short-handed, write it for the wire. New lead. Put Meedy's name on it."

"Meedy's covering it?"

"Covering it, hell. He probably did it."

"I'll be here all night," Mobley said. "I was fixing to get my ashes hauled."

"Bring her up here and do it at your desk. I'll authorize overtime."

"You'll pay an entertainment tax, too," Mobley said. "You want a lead right away?"

"Oh, no," Levine said. "We're only forty-five minutes behind AP now. Take your time. I'm already in a jackpot with Lamin because I didn't check something Meedy phoned in earlier."

"All right," Mobley said. "If I write 'by Gerald Meedy' one more time people are going to think I'm pimping for him."

"I got news for you," Levine said, nodding his head in agreement. "Oh-oh, my phone again. I quit."

"You say it," Mobley said to him, "but you won't do it." He bent over the typewriter and began to work.

Chapter Six

Jon Day Griffith, editor of the New York *Sentinel*, was given to claiming that he owed nothing to any man, save his father, who had taught him how to drink. At the age of forty-two, he estimated he already had spent thirty-five thousand dollars on whisky, most of it Dawson scotch, which he drank always with plain tap water. Griffith possessed a massive distrust for bottled water, a distrust dating back to his tenure as editor of the Chronicle, the Kyne paper in Chicago; in Chicago, the swankier restaurants served bottled spring water, and it was there that Griffith experienced adhesions of the intestinal wall. The ailment required surgery and kept him away from work from mid-October to mid-November of 1948. Thus he was not able personally to take credit for the fact that the Chronicle was the only Kyne paper which did not elect Thomas E. Dewey president of the United States.

Griffith derived an additional degree of pleasure from the fact that he drank against doctor's orders. As he pointed out to Carlo, the bartender in the Dell, whisky was a necessary adjunct to working for Kyne. This was true when Cyrus McCrady was alive to do the work for Walter Kyne, and it was excessively true tonight, with Kyne acting as the interim McCrady and bloody axes being found in basements.

"Carlo," Griffith said, "I got news for you." They were alone in the Dell, a long, blue-lit place with a juke box and a little room behind the bar where Carlo kept a hot plate and an assortment of canned foods in respect to the state law that said every saloon must be a restaurant as well. Carlo had, for added protection, an arrangement with the luncheonette on the first floor of the O.K., so that whenever the food inspectors entered the building, the Greek in the luncheonette would rush ham, cheese, and bread downstairs, so that when the inspector got to the Dell, read Carlo's menu and asked for a cheese sandwich, Carlo could give it to him.

Now Carlo set Griffith's scotch before him. "I didn't see you since the funeral. It was all right?"

"Beautiful," Griffith said.

"I was going to send flowers," Carlo said. "I was going to call up, send over McCrady a six dollar bunch."

"A sweet thought."

"Well, anyway," Carlo said. "I didn't."

"Mr. McCrady would have wanted it that way," Griffith said. He never failed to be impressed at the way Carlo dated his subject matter back to the last time he had seen you, just as if McCrady's funeral had been earlier today. "Carlo," Griffith said, "do you know why I like you?"

"Yes, sir," Carlo said. "Was it wet there in the rain?"

"Because you kept 'Heartaches' on the juke box for seven months," Griffith said. "My wife said to me, 'I'm going to kill that Ted Weems,' she said. But you were a man, Carlo. I'll never forget it. It was wet as hell."

"How's Mrs. Griffith?" Carlo said.

"Who knows?" Jon Day Griffith said. "She woke up this morning, she said, 'I'm sick.' I said, 'What do you mean, you're sick?' 'My feet are cold.' 'So you slept with your feet out of the covers all night.' 'I wouldn't have done that if I wasn't sick.'"

"I'm sorry to hear she's sick," Carlo said. "You ready for another?"

"Yes," Griffith said. "I've been upstairs with the one and only Walter Kyne, Carlo. You know the great man?"

"A fine man," Carlo said.

"A weak-spined, blue-eyed son of a bitch, you ask me," Griffith said.

"I don't know him too well," Carlo said.

"You ain't really missing a hell of a lot," Griffith said. "Let me tell you something about Walter Kyne. What he doesn't know about people, you could put it cover to cover in the Manhattan phone book. He just *doesn't know*, Carlo. You know that wife of his?"

"She's a pretty woman," Carlo said.

"She is that." Jon Day Griffith nodded his head profoundly. "And she's sleeping with somebody on the side. I'm not saying I know that for a fact, I'm just saying it's likely. I'm only saying it's probable. I'm simply saying it figures. Probably one of Kyne's friends on the Republican Lost Inventory Committee."

"Well," Carlo said, "I hope you didn't tell Mr. Kyne that."

"No," Griffith said. "We had other things to talk about. I call Mr. Kyne Walter, you know, and he calls me Jon. 'Well, Jon,' says Walter, 'a little girl's been murdered.'"

"That's terrible," Carlo said.

"When Walter Kyne's interested, you bet your ass it's terrible. What time is it?"

Carlo bent under the bar. "Ten-thirty," he said, still bent over.

"Well, you'd better give me one more," Griffith said. He looked along the bar to his left, to the base of the stairs leading up to the street. "No, you'd better make it two. Mobley's here. No, make it three. He's got somebody with him."

Edward Mobley and Nancy Liggett came over to where Griffith was sitting. "Here's tall, dark and handsome," Griffith said. "And the beautiful Miss Boo. Here, no, let Nancy sit here in between us. Then you and I can indian-wrestle under the bar."

Nancy said, "I want rye and soda and I'll be back in a minute."

"Watch out for Suzy in there," Carlo said. Mobley said, "Who's Suzy?"

"The cat," Griffith said. "She now lives in the ladies' room." He and Mobley watched Nancy walk toward the dark-curtained doorway at the far end of the bar. Griffith looked at Mobley. "You score yet?"

"Ah, don't ask questions like that," Mobley said. "You give me gooseflesh. It's the funniest prickly-wickly feeling."

"Yeah," Griffith said. "So ask me."

"Ask you what?"

"Ask me what did Kyne say and am I going to get the posisshon."

"Look," Mobley said, "you're the big editor in the mighty chain of newspapers on which the sun never sets and I am merely thine humble servant and you want the truth, I couldn't care less. Eight hours I been going on the kidnap thing. What do you want?"

"It's no kidnap," Griffith said. "It's murder. The ball game."

"Who told you?"

"W.K."

"Kyne?"

"No, water-kloset. Ed, it's the damnedest thing I ever saw. The chicken-necked bastard is up there running around and screaming like hell about this little girl's been murdered and justice must be done and what ever happened to enterprise in the newspaper business. 'Send out your best men!' he hollers. 'Get the dossier!' Wha? What'd he say? What dossier? 'Find thè killer!' he yells. 'This is everybody's job! Reporters, editors, feature men, wire service men, photographers! Get me the man!' " Griffith communed with his scotch and water. "Well," Mobley said, "I pass."

"Not me," Griffith said. He curled a lean white hand around his glass and stared at the row of bottles back of the bar. "Ed, who'd you bet on?"

"You mean the derby?"

"Yes," Griffith said, "the McCrady 'Cap. Apprentice allowance waived. Weight for age. Weather clear, track miserable."

"I only bet eight bucks," Mobley said.

"On who?"

"Lamin."

"Oh-ho," Griffith said. "A chalk player."

"He's seven to five," Mobley said.

"Sure he is," Griffith said. "Lamin's smart, Lamin's fast, Lamin knows an awful lot of right people. People in South Diaphragm, Iowa, they never heard of you or me or McCrady, they heard of Arnold Lamin." Griffith lifted his glass again. "You know something, Edward, I've been nice to you."

"I still bet on Lamin."

"The hell with that. Ed, I've been nice to you. Mainly because I like you. Give me one of those cigarettes. Carlo, you got a match?"

"He never has a match," Mobley said.

"Never mind," Griffith said. "Carlo's all right. He kept 'Heartaches' on the juke box seven months. Here, I got matches." He lit their cigarettes. "Mainly, as I say, because I like you. Now I'm going to tell you something. Lamin doesn't get this job."

"No?"

"No. For one reason. For one jim-dandy reason. Because I'm going to get it. And you know why?"

Mobley said, "You know what the doctor told you."

"You know why?" Griffith said. "Because you and I are going to work together and crack this kid being murdered. Exclusive. You and me, Ed, my boy, you and me."

"Why me?"

"Because you're the best man I got. Because I know what's running through the feeble, infernal brain of Walter Kyne, Esquire. He's excited about this. So excited he might forget about the next order of business, which is picking the new McCrady. So excited he might just conveniently just slip off the hook and not have to pick anybody at all. So excited he might just set us at each other's throats like rats, everybody trying to crack this story and the first one who does it gets the big reward."

Mobley began to laugh. "I can see the four of you. You and Lamin. Loving. Poor Harry Kritzer."

"Honest Harry," Griffith said.

"It's all right," Mobley said. "It's neat. It does credit to a finer brain than Walter Kyne's. If he wins, he's got a hero, he's got a scoop, and he's got a made-to-order new McCrady without having to make up his mind. That's why this big act lately. So what happens? Nobody's feelings are hurt. It's sensational. There's only one thing wrong. . . ."

Nancy came back and sat in between them. "I don't know what you're talking about," she said, "but from the looks of you I hope it doesn't include me."

Mobley put his hand on her wrist underneath the bar and ran his index finger along it. "You know what we're talking about."

"How's Lamin?" Griffith said to her.

"I find it a privilege to be Mr. Lamin's secretary," Nancy said.

". . . So what," Griffith said to Mobley, "could be wrong?"

"Suppose we don't find the killer? Suppose it's the police? It's possible."

Griffith shrugged. "So we find the right policeman— and do our damnedest to get there first. What the hell, the worst Kyne can do is lose a little time before he has to make up his mind. With him, that's a pleasure."

"Oh," Mobley said, "I meant to tell you. I talked to Kaufman.

My guy down at headquarters."

Griffith's eyes moved to attention. "Did they find the..." He noticed Nancy. "You know. On the floor?"

Mobley shook his head. "No."

"So what makes them think the same guy did it as did the other two?"

"Why ask me?" Mobley said. "You read the Kyne papers, you'd think so."

"The fine hand of Arnold Lamin," Griffith said. "No, but I got the feeling it is the same guy."

"It might be," Mobley said. "After all, this is the first time he took the victim out of the room with him. Maybe he didn't have time."

Griffith brought his fist down on the bar. "Damn it, it's a story, Ed. That sleazy bastard Kyne, he uses it as an excuse for the fact that he's a coward, and it turns out he was right. He told me coming back from the funeral the same guy did it. I figure, he's just talking to cover up that he's got to pick a guy for this job. So maybe that's how he started out. But what are you going to do? He's right."

"*All* right," Mobley said, "I'm with you."

"I mean it," Griffith said.

"All right," Mobley said. "I said all right."

"Just because I know what Kyne's up to, that doesn't mean the others haven't figured it out too. Lamin and Loving and Kritzer come to you, you tell them to..."

Motley put up a finger. "Language. The lady."

"Don't mind me," Nancy said. "I'm not at all afraid. Nobody can tell me the big managing boss of the Kyne newspapers uses nasty words."

"I only manage one of them, you want to be technical," Griffith said, and leaned forward so that he could see Mobley sitting on her other side. "I mean it, Ed. I want this job. I need it."

"All right," Mobley said.

"We get this story," Griffith said, getting up from his stool, "don't worry about yourself. Everything's going to be great."

"Things'll be fine," Mobley nodded.

"Okay," Griffith said.

Mobley said, "One thing before you go."

"And?"

"Suppose there's no body? Suppose it wasn't a murder."

"It's a murder," Jon Day Griffith said.

They heard the sound of a woman's high heels on the stairs coming down to the Dell, and Mildred Donner, the Kyne women's feature writer, came in. She was in her early thirties. She wore glasses with loud-colored rims, and her forehead was too high for the rest of her face, but her walk and her bosom, the one as aggressive as the other, made her an arresting woman to watch and to be with. She wore a mink coat, supposedly purchased by an unknowing group of men that included Mark Loving, the director of Kyne World Features. It might have been that Loving bought her the whole coat. He was connected with sales and with the columns and puzzles and comics that Kyne sold on either a piece or package basis to newspapers throughout the world, and he could afford a mink coat. He could also afford what went into one.

Mildred Donner's voice was throaty and loud. "I'd known all along," she said. "I just knew I was going to find a friendly face down here."

Griffith patted the stool next to him. "I can't speak for anyone else," he said, "but my face is friendly. Sit down.

Have a rum on the rocks, or something."

Mildred made a face. She said to Carlo, "Rhine wine and seltzer."

Jon Day Griffith said, "For God's sake," and leaned backwards so Mildred could gaze in front of him at Nancy and Mobley. "Hello, you good people," Mildred said. "I always see you together."

"You could do a column about it," Mobley said.

"I could think of worse topics," Mildred said. "I have a terrible feeling I'm going to end up doing sob stories about these murders." The mink coat shuddered. "Aren't they awful? Mark's been up there arranging feature material on it all night. He was supposed to leave an hour ago, but then you-know-who called him in and they've been talking ever since. I finally came down here to wait for him."

Griffith drummed his fingers on the bar. "Who is you-know-who?"

"Oh, Jon," Mildred said. She put a hand on his arm. "Walter

Kyne.”

“Well,” Griffith said, “he couldn't have picked a finer man to talk to.” It seemed to Mobley, looking at him from behind, that Griffith's overcoat had come to attention.

“Now that you say that,” Mildred said, and nodded her head, “you just ought to see Mark. Why, you'd think this was the first murder in history. He's like a . . . like a fire-horse. You know, I rather admire him. He's just a police reporter at heart.”

Chapter Seven

"The good thing," Mobley said, "is to find out before you're married." He and Nancy were walking along Twelfth Street, coming to Seventh Avenue. Nancy's apartment was at the corner of Twelfth and Greenwich. They held hands as they walked; tonight it was not cold for December, and she wore a gray sweater and skirt and a tan coat of light wool. Mobley looked at her. "You know," he said, "you got nice legs."

"You're sweet."

"And nice nylon stockings. What holds your stockings up?"

"There's a lot," Nancy said, "that your mother should have told you."

"The hell with my mother," Mobley said. "I mean you personally. Yourself."

"Well," Nancy said, "don't tell anybody, but I hold my stockings up with garters."

"Garter belt?"

"You sound excited. No, a girdle."

"The panty kind or the other kind?"

Nancy laughed. "The other kind."

"Oh. Well, how does it come off?"

"The opposite from the way it goes on."

"I mean with zippers or snaps or something? I knew a broad in Boston one time that had one with hooks and eyes. Damnedest thing I ever ran into."

"That was before they banned you in Boston," Nancy said. "What were you saying before you got interested in my girdle?"

"I can't remember when I wasn't," Mobley said. "Oh. About the good thing is to find out before you're married."

"Not everybody does," she said.

"No," Mobley said. "That's one good thing about us. We're matched in size. You ever see these married couples where he's six foot eight and she's four foot nine? How do you suppose they get away with it?"

"Maybe they had to get married to find out."

"Let's get married," Mobley said.

"You never say that unless you've had five drinks."

"I've had six." They walked into the lobby of her apartment house. The doorman was asleep in & chair next to an imitation mahogany desk over by a wall. The desk was flanked by potted palms. "Look at him," Mobley said. "He's married."

"Sssh," Nancy said. They went into the self-service elevator and Mobley pushed the button that said 3. Like all self-service elevators, this one moved at a crawl. Mobley reached for her and kissed her slowly, and with tenderness, on the forehead.

"You are my angel," he said. "My sheet-rock pie."

"Your what?"

"My delicious dumpling. My steaming cluster of yams. My Esther Jack."

"Your who?"

"Esther Jack," Mobley said. "She is in every fifth chapter of everything Thomas Wolfe ever wrote."

The elevator stopped and Mobley pushed open the heavy door. "You're not well enough read," he said to her. "It comes from being Lamin's secretary. I think he discourages reading."

Nancy smiled, a trifle sadly. She herself had had just enough to drink so that she was willing to give more pause and more attention than was usual to topics such as this one, topics which thus gained certain weight and rolled on their own momentum. At her door, she went into her purse for her key, and Mobley, watching her, knew suddenly the unfriendly feeling he had had that day at his typewriter in the office, thinking of how her door opened and how someone who entered women's apartments—maybe the same someone now with the little girl who was missing—was a someone who killed, a someone who was still at large.

She went in ahead of him, turning on the lamp on the little gray bookcase, and then, turning so that she faced him in the foyer with the darkness of the rest of the apartment behind her, she said, "Come on, drunk." She held out her arms and Ed Mobley went to her and kissed her at length, and with more gentleness than she had known from him before.

It was a kiss that lasted as long as it lasted, being terminated neither by him nor by her nor consciously by both of them together, but simply by being over when it was over. He put his hands on her shoulders and said, "You know, like that it makes me feel like an explorer."

"Oh?"

Mobley nodded his head up and down solemnly. "I feel like I ought to have a permit."

"What? To kiss me?"

"No. To explore."

"Do explorers have to have permits?"

"They should. Especially when they go after uncharted mountains."

Nancy put her head up so that her hair danced quickly and softly at the back of her neck. She turned and walked into the living room, snapping on the light on the table beside the couch.

"I don't want to hear any of your talk about mountains," she said.

Mobley followed her. "I," he said, "was talking about uncharted mountains."

"You think I go around handing out maps?"

"No. But people have been there."

She looked at him quizzically. "People?"

"Oh, baby," Mobley said. He took off his coat and put it on the chair across from the couch. "Forgive me, sister, for I know not what I say."

"Well," Nancy said.

"What I meant," Mobley said quickly, "was like Mount Everest. Now, would you like to hear about Mount Everest? Do you know that at twenty-two thousand feet there reportedly lives a breed of half-beast, half-man called the abominable snowman? I ask you."

"Ask me nothing," Nancy said. "If you want to mix yourself a drink, go ahead."

"You too?"

"No."

"Ah," Mobley said. "Nancy's mad."

She took her coat off and went to the hall closet with it. She came back, smoothing down her sweater in front, and sat down on the couch; she took a cigarette and lit it, and watched him as he watched her cross her legs.

"Yes," she said at last, "Nancy's mad:"

He was standing in front of her. He bent over and kissed her on the forehead; she put her hand against his shoulder and pushed him back away from her.

"What a way," Mobley said, shaking his head, "for my bride to talk."

"Bride," she said. "Your illiterate common law wife would be better."

"No," Mobley said, and she marveled, as she always did, at the way his soft, non-geographic accents became subtly clearer the more he drank. "No, my bride. You wrong yourself. What you are, really, is a lion. A lion on a street in Jena."

"Where?" Even as she said it she could see herself falling in love with Ed Mobley. It was a wonderful, repeated, consecutive, continuous process. Get mad at him for something, and he would look at you and say something like calling you a lion on a street in Jena, if that was what he had just said, and you could not help but wanting to hear him say more. Either you loved him because this was so, or this was so because you loved him.

"A lion on a street in Jena," Mobley repeated now, almost dreamily. "Friedrich Nietzsche. He went crazy, see, and they had him in this nut house under observation, and he was writing about it all the time in his diary. Here, see now, I can recite it to you. This one morning the keeper comes and finds Nietzsche looking out the window and asks him what he's looking for, and Nietzsche gives him that crazy look and says, 'You have only to follow my eyes. If you see me looking into the sky you must know that it is an eagle I am looking for. But if my gaze goes downward the quarry I am hunting is a lion.' So then the guy says, 'But can you really expect to see a lion on a street in Jena?' And Nietzsche says, 'If you have the eyes to see him with, why not?' "

Nancy looked up at him, smiling. "So I'm a lion?"

"Or an eagle," Mobley said. "Will you let me fix you a drink?"

"No," Nancy said. "I don't want to get drunk with you."

"You accent the get-drunk. Something else you'd prefer?"

"No," Nancy said, this time although she no longer wanted to say it. "If all you want is whisky and sex you ought to find somebody else. What about that Mildred Donner? She's just your type."

"Not bad," Mobley agreed. "Built like the proverbial brick

outhouse, if I may say so. Except one thing."

"What's that?" Nancy said. "And tell me. Don't go quoting any of your off-brand authors."

"Yeah," Mobley said. He sat himself down on the floor in front of her and rested his head back against her knees, looking up in a quickly-abandoned effort to see her face as he talked. "The one thing is this. You don't sit there and tell me what's my type, you verstehst? Kapish, you have to understand one thing. If you're worried about my type, you don't bring me home with you. If you do bring me home with you, you assume one thing going in. You're my type. You mind? You mind dreadfully? You think I should have better taste? You think I really get stone drunk, like a boiled owl, on half a dozen hightails? Martinis, all right. But highballs."

Nancy's fingers touched his hair. "You talk too much for a man," she said softly. "I read in a magazine where a man isn't supposed to do the talking. He's not supposed to talk a lot about what he feels. He isn't supposed to cry."

Mobley pulled his head away and turned to look up at her. "Who's crying?"

She shook her head. "That isn't what I mean."

"I know what you mean. All right, let me talk just a little bit more." His fingers moved expressively. "I will quote no authors. Ed loves Nancy. Very much. Very early. Ed wants to marry Nancy. Ed is not drunk." She leaned forward and took his face in her hands and kissed him on the mouth. This time the kiss was assertive, and Nancy was the aggressor. She said, "You know what you remind me of?"

"In this position, probably John the Baptist."

"Darling," she said, "aren't you comfortable?"

"If I said yes," Mobley said, "I'd be an idiot." He got to his feet and came next to her on the couch. "Let's get married."

"I wish you meant that."

"Ah, here we go again," Mobley said. "I mean it, I mean it, I mean it. I'd give you a ring only I can't afford one. You'll have to have one of those combined wedding-and-engagement rings, like Griffith gave his wife."

"I don't mind," Nancy said, "if it has a wide band."

"So?"

"So what?"

"So will you marry me? You got a pencil? You want me to put it in writing?"

"Think of it." She kissed him on the cheek. "The great reporter without a pencil."

"A pretty damn good reporter, you want to know the truth," Mobley said.

"I know," Nancy said. "Lamin's aching to get you on his side."

"Lamin'll make it without me and I'm still a pretty damn good reporter," Mobley said. "And it doesn't answer my question."

"Yes." She whispered it.

"You will?"

She nodded, happily, and then she thought she was going to cry. She said, "Should we telephone my mother and father?"

"At this time of night? In Moline?"

"They don't live in Moline."

"All right," Mobley said. "Davenport. Playground of the world."

"Rock Island," Nancy said.

"It's still too late," Mobley said. "My God, I'm engaged. Now will you tell me?"

"What?"

"How your girdle comes off."

"Fix us both a drink," Nancy said. "Then come back here to me."

Mobley stood up and went into the kitchen. Then he came back to the archway that led into the living room and said. "Nance."

"What?"

"I want you to do something for me."

"What's that?"

"Put an inside latch on your front door. You know, one of those chain things. I'll get one for you."

She laughed. It was a sound of which, he knew, he would never tire. She said, "Are you thinking of a chastity belt, too?"

"What do you know about chastity belts?"

"I read more than you think."

"I would like to join your lending library," Mobley said, and went back to fix the drinks. When he brought them out into the living room, the lights were out.

He said, "Where are you?"

"Here."

"I can't see you."

"I can see you."

"Oh? What do I look like?"

"A lion," Nancy said.

Chapter Eight

Arnold Lamin got home about nine-thirty. The letter, bearing the return address of the *Tribune*, the Kyne paper in Philadelphia, was propped up on the little telephone desk inside the door, where he would be sure to see it. He stood there, the door still open, and stripped the end of the envelope, putting the resultant sliver of paper in his mouth and chewing on it. Then he took out the letter and, as was another of his habits, looked first to see who it was from; though he knew, almost of a certainty, who the sender would be. Of his good friends in the newspaper business, none was more constant than Ellis Leeds, executive editor of the Tribune. It was from Leeds:

Dear Ann,
I trust neither the telephone nor the New Jersey turnpike. So I tell you by mail: You have one man to look out for, and don't ask me in connection with what. His name, in case you don't know and in case I am Juan Peron of Argentina, is Griffith. He's smart. I'm betting you're smarter. Am going to let Kyne know so, too. Sometimes I wish I were an electrician.
Seriously—I hate people who start sentences with the word seriously—watch this guy. Watch him good.
Best,
El

Lamin's wife came out to where he was standing, the front door still open. She was a tall woman with large gray eyes and a face that seemed capable, not unattractively, of perpetual surprise.

She said, "You're late and you look tired."

"It's probably the other way around," Lamin said. He kissed her without perceptible enjoyment. "The rat race is on."

"The McCrady business?"

Lamin nodded. He closed the door and took off his overcoat.

"Sometimes," he said, "I just get tired."

"Where did you get that paper?"

"What paper?"

"The paper you're chewing."

"Sweetheart," Lamin said, "do you want to hear about this or not?"

"Certainly," Betty Lamin said. "Of course. I don't suppose you ate. I can give you some supper. The doctor said Dolly's got conjunctivitis."

"What's conjunctivitis?"

"It isn't anything bad, but it's uncomfortable. The eyes get filled with sleep and then when she wakes up she can't open them. You have to use boric acid and penicillin ointment."

Arnold Lamin was at an age where he thought seriously about his trains of thought. The train of thought that he now had was that one should not use boric acid and penicillin ointment in conjunction (not even in conjunctivitis), that the word to describe it was that one contraindicated the other, that once, when he was thirteen years old and wanted to get out of playing basketball in high school he had his doctor write a letter to the teacher in charge of tardiness and illness excuses at the school. The note, said Arnold Lamin was having trouble with the cartilage in his left knee, a fact more or less the truth, and that any exercise was contraindicated.

By the time he was in the kitchen, he said to his wife, "My knee hurts."

"Maybe you bumped it," Betty Lamin said.

"No." Lamin sat down at the kitchen table and his wife set a plate and a knife and fork in front of him. "No, it comes from thinking too much. You know who that letter was from?"

"What letter?"

"The one you left for me on the telephone table."

"Oh," his wife said, "that letter."

"The hell with it," Lamin said.

"Do you want some eggs?" his wife said. "The ,egg man's all upset with his layers."

"Damn it," Lamin said, "can't you take an interest in this? Just for once?"

"An interest?" She opened the door to the refrigerator. "An interest in what?"

"In the business downtown, that's what. You think I'm doing this just for me? You keep telling me Dolly's got to go to Miss So-and-so's school, we have to have a house in Rye with a gardener and every other damn thing. Where do you think the money's going to come from?"

"Well," Betty Lamin said, "I'm sure I don't understand it. Doesn't Walter Kyne like you?"

"He loves me."

"Then why doesn't he just give you the job and stop this nonsense? Aren't you the best man?"

"The very best."

"Well, I don't understand it," his wife said. "Throw away that silly piece of paper in your mouth. You'll poison yourself. You know I don't think a wife should mix in her husband's business affairs."

"For Christ's sake, aren't you even interested?"

She reached out and patted him on the head on her way to the stove. "Of course I'm interested. It's just that I can't follow all the ins and outs of your business. It's so technical."

"There's nothing technical about this. The next McCrady is going to be the man who solves the murder."

"What murder?"

"Never mind what murder."

"You see," she said. "There you go."

"A given murder," Lamin said tiredly. "Two babes were killed and now a little girl's been kidnaped and they found an axe and a lot of blood in the basement and maybe she's been murdered too. So Kyne lets on that the one who gets there first with the big news is the one who gets the job."

"You all act like a bunch of little boys."

"And you act like a little girl talking all the time, get you more money, get you more money."

"Arnold," she said.

"Yeah," he said. "Arnold."

"You know I have confidence in you," she said. "If you want something, you'll get it. You always have."

"That's why you don't pay any attention to any of this."

"If I felt I could be helpful," she said, "it would be one thing. I don't like to talk just for the sake of talking."

"No?" he said. "Well, then, for one night in your life, listen."

"All right," she said. "Now, what about the letter?"

"It's from El Leeds in Philly. He's on my side in this thing. Of course, he doesn't know about the new development, the find-the-killer routine. Or, knowing him, maybe he does. Anyway, he seems to think the chief competition is Griffith. Here. Read it."

Betty read the letter. "I always thought," she said, looking up, "that Jon Griffith was a nice man. He drinks too much, but he's nice."

"He's nice," Lamin agreed. "He also swings weight. You know?"

"You think the letter is right?"

"Yes," Lamin said. His tone mimicked that of his wife, though he did not intend it so. "I think the letter is right. This new stunt of Kyne's, about the killings, is only a few hours old and already Griffith's got the best man in the joint working for him."

"Who's that?"

"Guy named Mobley."

"I thought you were the best man."

"I am," Lamin said. "Do you know what I'm going to do?"

"Your eggs are ready."

"I," Arnold Lamin said, "am going to counteract—to contraindicate—this clever little move of Griffith's. I have a gentleman of my own. A reporter. His name's Gerald Meedy."

"I've heard of him," his wife said. "Wasn't he your secretary before you got that Nancy person?"

Lamin nodded. "He's brash, untutored and unkempt, but he's got a primeval kind of guts. I'm going to sic him on this story."

"But you don't like him."

"No," Lamin agreed, almost cheerfully. "But while Griffith's man Mobley is chinning around my secretary and making those moo-cow eyes of his through the glass window, I am going to have my man Meedy out buttering up cops. You know something, in my own little way I'm smart too. We'll make it yet.'

Betty nodded. "And we'll have a big house in Rye with a big kitchen. Did you want toast too?"

Chapter Nine

Mark Loving was involved this night with a letter, too, but it was one he did not receive. He wrote it. It was addressed personally to an old friend who ran a radio station in St. Louis. In the days just following the war, Kyne had experimented with a wire service that went exclusively to radio stations. This station in St. Louis was one of the original clients of this service, paying $85 a week for the wire.

The station was owned by a corporation that also had radio stations in Dallas and New Orleans, and a man named Webster, who in those days was sales manager for Kyne, had signed these stations to contracts, too, charging them a similar $85 apiece.

What had happened then was that a rival service—INS or UP, Loving disremembered which—had moved in on the St. Louis station and tried to undersell Kyne. Kyne cut its price to keep the St. Louis station, but when the sister stations in Dallas and New Orleans heard about it, they in turn refused to keep on paying $85 each. They could press their point, too, for Webster, the sales manager, had signed all three stations originally to the same over-all contract, instead of separately.

In fee simple, Kyne had lost all three stations. That was the result, and the sudden collapse of the revenue which from the three sources totaled $13,260 annually brought about the end of the short-lived Kyne service for radio.

McCrady had fired Webster) the sales manager, because of this; fired him with a seven-word salute: "Didn't you ever hear of separate contracts?"

But now some years had passed, and this old friend of Mark Loving's, on this radio station in St. Louis, was a nut on unsolved murder cases. This much Loving knew.

So tonight Mark Loving, director of Kyne World Features, wrote his old friend a letter. Mark Loving knew what was on Walter Kyne's mind, and he was determined to miss no bets. All facets of the Kyne operation, he knew, would now be attuned to all-out coverage of New York City's unsolved murders. And the kind of service that this concentration would produce—this he) put in his letter—might be of enduring value to a radio station.

Chapter Ten

Two mornings afterwards, the first part of Laura Grabowski's body was found. It was the head and torso and left leg. The right leg and the arms were missing. The discovery was made by a Consolidated Edison worker who descended into a manhole in the center of a street one block away from the missing child's home and saw what he assumed to be a package, wrapped in newspaper and tied with string, at the base of a short ladder leading from the street to a shelf of piping below. The newspaper was wet from the underground moisture, and when he touched it with his foot it gave through.

Within moments after the Con Edison man had come babbling to the surface to blurt his dreadful finding, the Kyne newsroom, seven miles away in downtown Manhattan, began to rock. The news came on the special teletype printer from police headquarters:

zzzzz slip 102
231 pct. part of child's body found in manhole
front of 23083 e. 194 st. det's assigned.
zzzzz

It was eleven o'clock in the morning. Burt Healey, the city editor of the *Sentinel*, had just come to work. Out of long habit, he looked at the police ticker on his way to his desk. It was a copy boy's job to mind the ticker, but from time to time it went unwatched. This morning, the boy had just finished tearing the long strip of paper from the machine. Thus what Healey saw coming in now was the first item in another series that might have gone un-minded for another hour.

Healey had, in fact, been thinking of the murders—specifically, of the lipstick handwriting on Judith Felton's bathroom wall—when he came to work. Now his teeth came down hard onto his cigar. He tore the piece of paper from the machine and called out, "Joe!"

Joe Levine, in charge of the desk of the wire service on the other side of the room, looked over. Despite the competition between the paper and the wire service—competition strongly accentuated now with the unspoken battle for promotion between the *Sentinel's* Jon Day Griffith and Arnold Lamin of KPS—Healey did not hesitate in calling the police flyer to the attention of the wire service. It was the wire's story, for now; the *Sentinel's* deadline for the first edition was still some seven hours away. Now Joe Levine saw Healey coming toward him, turning sideways to get between a couple of desks. Levine got up and met him a few steps away.

"They found the kid," Healey said.

"Let me see." Levine read the police flyer. "Give me this, Burt. Tell Lamin." He stepped back to his desk, ran a fold of carbon-sandwiched sheets of paper into his typewriter. Out loud, he said, "Hal, who's sending?"

Hal Laferty, the wire filer who sat a few feet away from Levine at a narrow table separating him from the operators who punched the teletype transmitters of Kyne Press Service, said, "Washington. Who else?"

"Break them."

Laferty leaned across the table to get a look at the copy coming in on the machine. "They're almost through."

"Break them anyway. Here." Levine threw the short paragraph he had written onto the filing table. Laferty read it silently and handed it to the teletype puncher, the index finger of whose left hand now depressed the "break" key that automatically stopped whatever was being transmitted from any point on the wire.

"Four bells," Laferty said.

The operator put the piece of copy on his paper stand and hit his bell key four times, the signal for a bulletin. Then, along eight thousand miles of leased wires, feeding into a score of other Kyne bureaus and into the telegraph rooms of two hundred newspapers, the news cut its swath of urgency.

BULLETIN

NEW   YORK—(KPS)—POLICE   REPORTED   TODAY

DISCOVERY OF PART OF A CHILD'S BODY IN A MANHOLE IN THE BRONX NEIGHBORHOOD WHERE EIGHT-YEAR-OLD LAURA GRABOWSKI DISAPPEARED TUESDAY.

Joe Levine turned away from his typewriter and saw Arnold Lamin standing there. "Did you phone Meedy?"

"No," Levine said.

Lamin turned to Wes Collier, an old war correspondent who now did rewrite for KPS. Collier was an immensely gaunt man who had been a close drinking companion to the late Cyrus McCrady and who as a result had a fund of McCrady stories, including one which claimed McCrady insisted all his foreign correspondents wear a patch over the eye. Wes Collier never moved fast, but he was incisive.

"I'll get Meedy," he said to Lamin now, and picked up his phone.

"All right," Lamin said. "Then get up there yourself. Take Gusskind and Hamilton with you. Let me see that police flyer."

The Kyne operation had a direct phone line to Gerald Meedy at police headquarters. Collier let it ring four times and then hung up.

"I guess he's on his way up to the Bronx, too," he said. "He doesn't answer, Arn."

"What about Photo?" Lamin asked. "Did anyone call them?"

"They'll get it on their machine," Joe Levine said.

"They never look at their goddam machine. Phone them anyway." Lamin himself now picked up a telephone on the desk. "Get me Mildred Donner."

Mildred Donner, the phone operator informed him, did not get to work this early in the day.

"Then get her at home," Lamin said. He set down the phone. "Joe, when Mildred calls tell her to get up to the house where the kid lived and interview the parents."

He turned and walked to the *Sentinel* side of the room, going into a small glass-enclosed area in the far corner where the wire services of the Associated Press and the International News Service, to which the *Sentinel* subscribed in addition to its own service, came in.

Williston James, a tired, stooped old man who had been

with Kyne for thirty years, was in charge of the little wire room. In this small area filled with chattering teletype machines, he worked day in and day out, tearing the copy off the various machines and then scissoring it according to content and hanging it on a row of spikes next to the doorway.

Lamin said, "How'd we break?"

"Even with INS," James said in a gravel voice. "Minute ahead of AP. We timed off at 11:02. AP 11:03."

"What do they say?"

"Same thing we say."

"I want to see all their copy."

"I'm not supposed to do that," James said in a high, complaining voice.

"I know," Lamin said. KPS was not privileged to use, or even see, opposition copy. "Fight with me tomorrow. Meanwhile I want to see the copy. All of it."

He went out of the wire room and diagonally across the newsroom to his own office. He leaned in his door and said to Nancy Liggett. "Where's your boy friend?"

"He's off," she said. "Today's Thursday."

"Uh-huh," Lamin said, and went back over to Levine's desk. "Anything else?"

Levine shook his head. "Nothing."

Arnold Lamin bit off a large hunk of copy paper from a stack on the desk and began to chew it, violently. He looked across the newsroom, confirming that Jon Day Griffith was not at his desk. Griffith, with a morning paper to put out, came to work at noon. The edge would be off the story for a morning paper—the discovery, coming at the time it did, was in the province of the pm's. Still, they had only found part of the body.

...

Lamin swung back to Levine.

"Joe."

"Yes, Arn."

"If you found part of a body in a manhole, where would you look for the rest of it?"

"The next manhole."

Lamin picked up the phone. "Get me reference." He removed the paper from his mouth, working it swiftly between the fingers of his free hand into an outsize spit-ball. "Hello,

Charley? How you feel? This is Lamin. No, Christ, I don't want to hear about your fistula. Listen. See if we have topographical maps of the city of New York. Not, not typographical. Listen, you bastard, I want the map that has where the manholes are. How the hell do I know? Maybe the Department of Water Supply. You know the maps, in the big loose-leaf things. I want the one with the twenty-three hundred block of east a hundred and ninety-fourth. Bronx. Get it up here. Yeah, I heard the joke about the manhole. And right away." '

When he turned around again, Lamin saw that Jon Day Griffith had come into the newsroom. Lamin looked at the clock. It was just shy of eleven-thirty. It was something he had noticed before in Griffith, a kind of animal sense of danger. Nineteen Thursdays out of twenty he would be late to work. Today he was early.

Lamin moved quickly across the newsroom. Griffith was standing at his desk, a large walnut beauty set against the far window at the end of the newsroom opposite the little glass-enclosed telegraph room. Griffith had not removed his overcoat or hat; he was standing at his desk, in an area set off from the rest of the room by a little inner fence of walnut stain, about three feet high. He was reading the bulletin on Laura Grabowski.

Lamin came through the little spring-door in the wooden barrier and said, "That's all we have so far, Jon. I've got three men on the way up there, and I think Meedy's going too. I can't raise him at headquarters."

Griffith turned to look at him. He was taller than Lamin, though not so good-looking, and he had a way of peering as he talked.

"Boy," he said now, "am I hung over."

"You don't look it," Lamin said.

"That's the worst kind of hangover. You should have seen me last night. I got blind as a hawk with Kyne and that blonde bitch he's married to."

"Where was this?"

"Downstairs," Griffith said. "Harry Kritzer was there. He came in with them and went out with them. I was just part of the furnishings. I don't like the way that Kritzer pals around with the Great God Pan."

"Neither do I," Lamin said. "Neither do I." If they had been able to read each other's mind, they would have known, Lamin and Griffith, that they were each thinking of the same thing: the idle conversations between Charles and Roger in John Marquand's *Point of No Return*. Charles and Roger worked in a bank, but they were candidates for a dead man's job.

"Well," Griffith said now, "I suppose we're in for a dandy day of it. You know what I'd like to do, Am? I'd like to get that big-chested women's writer of ours out to this kid's house to talk to the mother and the father."

"I already set that up," Lamin said.

"I would also like to check the rest of the manholes in that neighborhood."

"I sent downstairs for the city map on that, so we can locate them."

"You're a busy little bee," Jon Day Griffith said.

"It's a hell of a story," Lamin said. "You all right?"

"I'm fine," Griffith said. "Hung over, as I say, but fine."

"Well," Lamin said, "I'll be in my office."

The competition between them now was something almost alive.

Jon Day Griffith watched Lamin walk back across the room. Then he picked up his telephone and said, "Get me Ed Mobley at his home."

Sam Knight, the chief makeup man for the *Sentinel*, came through the swinging wooden half-door and said, "It's in the fan, Jon. I'm saving seven and eight on one and leaving six open." Knight reported to Griffith daily in this fashion, though usually not so early in the day. What he was saying was that he would, in entering the day's makeup for the first edition of the next morning's *Sentinel*—an edition that would hit the streets at seven-thirty in the evening—leave open the seventh and eighth columns, or the choice right-hand space, of page one, plus the entirety of page six.

"No," Griffith said now. "I'll take four and the top half of five. The hell with six. And get that Ukrainian that works for Mark Loving to draw us a map of the area with all those beautiful black German crosses he uses."

"I got a big menswear ad for page four," Knight said.

"Well, combine it with the jockstraps on page twelve,"

Griffith said. "And tell Archie to come over."

The phone rang. It was Mobley.

"Ed," Griffith said into the telephone, "I'm hung over and they found the little girl's body and Lamin's got everybody in Christ's creation out covering it. What do you mean, you got engaged? That was two nights ago. When I got engaged, I didn't even know it. Yeah, fine, you've been engaged for forty-eight hours almost. It's delicious, that's what it is. I am putting you in for the Croix de Guerre. Now do me a favor please and get your ass up to the Bronx."

Archie Ginsberg, the telegraph editor of the *Sentinel*, came in and stood beside Griffith's desk.

"Listen," Griffith said, still talking into the phone, "quit threatening me with a mandamus from the Newspaper Guild. I know it's your day off. Ginsberg is standing here whistling in my ear, I haven't even had a chance to get my coat off, I'm hung over like no poor unhappy bastard in history, and Lamin's off and running like Man o' War. Yes. I been trying to tell you that. Wait a minute." He consulted the bulletin in his hand. "Twenty-three-oh-eight-three East one-nine-four. How the hell do I know? Get a cab. Call me when you get there."

He hung up and turned to Archie Ginsberg. The latter was a small, young, round man who, at the age of thirty, had a wife, three children, and a promising future in the newspaper business.

"What you got?" Griffith said to him.

"A fair story from Iran," Ginsberg said. "Two or three medium stories from Washington. A lousy plane crash in Oklahoma, and the Far East."

"Good," Griffith said. "I want nothing over three-fifty." He paused for a moment. "No, that's too much. We have a crime hearing here in town, too. Keep all your stories to three hundred words or less."

"My pleasure," Archie Ginsberg said.

"And use a little Kyne copy for a change," Griffith said. "The boss is getting tired of seeing nothing but AP and INS in his paper."

"KPS stinks," Archie said.

"Give me a memo to that effect," Griffith said. "And while you're at it, pin the responsibility on Mr. Lamin. I shall send it in to Mr. Kyne for his inspection. Maybe you'll get a raise."

"Maybe you'll get a raise, too."

"The significance of that," Jon Day Griffith said, "escapes me for the moment, but I am assuming you are on my team. Who'd you bet on?"

"Lamin," Archie Ginsberg said.

"Well," Griffith said, "I don't blame you."

Burt Healey came over to the little wooden partition and said, "They're getting more now. Wes Collier just phoned in."

"What've they got?"

"We won't know till they put it out. Lamin's treating this one like the Hope diamond."

"Have AP or INS got anything?"

"Not yet."

"Well, Mobley's on his way up there," Griffith said. "When he calls in, we'll sit down, you and I, and figure this thing out for the first run."

A copy boy came over with a bulletin. He handed it to Griffith.

NEW LEAD BODY

NEW YORK—(EPS)—THE ARMLESS BODY OF EIGHT-YEAR-OLD LAURA GRABOWSKI, MISSING FROM HER BRONX HOME SINCE TUESDAY, WAS FOUND WRAPPED IN NEWSPAPER IN A MANHOLE A BLOCK AWAY TODAY.

(MORE)

Across the newsroom, another copy boy was handing Joe Levine, Lamin's desk man, a copy of the rival INS bulletin on the same subject.

Levine read it, exclaimed in a guttural voice, and strode into Lamin's office. "Arn," he said, "INS has a leg missing, too."

"What have we got? Just the two arms?"

"That's all."

"Damn that Collier," Lamin said. "I always said he took dope."

"Maybe INS is wrong," Levine said.

"Yes," Lamin said, "and maybe I'll be working for INS in the morning."

The phone buzzed at his elbow. He picked it up. "Hello? Yuh, Bill." He looked at Levine. "It's Bill Gusskind. Yes, Bill, all right, Joe will be back at his desk in a minute and he can take it from you. Listen, Bill, did you see the body? Well, listen, INS has got two arms and a leg missing and all we got is two arms. Yuh. Yuh. You sure? All right, all right, I know Collier was in a hurry. Here. I'll switch you over to Joe." He took the phone away from his ear. "Take Bill on your phone," he said to Levine, who started out the door. "And take a leg off," Lamin called after him.

It was not too bad a mistake. More facts would be rolling in, and this first version of the story would be subbed out completely before long. Still, Lamin was distressed at the way the armless lead read. It was written so a simple correction would not fix it up.

His phone buzzed again. This time it was Gerald Meedy, the Kyne headquarters man. Lamin said, "Where are you? Police headquarters? I tried to get you there an hour ago. I thought you'd gone on up to the Bronx. What? Oh, for God's sake." Lamin grabbed a pencil and began to write, bending over his desk and cradling the telephone receiver against his shoulder.

When he came out of his office, he saw that Walter Kyne had come into the newsroom. Kyne and Griffith were holding conversation over on the *Sentinel* side of the room.

Lamin stopped for a moment, the notes he had just finished taking clustered in his hand. Then he walked over to them and said, "We've got something big. We've got it exclusive. I'll tell you what it is damn quickly, and then I'm going to roll on the wire with it."

Kyne's blue eyes swung to his wire chief. "Well?"

"The same man that killed this kid killed those two dames."

For a moment, Walter Kyne's face shone brightly in unmistakable, terrible triumph. It was all the more noticeable to Lamin for the look on the face of Jon Day Griffith, whose paper had broken the fact that the two women, before the little girl, had been killed by the same man.

Griffith said, "How do you know? I thought there was no..."

"Prints," Lamin said swiftly. "Good old-fashioned fingerprints. The ones on the ladder match the ones on that Judith Felton girl."

Kyne said, "How did you find out?"

"Gerald Meedy down at headquarters," Lamin said. "He just phoned me." He took care not to put undue stress upon the word "me."

Griffith said, "I thought Meedy went to the Bronx."

"No," Lamin said. "He stayed at headquarters. Apparently he's the only one who did. He went upstairs and got to talking to one of the detectives and asked the obvious question—so obvious, nobody asked it before now, or at least they never got an answer—and we've got it."

Walter Kyne put his hand on Lamin's arm. "Arn," he said, "that's damn fine work."

"I'm going to get it out," Lamin said. "If the police were just keeping quiet about this till they found the girl's body, then everybody'll have it in a little while. If it's something Meedy's got on his own, then maybe we'll still have it exclusive by the time the *Sentinel* goes in."

Griffith said. "We don't go to press for seven hours."

"It may stand up," Lamin said smoothly. "Never can tell."

Chapter Eleven

Edward Mobley wondered what fire engines would be doing here, and then he realized that they were not fire trucks, but red emergency trucks from Con Edison. The police lines were already up. He pushed his way through the crowd that swamped the avenue exit to the side street and held up his press card so the cop by the longhorse barrier could see it.

"Stick that in your hat," the cop said.

"I haven't got a hat on," Mobley said.

"Well, tie it on your lapel," the cop said. "With what?" Mobley said.

"You're a reporter," the cop said. "You're smart, not me. I'm just a cop."

"All right," Mobley said. "Dandy, and thank you." He bummed a bobby pin from a woman standing back of the barrier and clipped his press card to the lapel of the brown suitcoat he wore. Then he clambered over the police longhorse and started walking up the middle of the street.

Every manhole in the street had been thrown open. Edison workers were down inside; on either side of the street, cops were working the houses methodically, checking the basements. Against the dirty basement windows of the houses, windows that were small and precisely an inch above street level, the occasional dull sweep of a flashlight within could be seen.

Halfway down the block, Mobley ran into Hamilton of KPS.

"That's where they found it," Hamilton said, pointing at a roped-off manhole. "Found what?"

"The body. The head and torso and one leg."

"Tied together?"

"Sure." Hamilton nodded energetically.' "Only things missing are one leg and two arms."

"That's all, hey?"

"That's all. They're looking for them now."

Mobley kept on walking. He got to the end of the block, found the police lines extended in either direction so that the entire area was roped off from the public. The police were working in from the avenue where Mobley had first crossed the longhorse line, figuring the killer would work away from the avenue where the lights were.

Mobley turned to his right, walked another block, looked in to his right and saw another Con Edison truck and a police car parked halfway up the street. He started to turn into this block; as he did, a black police car, the kind the detectives used, gunned past him and, brakes squealing, turned to the right into the side street one block farther on. A green and white patrol car followed.

Mobley got there on the run, turned the corner, and found a group of cops and detectives circled around another manhole. Up close, Mobley could see the green-gray uniform of a Con Edison worker emerging from the manhole.

He held a soggy batch of newspapers, and when he lay them on the asphalt of the street beside the manhole they fell open, revealing their red-white contents.

A cry, a babble, went up from someplace above, and Mobley turned to see the white faces of women and men looking out of the apartment windows on either side of the street. He straightened up, turned, and saw Miller, one of the men from an opposition afternoon paper, coming toward him, running.

"What is it, Ed?"

"Look for yourself," Mobley said.

Miller looked. "Holy Mary," he said. "Holy Mother of Jesus."

"That's the rest of it," Mobley said. He was not looking. One look had been enough.

"Holy Mother of Christ," Miller said. "Where's the nearest phone?"

"Cigar store on the avenue," Mobley said, and gestured in the other direction. Miller took off at a run.

Quickly, evenly, Edward Mobley stepped up on the sidewalk. It would take Miller a full minute to reach the avenue and get his paper on the phone. Now Mobley stepped into the doorway of the nearest apartment house. On the window to the right of the doorway, a sign said, "G. GOLDSTEIN M.D." Mobley went into the lobby and found the door to the first apartment on the right. A brass plate on the door said "RING BELL AND WALK IN." Mobley walked in without ringing the bell. There was a small waiting room, with no one waiting there. Beyond it, there was a small corridor, and in a little room off the corridor, a room that was obviously a small laboratory, Mobley found the phone. He picked it up and dialed his office. There was a sound in the corridor, and a little man with a black mustache looked in on him inquisitively.

"Hello, doctor," Mobley said, and patted the card on his lapel. "Press."

Chapter Twelve

Kyne, Griffith and Lamin were still standing together in the newsroom, talking, when Burt Healey came over and said to Griffith, "Jon, Ed's on the wire."

"I'll take it here," Griffith said, and reached for the phone on the nearest desk. Lamin and Kyne stood there as he talked. Finally, he called over to Healey, "Burt, I'm giving this to rewrite." He turned to Lamin and Kyne. "Two blocks away," he said, "in another manhole." His voice was unsteady. "A leg and two arms. Wrapped in newspaper."

Walter Kyne said, "Oh, Jesus."

"Give me a copy of what you've got," Lamin said to Jon Griffith. "I'll give you a copy of mine."

"Son of a bitch," Griffith said. "How we going to fit all that into a headline?"

"I want to see it," Kyne said to him. "I want the works before it goes downstairs."

More than on the story itself, more than on the photographs of different aspects of the story that began piling on his desk, more than on the artist's drawings, the history of the other murders, the weeping yarn that Mildred Donner did on the dead girl's parents, the story of a twenty-five state police alarm, the fact that now page one was thrown open unlimited with three full jump pages inside —more than on any of these, Jon Day Griffith worked, all by himself, on the headline that would sell his newspaper.

Into the headline he had to get these facts: that Laura's severed body had been found, that she had been killed by the same man who had killed two other women—if, indeed, it was a man who had committed the crimes—and that, in the exquisite balance of deadline timing that had given the discovery of the body to the afternoon papers, it still had to be pointed out nonetheless, that Laura Grabowski was dead. Somehow he must identify the murderer as someone who had murdered three times, identify him (or her) immediately and forever in the mind of the forgetful reader public. And he must do all this in headline type so big that, stretching across a full eight columns, it would accommodate no more than fifteen letters or spaces in each of two lines.

But Jon Day Griffith had a bent for writing headlines. He made two or three false starts, alternately depressed and elated by the fact that Meedy's scoop linking the killer to the other murders—a scoop already credited by Kyne to Lamin—was still holding up. No one else had it.

On his fourth try, Griffith said it all, in four words:

LIPSTICK SLAYER BUTCHERED LAURA

Chapter Thirteen

Sweetheart," announced Mark Loving, the director of Kyne World Features, "that was one doll of a story you did today."

"It was terrible," Mildred said. "I cried and cried."

"It was beautiful," Loving said. "I picked up the paper tonight and there was my darling, smack on page one."

"I like the women's page better," Mildred said. They were drinking together downstairs in the Dell, and she had removed her hat so that her hair, only slightly the worse for chestnut rinse, shone, almost tawny, in the blue light from the ceiling.

There were two other couples in the Dell tonight, down at the far end of the bar. Loving and Mildred were standing near the end of the bar toward the front staircase. The juke box behind them was playing something by Les Paul and Mary Ford.

"You know how they do that?" Loving asked.

"How who does what?"

"Les Paul and Mary Ford," Loving said. "They do it on tape, and then they run the tape again and do it over again a different way, and then they do it again and so forth. What they finally record is the taped result, see, after they run it through four or five times."

"Oh," Mildred said. "Mark, why don't you dance with me?"

"To that?"

"You can dance to it," she said. "Come on."

"No," Loving said. "I feel like a hottentot or something dancing in here. Besides, I want to talk."

Mildred moved her head, so that she was looking straight ahead at her drink. "Well," she said, "little boy wants to talk."

"That's right."

"Is that why you won't go home to your wife? Won't she listen to you?"

"Do me a favor, don't start in on my wife. You know what it is with me and my wife. Leave it alone."

"She's got that money, doesn't she?"

"Leave it alone."

"You like a lot of money, don't you? That's why you want

Walter Kyne to give you the big job. Not for power or prestige or even . ..." She lifted her glass .... "or even for the good you might do if you had the job. No, not you."

Loving said evenly, watching her, "I'm glad you think I might do some good if I got the job."

Mildred Donner did not respond at once. Then she put her hand up to her face so that the fingers moved downward over her eye, almost wearily. She said, "Ah, I'm sorry, sweetheart. It was terrible today, and I guess I haven't got over it."

"Was it really bad?" Mark Loving did not particularly want to hear the details, but he knew she needed to talk it out.

He had known many women, and many women wished they had known him. He was tall, and a two-hundred pounder. His jaw was pronounced, and cleft by a deep, narrow dimple. His hair was short and curly, only a step away from being crinkly, and his wife's money had helped bring to him an air of jaunty worldliness that sometimes he felt even himself. Of the women he had known, however, none had given so much, demanded so little, nor appealed so to his masculine animal eye—at least, not these things together in combination—as did Mildred Donner. It was only infrequently, tonight being one of those occasional times, that she showed she needed him, if only to listen. She would have another drink, and another, and they would end up at her apartment. Somehow, listening to her now, the prospective enjoyment seemed heightened in Mark Loving's imagination. He quietly signaled Carlo, the bartender, for a refill, and turned, elbow on bar, chin in palm, to listen to Mildred.

"You know what was the most terrible thing?" she said. "The most terrible? It was when the mother found out she'd been strangled." Mildred's voice, which could be high and oppressive, was low now, and in the quiet of the room it sounded a little dead. "She began to laugh. She was happy. She was really happy."

"I don't think she was happy," Mark Loving said.

"No, but in this terrible way she was. Because . . . well, she was happy because she knew her little girl hadn't been alive when he ..." She stopped and reached for her drink.

"You mean when he chopped her up," Loving said, slowly and evenly, watching Mildred as she spoke. He had a feeling that he now was invading licentiously upon her privacy.

Some years ago he had gone to a doctor who shared a suite of offices with four or five other doctors, and the examining room his doctor used was separated from the examining room of a gynecologist by a thin wall, the top half of which was frosted glass. The doctor had left Mark Loving behind in the room to dress, and Loving, looking toward the voices in the next room, found suddenly he could, possibly more by a mistake in lighting than anything else, see through. For a long time afterward he used to wonder wryly what would have happened if his doctor had been aware of this while he was in the process of checking his pulse and blood pressure.

But this, now, with Mildred, was the same animal feeling of secret enjoyment, a clandestine spy game which he found, in its own way, necessary. It was necessary because he had to substitute something for the excitement of the chase, an excitement most profound and needful to him, and one that had driven him quickly from his wife. It might also, some day, drive him from Mildred. What meant the least to him, and possibly the most to her, was the having.

"Mil," he said now to her, "some day maybe we'll move you out of this. We'll get you an inside job where all you have to do is go to fashion shows and the operas and the Broadway openings and a coronation every once in a while, and when Lamin or Griffith or somebody tells you to go cover a murder or a suicide or a plane crash, you can just tell them to go to hell, and tell them I said so. We might even make you women's editor for the whole shebang."

She put her head back and looked at him. "Baby," she breathed. "I only hope so."

"Some day," Mark Loving went on, running his thumb idly over the rim of his glass of whisky, "somebody besides me will be in charge of the care and the feeding and screwing of Lola and Bat Mercury and all our other goddam comic strips. Some day the crossword puzzles and the bridge columns and the daily pithy sayings will be somebody else's worry, and I . . ." His face opened, almost petal-like, into a smile .... "will be able to take care of my sweetheart."

She smiled, a personal smile. "Do you think you have a chance?"

"I don't know," Loving said slowly. "Carlo, give us one more here. I wish I could think of some way to move in on this story of the little girl. Kyne's working a gimmick with it. I wish I *knew* somebody."

"Don't you know anybody?"

"Oh, sure," Loving said. "I know the headwaiter at the Stork and the Colony and Twenty-one, and they know me at Voisin and the Pierre. I know the fellow at the horse show, and he knows the fellow at the dog show, and the fellow at the dog show knows Farley and Farley knows the people at the Waldorf and the people at the Waldorf know me. So what? Walter Kyne knows everybody at the Colony and Twenty-one too. The thing is, I don't know any cops."

Mildred said, "I don't think Lamin or Griffith know any policemen either."

"No, but they've got people working for them."

"Why don't you get somebody to work for you?"

"Who?"

"What about Ed Mobley? I think he knows some policemen."

"Let me tell you the facts of life," Loving said to her. "Mobley's spoken for. He's Griffith's boy."

"Couldn't you talk to him about it? He always struck me as somebody you could talk to."

Loving began to rub his chin. "Honeybabe," he said, "you really want me to have this job of McCrady's?"

"Oh," she said, "you know I want it. You ought to hear the way I've been talking you up to people. Anybody who'd listen. How you know all about crimes and murders and how to catch killers and how to run Kyne the way McCrady did."

"Well," Mark Loving said, and stared thoughtfully at his glass. "Let me say something. Let me begin by saying you're right."

"Right about what?"

"About Ed Mobley."

"You mean, he knows policemen?"

"I mean, if I had anybody working in my corner, I'd want him."

"Well, talk to him, Mark," Mildred said. "Surely it won't do you any harm."

"It might do me a great deal of harm. If he reacts wrong,

what happens? He goes and blats it out to Griffith and then where am I?"

"I don't know," Mildred Donner said. "If it's such a long shot, the way you say it is; if you don't have a chance anyway, well, I certainly don't see what harm it can do you."

Loving raised his eyebrows. "You're right. I am a long shot. A long shot going in. And I would talk to Mobley. Believe me, I would. If I thought it would do any good."

"Don't you think it would?"

"No."

"You're afraid you don't know him well enough?" He nodded.

"You're being silly," Mildred said. "I'm not being silly," Loving said. He took her hand in his. "Mil, you want me to get this job?"

She patted his hand. "You don't have to ask that." Mark Loving leaned forward. "Go to Mobley for me."

"What?"

"You," Loving said quickly. "You know him, Mil, you know him much better than I do. You can tell him about me. He'll listen. I've seen him look at you."

He sat back now and watched her. She said what he had known she must say. She said, "You've seen him look at me?"

"Those eyes of his," Loving said. "Have you ever noticed those eyes?"

"Yes," she said. "I've noticed them."

It was an implied rebuke to his own charms, but now Mark Loving did not mind. "I think," he said, talking slowly once again, "that Mobley would do almost anything for you."

She sat still for a moment, not looking at him. Then she said, "That Nancy somebody in Lamin's office might not like it. I've seen her with him a lot."

"I wouldn't let that worry me."

"All right, then." She turned and looked him fully in the face. "I know what you want me to say. How far do I have to go to say it?"

Mark Loving smiled at her. There was nothing that appealed more to his intellect than what he credited himself with having, an ability to anticipate questions, to have the answer swiftly prepared, to channel conversations into a series, almost Platonic in concept, of alternate choices, one choice each time being impossible.

Smiling now, he said to her, "Mildred, we're adults. I love you, love you very completely. Anything you may do out of love for me will only make me love you more."

She shook her head, wonderingly, and smiled back. "I love you too, Mark."

"Let's get out of here," he said. "Carlo, a check."

"They don't have checks here," Mildred said.

"I get in the habit," Loving said. "Come on. I want to take you home."

She reached for her purse and gloves. "Do you want to stay tonight?"

"About an hour anyway," Loving said.

"My," she said. "What ever happened to three-time Charley?"

"He's two-time Tom tonight," Loving said. He grinned, and it was not until they were sitting close in the back seat of the taxicab, he with his hand on her underneath her coat, that he realized how suddenly and completely she had snapped out of her earlier mood, her mood of sadness and tears over the dead child. He realized, too, that the word for himself, Mark Loving, director of Kyne World Features, was panderer; and the bad thing about that, the unequal thing, was that he did not think Mildred Donner —with her full, sensuous body and the kind of wanton drive that could bring a strange dead-alive look to her eyes and foul, full-throated words bursting from her lips—realized what he was doing. The reason she did not realize it, he knew, was that she wanted Edward Mobley as she had wanted other men before, and that now she had the excuse, added to the wherewithal, to get him.

And now Mark wanted Mildred, and the fierceness of him, when they had reached her apartment, startled her almost into forgetting that the dark-eyed Mobley would be, by executive order, hers.

Chapter Fourteen

In the cool December midnight the editorial floors of the O.K. and the N.K. buildings cut a wide ruler of light through the blackness of the midtown office blocks. The clock behind Jon Day Griffith's desk showed five minutes to midnight. He said to Burt Healey, "Did you make that subhead for the three-star?"

"Just," Healey said.

Under the headline

LIPSTICK SLAYER BUTCHERED LAURA

in the first two editions of the next morning's *Sentinel*, a one-line subhead had read:

STRANGLED TOT FIRST

Walter Kyne had not liked it.

"An eight-year-old girl is no longer a tot," he said. "A tot is a toddler."

"I know a tot is a toddler," Griffith had said. "But if you call her a girl you automatically think of a broad in her teens or older, and you can't call her a child because it's too long."

"You could call her a girl," Kyne said. Through the entire day he had kept his suit coat on, his white shirt white, his tie tied. "Everybody knows who you're talking about."

"I don't like 'girl'," Griffith said.

"And I don't like 'tot'," Kyne said. "So get it out of there."

"Are you telling me to use 'girl'?"

"I'm not telling you anything. It's your newspaper. I'm just saying get 'tot' out of there."

So Griffith had gone back to his desk, to stare moodily at

STRANGLED TOT FIRST

"It is true," he said to Burt Healey. "Everybody knows who we're talking about."

"Sure they do," Healey had said.

So Griffith changed it for the three-star edition:

Now on his desk was a selection of pictures snapped by the men of Harry Kritzer's Kynpix. There was a question of psychology in choosing the right picture to go into the late morning editions of the paper. The early editions, on the street the night before, could shout blood, but the public preferred tears with its breakfast.

Kritzer had organized his cameramen well. There were any number of crying shots that Griffith could use to replace the vivid four-column picture that ran in the one-star and two-star: a picture showing a detective standing full length and looking down at a newspaper parcel that contained one of Laura Grabowski's arms. Above the parcel, expertly montaged at Harry Kritzer's behest, was a childhood head-and-shoulders shot of Laura laughing. Just enough of her dress showed in the inset to enable the caption writer to point out she would be buried in it.

Jon Day Griffith picked up the phone. "Get me Harry Kritzer in his office," he told the operator on the night board. She was new, and you had to tell her not only who you wanted but where he was most likely to be found. Even now, something went wrong. Apparently Kritzer Was on the phone and she had cut in on the line, because what Griffith heard next was Kritzer's voice and that of a woman.

"I've been at mother's since ten o'clock," the woman was saying. Her voice seemed momentarily familiar to Griffith but in his wearied state he did not give it much thought.

"All right," Harry Kritzer was saying, "all right."

"I can't stay with her indefinitely," the voice said.

Jon Day Griffith got the feeling he was listening unprofitably, and hung up the phone.

In a moment, it buzzed. He picked it up and the operator said, "Did you get Mr. Kritzer?"

"Not yet," Griffith said.

"Well, you can have him now," the operator said. There was a buzzing, and Harry Kritzer picked up his phone.

"I've got all the shots," Griffith said. "You got any ideas for the three-star?"

"Let me come out there," Kritzer said. "We'll hash it over."

Waiting for him, Griffith found himself thinking again, in tired, faint curiosity, of the woman's voice on the phone with Harry Kritzer. He knew the voice, and yet there was no placing it. Did Kritzer have a broad stashed on the side? There was no reason for him not to. Despite his relative shortness of physical stature, the slight but noticeable paunch, the red face and the measured, side-to-side walk, Harry Kritzer, Griffith knew, was not unattractive to women. "You know," Griffith's wife Helen had said after meeting Kritzer for the first time, "my first impulse was to hug him. He seems like such a good man, and so alone."

"He drinks worse than I do," Griffith had said.

"Nobody drinks worse than you do," Helen Griffith said. "I bet he's tender, too."

"Why don't you take a bite out of him and see?"

"No, I mean tender in the way he touches. He looks at you as if you were something very special, something to be handled … well, lovingly."

"He doesn't look at me that way," Griffith said, "but if you want to try him out, I'll try to set it up. He has a knockout of a darkroom down at the office. You could go in there and let him develop you."

"Well, I'd still like to hug him," Helen Griffith said.

By now, in his musings, Griffith had come to the conclusion that Kritzer was having an affair with whoever it was on the phone. He put a hand across his eyes and thought about it, but he could not place the voice. Nor, at the moment, did he want to.

Chapter Fifteen

These things Robert Manners wanted, these were the things for which he would wish upon a star, implore the black skies, claw upon the gates of the gods: To have the power to become satisfied; To be blessed with unending manhood; To be enabled to make himself invisible. In his daydreams of fancy, he would be invisible. He would walk through the doors of chorus girls' dressing rooms, of hotel rooms in Las Vegas, of apartments where lovely models lived. They would not see him, would awake to think they were dreaming, would find unreasonable the thought of crying out for help. Then would he wreak his will!

Then he would know satisfaction, and yet, should dissatisfaction return, he would have within him the virility and the will to commit anew the act; and remorse and reflection, and conscience, would be driven forever from him.

Now let us, he said to himself, be realists: let us confront the knowledge that no man can be made invisible. Let us as a secondary premise assume no man's virility is constant and unending.

But was it impossible, was it asking much too much, that he could be satisfied? Or, falling even short of that, could he at least be freed of the torment which came to him each time when a crime was done?

Now again, failing even in this, could he at least—at very least—be able to keep his word, to obey himself, when, after every time, he told himself: Never again?

The memory of the open garage, and the ladder, and the open window and the little girl who looked up at him as she said, "I'm sleepy," and what it was like in her room inside the open window—all of this was second to the memory of the short flight of concrete stairs, guarded by the rusted rail of cast iron, leading down to The back entrance to the basement; the old iron door that fell inward as he pushed it, and the wash tubs there, and the blade of the axe in the corner, sharp and shining in the musty environs of the old cellar.

The dead child in his arms and the blood that was thick

and promising, the great stack of newspapers in the corner, and the two trips he made with the newly-wrapped packages, the first manhole with its lid askew, the second one that he found a block away—all this was behind him in his mind, while at the forefront was the aged flight of concrete steps and the axe, glistening and gleaming and made bright.

If only, Robert Manners said to himself again now, if only I could be made invisible. And it came to him, thinking of it, that indeed they were looking for him everywhere, but were unable to find him, and that, indeed again, he was invisible.

No, only God was invisible. But then could not he, Robert Manners, be thought of as the agent and the functionary of the Lord? Was he not Jeremiah, listening to the wrath of God and carrying it with him? Did he not know the purpose and the words, know them by heart from days and nights gone by when his mother sat by him and read to him from the Bible? And was not God's wrath, as revealed to Jeremiah, the wrath against womankind of Robert Manners?

Jeremiah.

"Make bright the arrows; gather the shields: the LORD hath raised up the spirit of the kings of the Medes: for his device is against Babylon, to destroy it: because it is the vengeance of the LORD, the vengeance of his temple."

So, then, thought Robert Manners, and more:

"Set ye up a standard in the land, blow the trumpet among the nations, prepare the nations against her, call together against her the kingdoms of Ararat, Minni, and Ashchenaz; appoint a captain against her; cause the horses to come up as the rough caterpillars.

"And the land shall tremble and sorrow: . . ."

It was a walk of five blocks from the next-to-last stop on the Canarsie line of the BMT subway to the smallish brick houses where, when he was through with college classes at the end of the week, Robert Manners came home. His parents lived in the third house from the corner. His father drove a road-construction truck during the day. His mother was a small, sickly woman whose tongue was bitter, and quick, and repetitive.

This was Thursday night, and Robert Manners had no classes on Friday, so he had come home.

Be home, he said to himself, and that will make it harder for you to disobey your own command: for never, never, never will you do something like that again. You have gone thus far without being known. You will not go farther.

It was a little after eight o'clock at night when he got home. He met his father on the street outside the house. The father had been down to the candy store, at the end of the block in the other direction, to get the early edition of the morning paper.

They went to the front door together.

"Your mother had supper ready," the father said.

"I got tied up," Robert said.

"You should have called her."

"I was already in the subway. We waited for a long time at one of the stations. I don't know what held up the train."

His father grunted and found the key to the door. He kept his keys on a large ring, and when he brought them out of his pocket he moved his hand quickly away from his body, bringing it around toward the keyhole in a wide arc.

They went in and Robert's mother heard them and came into the living room from the kitchen. The apron she wore was tied neatly and tightly. Her black hair was beginning to gray, and her face was birdlike, seeming even smaller than it was in contrast to the large figure of her husband.

"Oh, Robert," she said, "darling," and, lifting her head and arms, drew a long kiss from his mouth. "I thought you were coming for supper."

"I got held up," Robert Manners said.

"George, did you bring a paper?"

"I got the *Sentinel!*" George Manners said. "All about they found the kid."

"It was on the radio this noon," the mother said.

"There's a lot of pictures," the father said. He unfolded the paper he held and Robert Manners, standing beside him, read:

LIPSTICK SLAYER BUTCHERED LAURA
New York Sentinel
STRANGLED TOT FIRST

Then, on either side of the four-column picture that ran in the center of the paper beneath the subhead, there were two-column stories. The one on the right hand side began:

by EDWARD MOBLEY

The dismembered body of eight-year-old Laura Grabowski, who disappeared from her Bronx home two days ago, was found today and a shocked and aroused police force stalked as the killer a person already responsible for the deaths of two New York women—the terrible, unknown "lipstick slayer."

The story on the left hand side began:

by GERALD MEEDY

Fingerprints found Tuesday on the ladder down which little Laura Grabowski was carried to death have been matched to those in the apartment of 44-year-old Lena Tally, strangled to death four months ago, the Kyne newspapers and Kyne Press Service learned exclusively today. As was also first revealed exclusively in the New York Sentinel, police already had! linked the killer of the Tally woman to the more recent death of Judith Felton, attractive library girl.

"Here," Robert Manners' mother said. "Let me see."

"I'm reading it," her husband said.

"I think they're crazy," Robert Manners said.

"You think who's crazy?"

"The newspapers."

"You don't think this is an important story for them?"

"It doesn't belong all over page one. Besides, look at that picture. Who likes to see a picture like that?"

"Let me see the picture," his mother said, and stood on tiptoe to look at it alongside her husband's shoulder. "You mean they found the body? In that?"

"Just one of the arms," the father said.

"Well, let me see it," she said, and craned her neck so that the artery stood out in her throat.

"Well," her husband said to the son, "I think *you're* crazy."

"Why? Because it's all cheap publicity to sell papers?"

"It's important," the father said. His voice had a shaggy, dogged quality. "You don't think things like this are important, you're crazy."

"And besides," Robert Manners said, "I'll prove it to you. Look at that headline. Whoever heard of calling an eight-year-old a tot?"

"What's wrong with that?"

"A tot is an infant," Robert said flatly.

"So why then did the newspaper call her a tot?"

"To sell more papers."

"Ah," George Manners said to his son, "you're 'way nuts, like I say."

"Well," Robert Manners said, "all I can say is I'm not going to read it."

"Listen to the big college man," his father said.

"I'm going up to my room," Robert said.

"Go ahead," his father said.

Robert Manners went upstairs to his room on the second floor.' It was a small room, quiet and sharply distinct from the room he had at the dormitory in the Bronx, where his books had strange, medical-sounding titles and the locked suitcase in the corner gave off the faint, musky smell of soiled feminine undergarments.

Now he lay down on his bed, snapping on the light on the bed table and reaching for the book on the under-shelf. He heard the faint rap on his door and said, "Come," and his mother opened the door and came in, sitting on the edge of the bed and smiling down at him.

"What are you reading, sweetheart?"

"Bible," Robert Manners said. "Jeremiah."

"Read it to me," she said.

Robert Manners turned his shoulder, lying on his side with the book on the pillow in the light of the bedlamp.

"'They shall hold the bow and the lance: they are cruel, and will not show mercy: their voice shall roar like the sea, and they shall ride upon horses, every one put in array, like a man to the battle, against thee, O daughter of Babylon.'

"'Behold, he shall come up like a lion from the swelling of Jordan unto the habitation of the strong: but I will make them suddenly run away from her: and who is a chosen man, that I may appoint over her? for who is like me? and who will appoint me the time? and who is that shepherd that will stand before me?' "

His cool, low voice seemed loud in the smallness of the room. His mother smiled dreamily, looking at his head, his shoulders. She said, "But you skipped a passage."

"What?" He said it sharply, turning his head quickly to look at her.

Was it possible, he asked himself now, to hate your own mother? Was it possible to think of hating her for a cause so unimportant as this—that he had skipped a verse because the verse had, to him, no particular meaning, and that she, exact and all-knowing and remembering and taking everything and giving nothing—that she would stop him to remind him, to have it her way?

"You skipped verse forty-three," his mother said. "About the king of Babylon."

"No, I didn't."

"Of course you did, darling. Here, let me see."

Robert Manners said levelly, "Get away."

"I only wanted to see it for a minute."

"Read it in your own Bible. Maybe mine's different."

"Well," his mother said, "I never heard of ..."

"Some Bibles are different."

Sitting there, looking at him, she felt a coldness, a tightness: a feeling she had had before, but one that seemed ever more strong. Nor was it entirely an unpleasant sensation. Now she smiled warmly at him and said, "Robert, do you know what I did today?"

"No. What did you do?"

"I went to Abraham and Straus and I splurged. Don't tell your father. I got stockings and handkerchiefs and heaven knows what else."

"What?"

"I don't understand you," she said. "What else did you get?"

"Oh." She put her hand out and rumpled his hair.

"You're a tease."

The trace of a smile played at the corners of his mouth. "Come on. What else?"

"Oh, Robert."

There was a subtle change in his voice. "Tell me."

"Oh, you know." Her hands played in the air. "A slip and . . ."

"And what?"

"Some panties," she said. She knew her face had reddened. Now the blood was rushing through him, pounding, and he turned his face away, wondering if she had noticed.

She sat there, looking at him. "Well," she said at last, "don't tell your father."

He did not look at her. "I won't."

"Are you tired, sweetheart?"

"A little."

"Well," she said, and sat there. After a bit, she resumed talking. "As long as you know everything I got, do you want to see them? I mean, I've been dying to show them to *somebody*."

"Sure." He said it casually.

She was gone only a few moments. She came back with the boxes, opened them on the foot of his bed, and he raised himself to look.

"Do you like the handkerchiefs, darling?"

He licked his lips, momentarily. "They're very nice. I have a very pretty mother."

"Well," she said, a little breathlessly, "don't tell your father. At least not right away. Let me tell him."

Robert Manners pointed lazily to the flat box that contained the handkerchiefs. "How many of those did you get?"

"Half a dozen."

"*It* doesn't look like half a dozen."

"Oh," she said. "No, there are five in the box. I already took one out." She put her hand inside the front of her dress to her small bosom and drew the handkerchief out. "See?"

He stared very carefully at the handkerchief and then he looked away.

"I'd better put the things back in the drawer," his mother said.

He nodded.

She went to the door. "Robert?"

"What?"

"I'm glad you're a good boy."

He turned to look at her over his shoulder.

"Just think," she said. "Some mother's son killed that little girl. Can you imagine how that mother feels tonight?"

He smiled. "I rather doubt she knows about it. And for all you know, it might have been somebody's daughter."

"I don't think a woman could have done all those terrible things."

Her son shrugged. His black eyes watched her.

"Anyway," she said, "I know I have a good son."

"Almost like I was your real son," he said.

"I've always thought of you as my real son."

"Okay," he said.

"Are you going to read some more in your Bible?"

He nodded.

"All right, darling," she said. "Don't tell your father about these."

"I won't," Robert Manners said.

Chapter Sixteen

Steven, the butler, was in his bathrobe when Walter Kyne got home. It was ten minutes after midnight, and Sutton Place was soft and still.

"Good evening, sir," Steven said.

"Hello, Steven," Walter Kyne said. "Is Mrs. Kyne back from her mother's yet?"

"Not yet, sir. Mrs. Kyne's mother wasn't feeling too well, I understood."

"Ah," Walter Kyne said, "her poor, deaf, ailing mother."

"Yes, sir," Steven said. "Shall I take your coat?"

"Please," Kyne said. "And if there is a drink in the house I will have one of those, too." He took off his coat and gave it to the butler, and then he walked up the splendidly curved staircase to the drawing-room floor of the house. When he walked into the drawing room, he found a light on beside the couch and a copy of the two-star *Sentinel* on the gold-fitted table. For a moment he gazed down at the paper. He said, aloud, "Griffith and his tots," and then: "But a good first page. Walter, you doll, you, a good first page. The best first page in New York City."

The butler came in with a highball on a tray. Walter Kyne smiled at him. "Steven?"

"Sir?"

"Tonight, Steven, I would not trade places with Bill Hearst."

"No, sir," Steven said. "Or any of his brothers," Kyne said. "That's nice, sir."

"I'm an only child, Steven," Kyne said. "I can't keep up like this indefinitely. I need a right-hand man."

The butler stood there in his bathrobe.

"A right-hand man, Steven," Walter Kyne said. "Who would you suggest?"

"I beg your pardon, sir?"

"Mr. Lamin?"

"If you say so, sir."

"Mr. Griffith? Mr. Loving? Mr. Kritzer?"

"They're all nice gentlemen," Steven said. "If I may be permitted to venture an opinion. . . ."

Kyne sat down on the couch, holding his highball, and waved airily with his free hand.

"I'd say, sir," Steven said, "that you were unusually fortunate."

"Why?"

"Having so many fine gentlemen working for you," Steven said. "May I get you something else?"

"No," Kyne said. "Thank you. Good night, Steven."

The butler went out, and Walter Kyne sat where he was, inadequately, thinking that in fact he did have many fine gentlemen working for him. What was it, he wondered, that made a man sure of himself? That made a man certain? Jon Griffith was alive and almost joyful in his work, and dedicated, and sure of himself. Arnold Lamin was a clutch hitter who rose without fail when the occasion demanded, and he was sure of himself. Harry Kritzer was quietly effective, a born pro, and he was sure of himself. And no one was more sure of himself than Mark Loving, the flamboyant, the eternal salesman. Even Steven the butler was sure of himself.

But Walter Kyne, born to the purple, wealthy and titled, married to a woman who acquiesced to his desire— a desire that had, since McCrady's death, seemed to have become more insistent, a desire whose fulfillment left him at least temporarily with a feeling of mastery, the same feeling he derived from quantities of whisky—Walter Kyne, with all this, was not sure of himself. Too often now, his fine-chiseled face was a mask, so that no one could see beneath.

Even tonight, a night of triumph, found him unsure and unsatisfied. He applied himself to his drink of whisky. When the phone rang, he got up quickly and went to answer it. It was his wife. He said, "Where are you?"

"I'm at mother's," she said.

"I thought she didn't have a phone."

"I'm in the one downstairs. What's the matter, darling?"

"Nothing," the publisher said. "Every once in a while I like to come home and find you here, is all. Especially when it's after midnight."

"Silly," she said, and paused. Then, "Well, I've got a good

surprise for you."

"What?"

"I'll be home in half an hour. Just as soon as I can get there. Mother wasn't feeling well, but she's asleep now."

The physical contemplation of his wife, had as always, a mollifying effect upon Walter Kyne. "If you hurry," he said, "you can see Steven in his b.v.d.'s."

"I'd rather see you in yours."

"That can be arranged, too. Did you see the paper?"

"It's wonderful," she said. "I got a copy at the stand on the corner."

"I didn't like that headline with the tots."

"What?"

"Where he called the girl a tot. My God, she's eight years old. Or she was."

"I thought the picture was marvelous," Dorothy said.

"I left Harry in the office," Walter Kyne said. "He'll be there for hours yet."

"Didn't you like the picture?"

"Damn right I liked it," Kyne said. "Are you coming home?"

"Fast as my legs can carry me."

"Maybe we can improve on that when you get here."

"You're terrible," she said, and hung up the phone.

Walter Kyne went back in the drawing room. Steven, as a retiring gesture, had left a fifth of Old Granddad and a seltzer bottle on a tray on the table. Kyne settled himself on the couch and picked up the *Sentinel* again.

"It is a good shot," he said aloud, looking at the picture Harry Kritzer had provided for the front page. "A good, good, good, good shot."

When he had sat there for another moment he took a resolute pull at his glass of whisky, got up and went to the phone in the hall again. He dialed the office and said, "Give me Mr. Griffith."

The night telephone operator at the other end said, "Which Mr. Griffith is that?"

"Oh," Kyne said. "Are you new there?"

"Yes, I am."

"Ring the phone where the man in charge of the *Sentinel* sits."

"Mr. Kyne isn't in."

"I'm Mr. Kyne," Kyne said. "I want Jon Day Griffith of the New York *Sentinel*."

"Oh, yes," the operator said. "I'll give him to you right away."

Griffith came on and Kyne said, "Jon, that picture on page one. You changing it?" Griffith said, "Certainly."

"It's a good picture," Kyne said.

"One," Griffith said, "I am not going to put a bad picture in its place. Two, it is not a late-edition picture. Three, we've been on the street with it since seven-thirty. We can use a replate."

"What are you using instead?"

"Same size," Griffith said. "Hell of a shot. The mother and father holding each other and crying. Then up in the upper left hand corner, the picture of the girl when she was alive. In the upper right hand corner, a picture of the open manhole. Contrast."

"That sounds good," Kyne said.

"It was Kritzer's idea." Griffith knew when to credit another man.

"Okay," Kyne said. "Good. Get some sleep when you're through."

"All right, Walter," Jon Day Griffith said. "Was there anything else?"

"Nope," Kyne said. "The paper looks good."

"See you," Griffith said, and rang off.

For the third time, Kyne entered his drawing room, sat down on the couch, and picked up the *Sentinel*. He put the paper down, mixed himself a fresh drink, and reached for the little silver bowl of peanuts on the table.

He took a peanut out and placed it on the table.

"Jon Day Griffith," he said.

He took another peanut and placed it beside the first. "Arnold Lamm."

"Harcy Kritzer," he said, and placed the third peanut centered behind the first two.

"And Mark Loving." Suffused as he was with the great moment of the big news story of the day, he was momentarily perplexed as to where the fourth peanut would go. The features that Loving was producing, features growing out of the string of unsolved murders in New York, were winning good display in papers across the country. And there were other considerations. Where the sales department of the Kyne empire had failed, Mark Loving had, little more than a week ago, signed an important, independent midwestern newspaper to a long-term contract for Kyne Press Service and Kynpix art work. The paper already subscribed to Loving's Kyne World Features.

The new midwest client actually had enough news and feature service without having to subscribe to KPS or Kynpix. But its publisher was an ambitious man. He wanted to become a member of the Associated Press' Board of Directors, an achievement that was to be accomplished through a vote of the AP membership. The ten Kyne papers all were AP members. That meant ten more votes.

Thus was the publisher persuaded by Mark Loving to subscribe to KPS and Kynpix.

"No big business," Walter Kyne said to himself now, "is complete without a blackmailer. A good blackmailer."

He lined all four peanuts up in a row.

"But who," he said, aloud, "is the best—I say best, Walter, b-e-s-t—of your men?"

He reached forward and, very carefully, inched one peanut forward from the rest.

"Lamm."

But the *Sentinel*, with its shouting, exciting front page, still stared at him.

"That Griffith," he said, and moved another peanut forward, even with the first.

The good whisky feeling was beginning to take hold of him.

"I have only," he said to the peanuts, "begun to fight." He smiled at the table. Almost gently, he murmured,

"'O Oysters' said the Carpenter,
'You've had a pleasant run'.
Shall we be trotting home again?'
But answer came there none—"

Then he ate the peanuts and washed them down with

whisky.

Chapter Seventeen

"I read someplace once," Nancy Liggett said to Edward Mobley, "that oysters and gin have a vitalizing effect on a man."

"They do," Mobley said. "And I need vitalizing." They were sitting, talking, in the inside room at Camillo's, where they had had a late supper. It was twelve-thirty, Friday morning.

"Well," Nancy said, "don't over-vitalize yourself."

"Be tough to do," Mobley said.

"Well," she said, "lay off the gin, anyway."

"It doesn't smack right," he said. He tore a small strip of paper from the cocktail napkin on the table and began to chew on it.

Nancy said, "What doesn't?"

"The business about the prints."

"The fingerprints?"

He nodded. "Look. If anybody knows anybody at headquarters, I know Kaufman. I grew up with him. We used to run from the cops together. I asked him about them. We've got a story in the paper says they matched a print on the ladder to the Tally killing. You know how many cops handled that ladder? How would there be any prints left?"

Nancy said, "You mean Gerald Meedy's story."

"Sure," Mobley said. "He says he got it upstairs from somebody downtown. I know who his somebody is. A bourbon-nosed old detective, name of Sullivan. Never moves out of his chair. All right. Now either Meedy made it up about the prints, or Sullivan is lying to him, or. . ."

"Why didn't you say something about it in the office?"

Mobley put up his hand ". . . or—just maybe—Sullivan's telling the truth. But it doesn't figure he'd tell, even if he did know. Hell, the cops have got to make an arrest. Whether it's the guy or not they've got to pull some people in. The town's running them nuts. Would a cop tell a newspaperman something like that? It's bad enough the public's killing them because they've got two killings on the blotter, they have to announce the third one was killed by the same guy?"

"You still didn't answer my question," Nancy said.

"What question?"

"Put down the drink for a minute. Why didn't you say something about it upstairs?"

Mobley shrugged. "They had the story on the wire before I found out about it. That's number one. Number two, there's a neat situation in that city room between Meedy's guy Lamin and my guy Griffith and anything you do looks like you're trying to move in. Number three, maybe the same killer did get all three. How the hell do I know? Maybe Meedy's got it."

Nancy laughed. She was wearing a grey suit tonight, with a dark blue sweater and a single strand of pearls, and the new warmth of being engaged to marry the man she loved had heightened the color in her cheeks.

"What," Mobley said, "is funny?"

"I was just thinking," she said, "about what you said about the situation upstairs between Griffith and Lamin and Meedy working for Lamin. Wouldn't it have been funny if someone had put that detective—that what's-his-name—"

"Sullivan."

She nodded briskly . . . "if someone had put Sullivan up to telling Meedy something like that just to make Lamin look bad."

Mobley shook his head seriously. "They wouldn't work that way."

"They wouldn't?"

"Damn it," Mobley said, "maybe they would, at that." His brow furrowed in concentration. "I'm trying to think who up there knows Sullivan, outside of me and Meedy and a couple of other beat men." He thought for a moment. Nancy took his hand in hers, holding it with gentle pressure and watching him.

"Oh, my God," Mobley said.

"What?" she said. "Who?"

"I know who knows Sullivan."

"Who?"

"Back from the old days when he was downtown."

"Well, who?"

Mobley began to laugh. "Harry Kritzer."

"Oh," Nancy said, "no!"

"Sure," Mobley said.

"He wouldn't do a thing like that."

"No," Mobley said, "he wouldn't."

"Well," she said, "that puts us back where we started from."

"I know," he said. "Well, you just watch this one thing. Maybe the same man killed this one as killed the other two and maybe he didn't. But you keep your eyes on those cops. They're going to arrest somebody quick, and when they do they're not going to let any Kyne exclusive about matching fingerprints bother them one way or the other."

Nancy said, "I feel sorry for Gerald Meedy."

"Why?"

"Nobody likes him."

"Because he steps on people to get what he wants."

"I don't know," Nancy said.

"He has no class," Mobley said. "A guy can be the worst bastard in the world, but if he's got something, maybe not even talent, maybe just a little class, then you have to go along with him. This guy—nothing."

"Even Lamin doesn't like him," Nancy said.

"He took him on as his beard man."

"Because he knew Griffith had you."

"Ah, it goes back before that," Mobley said. "Meedy latched onto Lamin a long time ago. He figures this guy is the up-and-comer in the organization, this is the man to work for. Tell you a funny thing. I dreamed last night I met you coming out of Meedy's hotel room."

"What? What hotel room?"

"How the hell do I know? It was the damnedest dream in history. There was one terrific line in there. You came out of his room and I said to you, "What did he do to you?' And you said, 'He canceled my subscription to *Popular Science.*'"

Nancy brought his hand up and put her cheek against it. "You're really whacko," she said fondly.

"All right," Mobley said. "It's a great line."

"I bet you dream that about all the girls."

"No. Only you and big-bust."

"Big-bust?"

"Mildred Donner. I'd like to put the blocks to her again, just to make it an even once."

"Oh," Nancy said, "you would, would you? And would you like it if I took you up on that dream of yours?"

"What? You and Meedy?"

"Yes," she said. "I'll subscribe to *Popular Science* in the morning."

"Are you going to keep Meedy on the side? He doesn't make enough to keep you."

"I most certainly am."

"'Most musical of mourners, weep anew!'" Edward Mobley said mellifluently. "'Not all to that bright station dared to climb.'"

"What bright station?"

"Your apartment."

"Who said that?"

"Shelley," Mobley said. "Is it all right if I have another drink?"

"No," Nancy said. "If we are going to be married, I don't want a drunkard for a husband. This is the time to train you. I can see you now, coming home drunk at night and beating me."

"If I come home at all. How long do you think it'll take?"

"How long do I think what'll take?"

"Training me."

"I don't know," Nancy said, "and that reminds me. In the confusion the other night the lights went out and we forgot to settle one little thing."

"I thought we remembered everything."

"Along certain lines," she said. "But just this one very small matter. Hardly worth mentioning, really."

"I know," he said, and nodded heavily. "When do we get married."

"Well?" she said. "Or are you already thinking up a way to quote John Dryden or Henry Wadsworth Longfellow telling me you've decided to back out?"

Mobley grinned. "'Since there's no help, come, let us kiss and part. Nay, I have done. You get no more of me. And I am glad, yes, glad with all my heart. That thus so cleanly I myself can free. Shake hands for ever, cancel all our vows; and when . . .'"

"Ed," Nancy said, "I warn you."

"Michael Drayton," Mobley said.

"All right," she said. "Now it's late and I have to be at work at nine and I want to know."

Mobley spread his palms. "We aren't going to get married

until we can have a honeymoon someplace. We aren't going to have a honeymoon until this murder business is over."

"As soon as it's over?"

"The minute I solve the case for Griffith and Lamin gets the job."

"All right," she said. She opened her purse and reached for her compact. "I hope they catch him."

"So do I," Mobley said. He grinned at her again. "Come on, babe, I'll take you home."

"And don't go getting ideas," she said. "It's late."

"Yes," Mobley said. "And we're both tired."

"Shut up," she said.

"Can I kiss you good night?"

"Yes."

"Did you get that lock for your front door?"

"No."

"Well, damn it," Mobley said, "get one."

Chapter Eighteen

It was ten forty-five that Thursday night when Gerald Meedy got home, He lived by himself in a half-baked apartment hotel off West End Avenue in the nineties. When he snapped on the light he saw that the maid had been there only to make the bed. The ash tray still was filled with chewing gum wrappers, and his scrap book still was open on the crumby old arm chair, where he had left it.

He took off his coat, went to the long table that he used as a desk, and picked up the scissors and the jar of paste. Of the two copies of the *Sentinel* that he had brought home, he began to run the scissors along the front page of one. He had been getting a byline for a year and a half now, and this was his third scrap book.

True, the front-page story that now he began with care to paste into the book was not his own creation. Some rewrite man in the office, sitting at the battery of desks on the *Sentinel* side of the newsroom, had done it from the facts he first had phoned to Arnold Lamin.

Still, the by-line was there:

by GERALD MEEDY

Fingerprints found Tuesday on the ladder . down which little Laura Grabowski was carried to death have been matched to those in the apartment of 44-year-old Lena Tally, strangled to death four months ago, the Kyne newspapers learned exclusively today....

Meedy stopped reading and looked, expressionless, at the wall over his bed. Some one long ago had painted the wall a hideous green. He thought of his exclusive story.

"All right," police detective Lawrence Sullivan had told him. "You asked, so I'm going to tell you. But you don't know where you got it."

"Right," Gerald Meedy had said professionally, bringing out his stenographic notebook. "You matched the prints."

"I didn't say that."

"You've got a lead."

"We have a fragmentary print," police detective Lawrence Sullivan said. "We believe it may be traced."

"To the Felton girl?"

"I didn't say that."

"The Tally woman?"

"Well," police detective Lawrence Sullivan said, "the Tally place was full of prints. If we were going to match a print, that would be a hell of a place to start."

"What do you mean, a hell of a place?"

"A good place," police detective Lawrence Sullivan said. "And remember, you don't know where you got this."

"That's grand," Gerald Meedy said, and slapped his notebook shut and left the room.

In the elevator of the headquarters building, on his way downstairs to the phone in the press room Meedy read over his notes. Something puzzled him. By the time he got down to the first floor, he realized what it was.

Police detective Lawrence Sullivan had not told him anything.

All right, Meedy, analyze it. If he didn't tell you anything, why did he tell you not to quote him?

Two reasons. One, he wasn't supposed to talk to reporters. Two, he wanted to make you think he was giving you something hot. If he wasn't supposed to talk to reporters, then chances were he only talked to you out of what he supposed were the best interests of the police department.

He wanted you to think that possibly they have a print off that ladder matched to a print in the Tally case. He wanted you to put it in the paper.

Why?

Gerald Meedy was in the press room by now. He slipped open a package of gum, wadded two pieces into his mouth, and thought.

This is why, he told himself. This is why: because a story like that will make it look like the police have a line on the killer. It will shut up the squeakers from the Board of Estimate on down for maybe forty-eight hours, and give them a chance to work.Ah, Gerald (Meedy said to himself), you're the smart one, you are.

Then why, he asked himself, on a new tack this time, did he only give it to you? Why not give it to everybody?

You were the only one around.

That's not a good enough reason.

Gerald Meedy thought some more and came up with the answer to this one, too. It was an answer not flattering to himself.

The answer (he informed himself) is that a group of reporters wouldn't have gone for a story like that. They would have asked more questions, wanted to see a check-run on the prints, phoned their desks.

Sullivan figured I wouldn't do that, Meedy said to himself.

And, he added, Sullivan was right.

He was smiling when he picked up the phone to call Arnold Lamin. If the police wanted this story planted, then they wouldn't deny it, true or false.

If it proved false, it could always be pegged back on that font of misinformation, the "police department spokesman."

If it were true, then Arnold Lamin was home free. And Arnold Lamin had made certain representations to Gerald Meedy. Only yesterday, Lamin had told him, "Gerald, I've been watching your work. I want you to keep it up, and if the time ever comes that I can do something for you in a positive way in this organization, I just might do it."

"You know I'm with you," Meedy had responded—it was in the narrow hallway of the N.K. building, just outside the spanking new men's room—and he had been rewarded by a leathery Lamin smile.

Even without proof—no more than the cryptic, quite possibly planted words of police detective Lawrence Sullivan—Meedy had a feeling that the same murderer had killed the two women and the little girl.

Nor was he, indeed, alone. Did not Walter Kyne, the publisher, think the same thing?

Now, carefully completing his pasting job in his furnished room, Gerald Meedy smiled anew. It was hot in his room: the radiator under the window served him mightily, winter, spring and fall. Under the matted brown hair by his ears and the top of his neck, he could feel the sweat, oily and heavy. He took off his coat and loosened his tie. Tomorrow on his way to work he would go first to the little place of Ah Wong, the laundryman on ninety-sixth street, and pick up the bundle of shirts. Tomorrow the maid would come and change the linen on his bed; perhaps vacuum the threadbare rug, empty the ash tray and the waste basket.

Tomorrow, perhaps, he would walk into the office, on his way back from headquarters, just in time to meet Nancy Liggett on her way down in the elevator. She would be wearing a low-cut dress, and she would smile at him, and he would take her out and get her very drunk, and under his spell she would return home with him, confess that Mobley was no more than a passing fancy, spend the night with him.

He had been a long time between women, Gerald Meedy. He was thirty-one and unmarried, and the fact that he never smoked, and drank only infrequently, put him, he reflected, at a social disadvantage.

But he would nurse one mild drink perhaps, while Nancy drank one after the other. She would drink because he would tell her things about Mobley—lies, perhaps, but Detective-Sullivan-type lies.

It was not hard to tell a lie. The business world, the newspaper world, was made up of liars. Walter Kyne was a liar. The important thing, the only thing that mattered, was to protect yourself, like Detective Sullivan and like, in turn, Gerald Meedy.

"I would suppose," (now he was talking aloud, rehearsing what he would say to Nancy) "that the most important thing about a husband ought to be his faithfulness. Not the question of whether or not he's faithful, but his *willingness* to be faithful."

And what would Nancy say to that?

"I'm not," (she would say) "worried about Ed."

"There may not be any reason to worry. What a man says is one thing. What he thinks is something else."

"What," (she would say) "do you mean by that?"

"Take me, for example," (he would say, in response). "What I've ever said to you has been practically nothing. Yet if you ever saw a faithful man—a faithful man—why, look at me. Relatively speaking, no, I hardly know you. And yet—well, sooner or later

I had to tell you this. I had to let you know. Just for the sake of being fair, I had to talk to you. You talk about the difference between men. All right, now you're looking at a guy who has been your faithful lover for—for I don't know how long."

Nancy would look at him searchingly and he would signal the bartender to pour her another drink.

The paste was dry now. Gerald Meedy closed the scrap book and placed it against the wall underneath the table he used as a desk. He stripped to his shorts and undershirt and got into bed, and the sleep that he had was long and undefiled by dreams.

One dream did come, but it was in the period of coming awake toward morning, and it was not an unpleasant dream. In the dream, Nancy was in bed beside him in the downtown hotel room she had rented for the night. The telephone was ringing, but Gerald turned to Nancy and said, "If we don't answer, they won't know we're here."

"Maybe it's Mobley," she said.

"The door's locked," he said to her.

"Then he'll come up and pound on it," Nancy said. "Kiss me. Kiss me, quickly, before he comes."

He moved warmly to kiss her, and the pounding on the door commenced. Neither of them said anything, and still someone—Mobley—beat on the door.

Then Gerald Meedy came more awake, out of his dream. The silver-gray light of New York's winter morning came through the slats of the Venetian blind at the window. He blinked his eyes and looked at his watch. The watch said ten minutes after six. The pounding on the door went on.

"All right," he said huskily, awake now. "All right."

"Meedy," said a woman's voice on the other side of the door. "Telephone."

Gerald Meedy found his bathrobe in the closet and opened his door. There was a phone on each floor of the hotel, a pay phone against the wall with a generation of phone numbers scrawled on the green paint beside it.

Meedy went down the hall and picked up the phone. "Yeah?"

"Get down to headquarters, Gerry."

"Who's this?"

"Lamin. Come on. Wake up."

"Hi, Arn," Meedy said. "What's up?"

"They pulled in a guy. Get down there as fast as you can. Get a cab."

"Who's the guy?"

"Charles of the Ritz," Lamin said. "How the hell do I know who he is? He's the superintendent of the building where the kid lived. That's all we know."

Meedy said, "What time is it?"

"Damn it," Lamin said, in irritation. "It's a quarter after six in the morning."

"Where are you?"

"Portland, Oregon," Lamin said. "Get down there now, and phone me when you get there." He hung up.

Gerald Meedy went back to his room, blinking his eyes and rubbing the sleep away. He would have to wear the same shirt. He would not have time to shave. In what shape was he to romance Nancy Liggett?

And now, in the light of the morning, he wanted her more than ever.

Chapter Nineteen

At three-thirty in the morning, three detectives' cars had gunned up in front of the house where Laura Grabowski, the dead girl, had lived. Two uniformed cops jumped out of the first car. Two detectives got out of the second. The Chief Inspector, Homicide, got out of the third, and the five of them took the steps of the three-story house, the flight leading to the front door, at the kind of soft-heavy run perfected by cops. One of the uniformed men rang the bell: four long rings, then a pause and three more.

At length, a gray-haired lady, her hair up in curlers, came through what seemed an eternity of dimly lit first-floor hallway, to open the door.

"Police," the first cop said. "George Pilski live here?"

"I'm his wife," the gray-haired lady said. "He's asleep inside."

"Let's go," one of the plainclothesmen said. He pushed the door open wide. "Reilly, you stay here."

"Yes, sir," the uniformed cop said, and he stood to one side as the four men entered.

George Pilski's wife paused doubtfully. "Is it about little Laura?"

The first plainclothes said, "Your husband the super here?"

"Yes," she said. "But he's asleep."

"Where's the apartment? In the back?" The plainclothes walked rapidly through the hallway to the blackness of the open door at the rear. The other followed him.

George Pilski's wife followed them. "What do you want with him now? At this time of night?"

They found themselves in the kitchen of the ground-floor apartment. The second plainclothesman snapped on a flashlight. "Where's the light switch?"

"Oh," the woman said, and she began to cry. The Chief Inspector squinted in the sudden light as the plainclothes found the wall switch.

"Come on," the Chief Inspector said, "let's go. We got work.

Where is he?"

"This looks like the bedroom," the second plainclothes said. He pushed open the door with his foot and shone his light inside. "Come on. He's here."

George Pilski sat up in bed.

"Pilski?"

He shook his head once or twice and stared at them. The uniformed cop turned on the bedroom light. . "Police," George Pilski said. "At this time of night." He saw his wife behind them in the doorway. "Vat, Frieda?"

She shook her head and pressed a handkerchief to her eyes.

"Get dressed, Pilski," the Chief Inspector said. "We want to ask you some questions—"

"Get dressed?"

The plainclothesman nearest to the bed went over and ripped the covers down. "Well, screw me," he said. "Look at that. Long underwear."

George Pilski sat up in bed. He made no other move. The plainclothes leaned down and slapped his face twice, going and coming.

From the doorway, the voice of the woman said brokenly, "You hit him."

"Get dressed, you son of a bitch." The plainclothes slapped him again, harder, one time.

"Downtown," the Chief Inspector said. "Come on. Come on, come on, let's do it."

"Come on," the plainclothes said. "You heard it. Come on."

Four minutes later they were outside again. George Pilski got into the middle car, a plainclothesman holding each of his arms. A radio patrol car had drawn up outside the building.

Now the patrol car cut in front of the first of the black homicide cars, its spotlight threading an elliptical pattern on the dark street ahead as they moved swiftly away.

Chapter Twenty

At twenty minutes after six, Edward Mobley's telephone rang. His apartment was on York Avenue, in the eighties, one of the new buildings where the rear apartments overlooked the East River and the Triborough Bridge.

Mobley had been dreaming of Nancy. He picked up the phone and heard Jon Day Griffith's voice. "They got somebody."

"Who?"

"The super in the building. He's down at headquarters."

"You don't go in for twelve hours. What are you worried about?"

"We may extra."

"Wait a minute," Mobley said. "If this is the super in the building, maybe he did this job and not the others. It'd make Lamin look bad."

"Why the hell do you think I called you?"

"Of course," Mobley said, "you ran Meedy's big scoop in your paper."

"Yeah," Griffith said. "But I got it from Lamin."

Chapter Twenty-One

At eight o'clock in the morning Mark Loving called Walter Kyne on the telephone.

"Did you hear about it, Walter?"

"Yes," Kyne said. "There wasn't a Kyne man or a Kyne photographer within ten miles of Centre Street when they hauled him in."

"We should have staffed Centre Street last night."

"You're telling me," Kyne said.

"Well," Loving said, "it's a good thing the *Sentinel's* a morning paper."

He smiled when Walter Kyne gave him the answer he wanted. The publisher was almost snarling. "There are morning papers on the coast, aren't there? We service afternoon papers, don't we? You think the *Sentinel's* the only paper I worry about?"

"That's what I was saying," Loving said smoothly, "when I said we should have staffed Centre Street."

Chapter Twenty-Two

They booked George Pilski. They fingerprinted him, shot him head and profile, and took him inside. His dirty white shirt was open at the throat. There was a cluster of hair at the top of his chest, showing where the shirt was open. He was unshaven, and he wore a thinning pair of old gray pants that once had gone proudly with a new suit. His face was gaunt and sharp-boned. The first photographer who got a shot at him told the second photographer he looked a hell of a lot like Bruno Richard Hauptmann. The news photographers got only a passing shot of him in the corridor. A plainclothesman said, "Later, boys," and they hustled the thin, gray suspect inside.

The first thing they showed him was the axe.

"Yours?"

He said it was his.

The blood-stained rags from the basement. The evidence of his fingerprints throughout the basement.

"Come on, George," one of them said. "What'd you used to do?"

"What I used to do?"

"Before you was super."

"That's fourteen year," George Pilski said.

"You were a butcher, weren't you, Pilski?"

Another cop said, "Knew how to cut meat."

"That cut between the arm and the body, now," the first interrogator said. "The right arm. Think now, George. The right arm."

George Pilski put his bony hands to his cheeks and looked up at them.

"All right," one of them said. "Bring her in."

A plainclothes went out the side door of the room, and when he came back he had a woman with him. She was short, and her legs were fat and swollen at the ankles. She wore a black coat and a faded, but improbably gay, flower-print dress. There was another plainclothes who came in the room behind her.

The Chief Inspector, Homicide, lit one cigarette from another, then reached out and took the woman's arm and steered her so that she stood before George Pilski.

George Pilski, sitting in a plain wooden chair like the kind that line the platforms of assembly halls in the public schools, put his hands on his knees and looked up at her.

He said, "Mrs. Kolal."

The Chief Inspector said, "Is that him, Mrs. Kolal?"

Her eyes shifted, large and alarmed, to the hand on her arm.

"There's nothing to be afraid of, Mrs. Kolal."

There was a silence. Then the plainclothes, the one who had followed her into the room, began to speak. He stood directly behind her, and his voice had a courtroom quality, like that of an educated bailiff. In speaking, he recited; his voice high and melodious.

"Mrs. Alexander Kolal, of two-three-oh-seven-seven Park Avenue, the Bronx, housewife, does here appear voluntarily."

There was a goose-necked light on a chrome-plated stand in the far corner of the room. A cop switched it on and pointed it at the wall over George Pilski's head. The only other light came from a dirty ceiling fixture in the center of the room. There was a long table against one of the side walls. The only other piece of furniture in the room was the chair in which George Pilski sat. The circle of the light against the wall behind the suspect silhouetted one of the plainclothes' head and shoulders.

The Chief Inspector said, "Tell us now, Mrs. Kolal." His hand remained on her arm.

The frightened woman looked back at George Pilski. When she opened her mouth, her voice, coming for the first time, was the voice of a glandular frog:

"Him."

The plainclothes behind her said, "Mrs. Kolal identifies George Pilski of two-three-oh-four-five Park Avenue."

"Him, the super," the woman said.

"And," the plainclothes said in his sing-song voice, "does state he is superintendent of the building at said address."

"The little girl," Mrs. Kolal said. She looked around, but no assistance forthcame. Three times then, she nodded her head, each time more profoundly than the last, almost like a pitcher winding up, and then she said, "I seen him. He watched her. I seen him, he come to the window and watch her. When she play in the street, he watch her. All the time he watch her. Candy he give her, and ice cream. He pat her on the head, he hold her arm."

"It is declared," the plainclothes behind her said, "that it is the belief of the witness that superintendent George Pilski did show interest unusual, abnormal and unique in the child named Laura Grabowski."

The hand tightened on Mrs. Kolal's arm, and she looked up wildly. She dug her free hand into the pocket of her coat and pulled out a large, wrinkled handkerchief, colored no less flamboyantly than the dress she wore.

The Chief Inspector said, "That's your statement?"

"She does so state," the plainclothes behind her said. "She'll say it again in court?"

"She so deposes."

"All right," the Chief Inspector said, and let his hand drop.

Now the woman, Mrs. Kolal, began to cry. Her face became lined and furrowed like an apricot, and her shoulders shook. She turned and let her plainclothesman spokesman lead her out the same side door she had come through.

The Chief Inspector swung his body so that he stood, veritably implanted, in front of the little grey superintendent.

"Look up at me, Pilski."

George Pilski tilted his face, but his eyes did not look up.

"Up," the Chief Inspector said. "Look up. Up, up."

A detective went behind the chair and put his hands on Pilski's face, fingertips at the jawbone. "Put your head up."

"Now," the Chief Inspector said. "Now. Say something, Pilski. I want to hear you talk."

George Pilski's hands gripped the edges of his chair. "How old are you, Pilski?"

The old superintendent spoke, at last. His voice was barely audible. "Sixty-four."

"Sixty-four?"

"Sixty-five March."

The face of the Chief Inspector was not a cruel face. It was a big face, and he was a big man, but the eyes, set far apart, were not without compassion. Either that, or they were too easily misread. When he smiled, the corners of his mouth turned down.

He smiled now. He half-turned his body and said, "Eddie, why is it always the old ones?"

Eddie was a lean plainclothes, the only man in the room who had kept his overcoat on. He said, "I knew a man eighty once, kept two broads on the side and killed one of them with a knife."

"The old ones," the Chief Inspector said again. He turned again to George Pilski. "Now, listen to me, George. I'm going to ask you questions. Eddie, have them turn off that goddam light. It's too hot in here. I'm going to ask you questions, George, and for each question I ask, I want an answer. Do we understand each other?"

"Lawyer," the old man said.

"Don't worry," the Chief Inspector said. "You're going to have a lawyer. This is what we call preliminary questioning. Now, let's go, George. The better we get along together now, the better it's going to be for you later. Now. Question number one. You used to be a butcher?"

The detective standing behind George Pilski's chair slapped the suspect's face twice with his right hand. "Answer up," he said. "Talk."

George Pilski raised his chin. "I was a butcher seven year."

"Did you cut meat?"

"Some times."

"Know how to make a shoulder cut?"

"I did, maybe."

"Did you like being a butcher, George?"

"I was tired."

"Where'd you get the axe?"

"I chop wood, sell wood. Some homes with fireplaces."

"I didn't ask what you did with it. I asked where you got it."

"I buy the axe."

"When?"

The old man spread his hands. "Eight, ten year."

"You ever been in trouble?"

"What trouble?"

"Any trouble."

"I never steal," the old man said.

"Any other kind of trouble? A morals charge?"

"Never," George Pilski said. He folded his arms across his chest. The plainclothes behind him said, "Put your hands down.'-' Pilski put his hands down.

"Any children?"

"Two boys," the old man said. "They're both dead."

"How long you been married, George?"

"Thirty-one year. Thirty-two year."

"You love your wife?" George Pilski did not answer.

The Chief Inspector said, "How old is your wife?" The old man's head came up again. "Fifty-eight."

"You sleep with her?"

Again there was no answer. The Chief Inspector said, "Look, George, this is important. Do you go to bed with your wife? No? When did you quit? How long ago? Come on, George, come on. We're all tired. Tired, understand?"

"I don't answer that," the old man said.

The Chief Inspector put his hand heavily on the old man's shoulder and leaned down. "You," he said distinctly, "answer every question."

"I don't answer that."

The plainclothes slapped his face from behind. The Chief Inspector said, "Why'd you kill Laura?"

"I don't kill her."

"What do you mean, you didn't kill her?"

George Pilski's voice became husky. "I love little girl. When I heard she gone, I cry. I sit down in my living room and cry."

"Who did kill her?"

The old man spread his palms expressively.

"Look, George," the Chief Inspector said. "Your fingerprints all over the basement and the axe."

"I find the axe."

"Sure, sure, you find the axe. You didn't have normal feelings toward that little girl, did you?"

"I love little girl," George said.

"A sixty-four year old man in love with an eight-year-old girl," the Chief Inspector said. His voice quickened. "You used to be a butcher. Where was the ladder? In the garage out back. Who knew where the ladder was? Who knew the garage door was open? Who knew the basement door was open? Who knew where the axe was, and the newspapers and the string and the rags? Who knew the manhole cover was loose? Who knew the locations of both the manholes? All right."

He stopped talking, and there was stillness in the room.

The Chief Inspector pointed his finger at George Pilski. "George, standing behind me is a police stenographer. Over on that table is a machine, that thing that looks like an adding machine. This stenographer's going to go over to that table . .." He stopped. "Eddie, see if you can get another chair." He turned back to the old man. ".. . and everything you say, he'll take down on that machine. You tell us how you did it, you confess, and I'll go for you. You'll plead insanity and I'll get up there on the witness stand and back you up, because only a crazy man could have done what you did, George. Only a crazy man.

"But one thing, George. One thing. You confess and you confess now. You understand me?"

George Pilski looked at the floor. The other men in the room eyed one another, waiting for him to say something. Then he looked up.

"I'm innocent. I don't confess."

The plainclothes behind him said, "Inspector, let me take him by his thumbs. Come on, you son of a bitch." The Chief Inspector stood there. "You won't confess?"

"I'm innocent."

"You don't want to confess?"

"I don't confess."

The Chief Inspector looked at him and smiled. "You'll confess, George. You're going to sit there and you're going to tell the truth for once in your blackhearted life. Eddie."

The detective behind him said," Sir?"

"I'm going out of this room for exactly two hours."

"He'll talk," Eddie said.

"Sure he'll talk," the Chief Inspector said. He smiled again. "You'll talk, George. I want you to believe me when I say this to you. You'll talk. If you can only take my advice, you'll do it right off, now, and get it out of the way."

He went out the side door.

Chapter Twenty-Three

The day went on past noon and into the afternoon. No lawyer showed up for George Pilski. George Pilski was somewhere upstairs, alone with the cops, and in the press room downstairs the waiting reporters and photographers played poker, examined the cameramen's pornographic snapshots, and wondered whether they would hang the Tally and Felton murders on Pilski, too.

Shortly after noon Harry Kritzer of Kynpix showed up to supervise the installation of a portable machine that would send the pictures of the suspect, hastily developed on the spot, direct onto the leased photo wire throughout the country.

At two-thirty in the afternoon Edward Mobley got a call from Jon Day Griffith and went back to the office to write the story when it broke. Geraid Meedy and two lesser lights from the *Sentinel* city desk stayed downtown.

At four-thirty everything but pages one, two, sports and financial were locked up in the *Sentinel* composing room downstairs. Financial went in at five minutes after five.

At five minutes of six, sports went downstairs. At 6:20 they locked up two. One stayed open.

Now they were riding deadline. The phone rang. It was 6:23.

From Centre Street, one of the local men said, "They've come downstairs. The photographers are in there and Meedy's in there with them."

Burt Healey, at his desk, had the phone switched to a headset. On the desk before him were proof strips of two headlines already set in type:

JANITOR CONFESSES QUESTION JANITOR

At Jon Day Griffiths's suggestion, another, a third, headline had been written. Now the copy boy placed the third proof on Healey's desk:

NAMES KILLER!

On a sudden hunch, Burt Healey scribbled a fourth possibility on a sheet of paper:

JANITOR NAMED!

The headphones strapped on, he waved the slip of paper at a copy boy, indicating it should be taken at once to Griffith.

Across the room, Joe Levine, Arnold Lamin's desk man for the wire service, cut into the open phone line with his own headset. The piece of paper in his typewriter said:

BULLETIN
NEW YORK—(EPS)—GEORGE PILSKI, 64-YEAR-OLD SUPERINTENDENT OF THE BUILDING IN WHICH EIGHT-YEAR-OLD LAURA GRABOWSKI LIVED,
THE GIRL'S MUTILATION DEATH.

It was 6:28.
Arnold Lamin was standing in his office, chewing paper, looking out into the newsroom.
Jon Day Griffith sat at his desk, the telephone at his hand opened to the composing room downstairs.
6:30.
Walter Kyne walked into his city room. To the untrained eye, the men at their desks throughout the great room would have appeared calm and unperturbed, perhaps even smitten by the routine character of their chores. The KPS machines still chattered their news. Copy boys filtered between desks. Far back along the *Sentinel* side of the room, two of the boys in sports argued loudly.
Walter Kyne felt in his breast a brief but powerful surge of pride.

6:34.

"Break the wire!"

Joe Levine called it out and listened momentarily at his headset, his fingers like talons over the keyboard of his typewriter.

All the way across the room, Burt Healey of the *Sentinel* bit down on his cigar and began to typewrite. The teletype machines had stopped. "Bulletin!"

Joe Levine threw the top copy at his wire filer. Arnold Lamin came out of his office. He said quickly to one of his cable men, "Get back to the wire room and check the opposition." The man got up from his desk.

Burt Healey ripped his bulletin from his typewriter. At his desk, Jon Day Griffith picked up the phone to the composing room and held out his hand, waiting for the copy boy to hand him the bulletin.

The wire moved it first.

BULLETIN

NEW YORK—(EPS)—GEORGE PILSKI, 64-YEAR-OLD SUPERINTENDENT OF THE BUILDING IN WHICH EIGHT-YEAR-OLD LAURA GRABOWSKI LIVED, WAS NAMED BY POLICE TONIGHT AS THE KILLER WHO CAUSED THE GIRL'S MUTILATION DEATH.

MORE

The add was out almost immediately:

FIRST ADD MURDER NEW YORK XXX DEATH.

POLICE SERGEANT TIMOTHY MALAR XXX POLICE SERGEANT OF DETECTIVES TIMOTHY

MALAR TOLD REPORTERS "THAT'S THE MAN."

THE STATEMENT FOLLOWED THIRTEEN HOURS OF QUESTIONING. OFFICIALS WOULD NOT SAY WHETHER PILSKI HAD SIGNED A CONFESSION.

MORE

The operation was moving swiftly now, automatically. It was 6:38.

Walter Kyne said to Arnold Lamin, "How'd we break?" Lamin saw his man coming back from the telegraph room. The man had a puzzled look on his face. "How'd we do?"

"We're the only ones who have it, Arn."

"Let me see that copy again."

"For God's sake, Arn!" Walter Kyne exclaimed. "We're ahead! We've got four minutes on the biggest story in th country!"

He turned to see Jon Griffith talking rapidly into his telephone. Walter Kyne walked quickly across the room. "We going, Jon?"

Griffith took the phone away from his ear. "No."

"What do you mean, no?"

"Wait a minute," Griffith said. He talked again into the telephone, apparently dictating a bulletin of his own to the composing room downstairs. Then he hung up the phone and got up from his desk.

Kyne said, "We got AP and INS. Four minutes."

Griffith looked at him. "Did that get on the wire?"

"What do you mean, did that get on the wire?"

Griffith shouldered past the publisher and walked to the battery of teletype machines, three of which were turned on. "I'll be damned," he said, half to himself. "It did get on. No, wait. Lamin's saving it."

The publisher came up beside him, and they both read:

BULLETIN K—I—L—L MANDATORY
EDITORS: KILL BOTH TAKES NEW MURDER BULLETIN (NEW YORK) ITEMS 126 AND 127.
KPS NY
REPEAT
EDITORS: KILL BOTH TAKES NEW MURDER BULLETIN (NEW YORK) ITEMS 126 AND 127.
KPS NY
NEW LEAD WILL BE FILED IMMEDIATELY.

Walter Kyne said, "What the hell goes on around here?"

Arnold Lamin came walking over from his side of the room. He was cursing.

"It's not my desk man's fault," he said. "The fault is at the other end. That damned Meedy. We should never have got that news."

"Didn't the cop identify him?" Kyne asked. "Did we have it wrong?"

"He identified him," Lamin said.

"Well then, what the hell's the matter with you? You're quoting the cop, aren't you? You gone crazy?"

"Nothing a cop says outside a courtroom is privileged," Jon Day Griffith said to him. "If this man didn't kill her, it's libel from here to hell and back again."

Walter Kyne stared at him.

"Libel," Griffith repeated. "You can be sued. Every paper that uses it from your wire can be sued."

"Wait a minute," Kyne said. He was looking up at Griffith's long, lean face. "Are you quoting a cop or aren't you?"

"It doesn't make any difference," Arnold Lamin snapped. "The copy is not privileged."

"Well, what was that you were saying about a courtroom?"

"Inside a courtroom is all right. There are certain places where anything goes. The United States Senate is one. The . . ."

"You don't have to read me the law of libel," Walter Kyne said. His voice was newly sharp. The mask was in place once again. "If it was libelous, what was it doing on our wire?"

"We killed it immediately," Lamin said. "Don't worry about getting sued."

"But AP and INS didn't carry it at all."

"Of course not."

"That," Jon Day Griffith said—he found himself hardly able to disguise his enjoyment of the publisher's wrath against Lamin—"is why we were ahead."

"Damn it," Kyne said to Lamin. "What kind of a wire service are you running, anyway?"

"Meedy's off the story," Lamin said. He said it loudly, not capable entirely of hiding his anger at the publisher. "I'm taking him off."

Jon Day Griffith turned and walked away from them.

"You didn't see *him* rushing into it," Kyne said, watching Griffith as he walked away.

"I didn't rush into it either. I killed it the minute I saw it."

"And that was just about one minute too late."

"All right, Walter," Lamin said. "It's killed. I killed it. I can't monitor those teletypes every second of the working day. I've got other things to do. I've been ahead every step of the way on this story so far and I'm going to stay ahead, and we're going to make the opposition look stinking, but I can't do it sitting on top of a teletype machine reading every word that comes over. You have to delegate authority. Once in a while, the best men you have will blow one."

"I don't think Meedy's the best man you have."

"I was talking about my desk man. The hell with Meedy. The big thing is, we caught it and we caught it fast. You don't have an editor in the place, there isn't an editor with a wire service anywhere, who would have caught that faster than I did."

"All right, Arn," Kyne said. "I wasn't talking about you personally. I just hate to see us kick one."

He was retreating, Lamin knew, because his position was unsound in one fundamental respect: Walter Kyne, as had just been demonstrated, knew about as much of the law of libel as Gerald Meedy.

But Lamin, observing the retreat, still was not a happy man.

Chapter Twenty-Four

Mobley had been on the Pilski story all day, and Nancy had not waited for him tonight, not knowing how long he might be. Thus he was alone at the bar in the Dell when Mildred Donner came in.

She wore a black dress, her hair done in an upsweep. She carried her coat over her arm. She sat down next to him and said, "Buy me a drink, Ed."

"Carlo," Mobley said. He looked at Mildred. "Going someplace tonight?"

"No."

"But all dressed up," Mobley said.

"What?" she said. "This?"

"Yeah," Mobley said. "This."

"Oh," she said, and nodded to him. "You like it."

"Very much."

"Well, thank you," she said. She paused for a moment. "No, I don't think I'm going anywhere. Not now that I've found you down here."

"Well," Mobley said. "Well."

"Some times," Mildred said, "I get in a mood where I like to speak my mind. Tonight is one of the times. All right?"

"Sure it's all right," Mobley said. "It's spectacular."

Mildred reached out and patted his hand. "You can be a spectacular guy," she said. "And I've known a couple of spectacular guys."

"In your time," Mobley said.

"Don't be cute," she said.

"I feel cute," Mobley said.

"Where's your lady friend?"

"Where's your man friend?"

"Let's have a drink together," Mildred Donner said. "I have just seen the lions loose upstairs, and I think you know what I'm talking about."

"Well," Mobley said, "I would say that the big Kyne scoop is still intact."

"Intact?"

"We said the same man killed the two women and the girl," Mobley said. "And if it turns out this super didn't do it, then maybe the same man did."

Mildred sipped at a glass of rye and water. "That's not what the lions are loose about."

"I know it."

"This libel thing tonight was a terrible blow to Lamin."

"It wasn't his fault. He caught it."

"But it got out," Mildred said. "Do you know what that did to his chances?"

"Well," Mobley said, "maybe your man will get in yet."

"I wish you'd stop calling him my man," she said. "Mark Loving is not my man."

"Well, he certainly ain't mine," Mobley said. "And I thought he was yours. I'm sorry."

"If I told you about Mark and myself," Mildred said, "you might change your mind."

It occurred to Mobley, for the first time, that she had been drinking before she came downstairs. His feeling now was nothing but a sort of patient tiredness, a state wherein he was weary but not sleepy. In this state, he had discovered, he could consume a continuous quantity of whisky without becoming drunk. Withal, the presence of Mildred here, with him now, was not lacking in appeal.

"Let me put it this way," Mildred said. She inspected her fingernails; she had long fingers. Edward Mobley liked women who had long fingers. "The way I would put it," Mildred said, "is that I would do almost anything for Mark. I want to see him prosper, I want to see him happy. I would like to see him get McCrady's job. But if you sat there and called it love, I would say I just don't know."

"'Tell me not, sweet, I am unkind,' " Mobley said. "If you are in a confessional mood, you had better have another drink."

"Love has a physical side," Mildred said.

"Ah," Mobley said.

"Don't disparage Mark."

"Who said anything?"

"Well, I didn't mean that," Mildred said.

"What did I call him?" Mobley asked. "The court eunuch?"

He asked this last of Carlo, the bartender.

Carlo said, "What was that, Mr. Mobley?"

"We were speaking," Mobley said, "of manhood. So far as I gather, we were still at the stage of discussing it in quite general terms."

"Well," Carlo said, "it's something to think about." He set down two new drinks and went to the other end of the bar.

"Some women," Mildred Donner said, "are more demanding than others. Do you understand that?"

"Yes," Mobley said. "And some Oldsmobiles are blue."

"All right," she said. "I'm sorry."

"Don't be sorry."

"I am sorry. I wish I could tell you why."

"You can tell me why."

"No, I can't," she said. "I might tell you an hour from now, but I can't tell you now."

"Carlo is going to have an active night of it," Mobley said.

Mildred looked at him carefully. "Ed," she said, "am I attractive to you?"

"The shape I'm in," Mobley said, "I could use a snake. But I would say, objectively, yes. Yes, you are. On the other hand, this is a dismal and a fearful night. Do you know the works of Abraham Cowley?"

"Who?"

"'It was a dismal and a fearful night,'" Mobley said. "'Scarce could the morn drive on th'unwilling light.'"

"You're full of poetry," Mildred said. "Aren't you?"

"To the ears," Mobley said.

"It's a defense mechanism," she said. "You're afraid of something."

"Okay," he said.

"On about three more drinks," Mildred said, "I would say you were afraid of me."

"On about two more drinks I'd agree with you."

"Drink up," Mildred said. "Let's have another."

Mobley thought of Nancy. He said to Mildred, "I am a poisonous, black-souled, nefarious, weak-kneed, gutless son of a bitch. So all right. Let's have some more to drink."

Chapter Twenty-Five

"I keep telling you don't worry," Gerald Meedy said to Arnold Lamin over the telephone. "This guy did it. They've got him. They'll have a confession by morning."

"I hope so," Lamin said. "For your sake, Gerald."

Chapter Twenty-Six

Mobley's mind was clear, he told himself, but he had had too much to drink. He hailed a cab with Mildred outside the O.K. building; it was after midnight, and they had just come upstairs from the Dell.

Inside the cab, Mildred gave the driver her home address and leaned back with her head on Mobley's shoulder. She said to him, "You could help Mark."

"Could I?"

"And he could help you," she said. "The queen of England can help me, too."

"Well," she said, "maybe I can help you." She pulled his face down to hers and kissed him thoroughly. After a while, Mobley said, "That was no help at all."

"Didn't you like it?"

"I liked it. I just said it wasn't any help."

"Maybe I'm really not very helpful."

"Maybe."

"Your hands are cold," she said. Mobley said nothing.

"Here," she said. She took his hand. "Now, there." They kissed again, and she smiled lazily at him. "I hate people who neck in taxicabs."

Mobley said, "You do?"

"It's more fun at home."

"I didn't know you graded things like that."

"Sure you do," she said.

"I must speak to Loving about this in the morning."

"You won't speak to Loving," she said, "and I won't speak to Nancy."

"I'm plastered," Ed Mobley said, and realized it was true. He felt sleepy, and a little sick.

"Now you take Mark, for instance," Mildred said quietly. "He has all kinds of particular preferences."

Mobley wished deeply he could become more interested. He wanted to concentrate on what she was saying.

"Some men," Mildred went on, "want to undress a girl and

tear her clothes. Others like to watch them undress in front of them. Or others, they like you to go in the bedroom and call them when you're ready, or to come out wearing a nightgown."

The motion of the cab was inimical to Edward Mobley. He found himself fighting a circular motion in his head.

"What," Mildred asked, almost idly, "is your pet way?" Mobley's lips were dry. He said, "What? Ask me that again."

"How do you like your women?"

"In purple pajamas," Mobley said, and lurched away from her as the cab came in to the curb-line in front of the east midtown hotel where she lived.

The air outside felt good. Mobley paid the driver and said to Mildred, "I'd like some coffee. Can we get some coffee?"

"I'll make you some," she said.

"Don't you want to get some downstairs?"

"Don't be silly," she said. "Everything's closed at this time of night."

He followed her into the elevator and they went upstairs. She had a two-room suite with a kitchenette. When he closed the door behind them, she said, "Stay out here for a minute," and went into the bedroom. Mobley took . off his coat and loosened his tie and sat down on the couch. He found he was sweating.

He did not observe the passage of time before she was back, standing before him in a crimson satin dressing wrap that reached to the floor.

She said, "You want to see my purple pajamas?"

"My God," Mobley said, "you mean you've got purple pajamas?"

She smiled at him and loosened the robe. It fell away and he saw she was wearing nothing underneath. "The next best thing," she said.

Edward Mobley did not say anything. He looked at the fullness of her, and the ripeness, and the hollows.

Still smiling, she fastened the wrap again and reached for a package of cigarettes on the table that separated them. "If you think I'm doing this to get you for Mark," she said, "I might as well tell you you're right. But I'm also doing it for myself."

She had told him about Mark Loving, he knew, because her feeling of the moment was a feeling not for Loving but for himself. But Mobley felt neither exclusive nor privileged in the knowledge.

"Well," Mobley said, "out of honesty as much as anything else, I ought to tell you the answer on Loving is no."

She looked at him. After a moment she said, "Maybe it doesn't make any difference. To me, I mean."

"And," Mobley said, "not out of honesty, or principle, or faithfulness to the bride-to-be, or any other thing, I ought to tell you this. I got no sleep last night, damn little the night before, now I'm drunk and I'm tired, and on top of everything else I'm sick. I'm talking at great lengths here to keep from thinking about being sick. You want me to quote you some poetry?"

"All right," Mildred said. "Unless you work with Mark, he'll make something out of this. He'll get it back to Nancy."

"I only wish I could care," Mobley said. "When I tell you I'm sick, I'm sick. I'm human. Human beings get sick."

"You didn't act very sick in the taxicab."

"The more you talk about it, the sicker I get," Mobley said.

Her hand moved to the fastening on her robe.

"Ah," Mobley said, "the second show." A new wave of nausea came upon him, and he barely reached the bathroom in time. He was in there for a long while.

When he came out, she was no longer in the living room. He picked up his coat and put it on. He heard her voice from the bedroom.

"How do you feel now?"

"Terrible," he said. "I'm going home." He went to the door of her room. She was lying on the bed naked, and it meant nothing to him. "I'm sorry," he said. "Tell Loving to blackmail me in the morning."

She ran her hands along her body. "I will," she said.

Chapter Twenty-Seven

Saturday night, Robert Manners had a date with a girl, He had a date with Evelyn, the thin girl who was his classmate at the University. He met her in Manhattan, on the upper West Side, at the home of another of the students, a pudgy youth named Klemfeld whose father was an importer. Klemfeld played the clarinet, and the gathering there was one of three girls and five boys. One of the boys played the drums and another played the piano, and the three of them were there in the large living room of the large apartment, playing blues.

There was a newspaper on the table in the foyer—a paper which said that George Pilski, the superintendent, had been freed. There now had been formed, the account continued, a Neighbors' Committee to Secure Justice for George Pilski, and it appeared that George Pilski was going to sue the city.

All this Robert Manners already had read while riding the subway from Brooklyn. He felt depressed tonight, and when the host, the boy named Klemfeld, broke open his father's whisky, Robert Manners drank it straight, without chasing it with anything. He and Evelyn sat on the couch for a while, listening to the music, and after a while they and another girl, Klemfeld's girl, and the three musicians were in the room while the other couple went down the hall into one of the bedrooms. Klemfeld's girl was a brunette, small but cute. She stood in front of the piano listening to the music, and letting her hips roll subtly, not quite in time to the beat.

Klemfeld took the clarinet away from his lips and began singing to the accompaniment of the piano and the snare, looking directly at his girl as he sang:

> "Ashes to ashes, and dust to dust;
> Ashes to ashes, and dust to dust;
> If that girl don't let me,
> I know I'm gonna bust."

The girl at the piano turned to a low table on her left and took her drink and sipped at it, her hips still moving to the music. Klemfeld looked at her and began to sing,

"I got a gal, she live up in a tree;
"Oh, I got a gal, she ..."

The boy playing the piano, lean and black-haired, said, "Tell her to do something, Pete. See if she'll take off some clothes."

"Play 'Can't We Be Friends', Pete," the drummer said. "That's real strip music, like at the Palace in Buffalo."

"Let's get some lights off," Pete Klemfeld said. On the couch, Evelyn looked at Robert Manners. "Let's go inside," he said.

"All right," she said, and got up with him. They went down the hall. There was a small bedroom to the right. The door was open, and looking in, Robert Manners could see the other couple, the ones who had left the room first, lying on the bed. They were side by side, the boy on the side nearest the door. They seemed fully clothed, but Robert Manners could not tell whether or not the girl's skirt was up.

"Come on," he said to Evelyn, and they went into the next bedroom.

Robert Manners closed the door.

"Bob," she said.

"What?"

"Leave it open."

"I thought you wanted to get away from them."

"I do." Evelyn sat on the bed. She wore a simple black dress tonight; her throat was long and white. Her figure was too vertical to be good, but when she sat on the bed he looked at the sweep of her legs and felt pleased. "I didn't know," Evelyn said, "that the party was going to be like this. I didn't know Pete was that kind."

"What kind?"

"You know," she said.

The door had remained closed. He went over to the bed and sat down next to her. "I should have brought our drinks."

"Oh, no," she said. "I had too much as it was."

"You didn't even have a whole one." She giggled. "That was plenty."

Robert Manners folded his hands over his knees and stared at his shoes. "I was going to pick you up tonight."

"Oh, I understood," she said. "There's no reason for you to come all the way from Brooklyn. It isn't as if you weren't going to take me home."

"I know," he said, "but I wanted to pick you up anyway. I got strung up at home. My mother wanted to talk."

"I'll bet your mother's a nice woman."

"Nice?"

She looked at him. "Is that so strange?"

"I don't know," he said slowly. "I don't know. She drives me nuts sometimes. She's always reading out loud from the Bible. She's got me so I've memorized whole parts of the Bible."

"I could never do that," Evelyn said.

"The hell with it," Robert Manners said. "Sometimes I just wish she'd leave me alone."

"It's because she loves you," Evelyn said simply.

"Yeah," Robert Manners said.

"You're her only boy," Evelyn said.

"Yeah, I know it."

"Anyway," Evelyn said, "you graduate from college, leave home, go in the army, get married, and, you know, she won't be seeing you. Not so much as she does now."

The whisky was going around and around in his head now. From the other end of the apartment came the sound of loud, wailing clarinet, the drive of the drums, the grinding of the piano.

Robert Manners got up and walked over to the window, looking out over Riverside Drive and the parkway and across the Hudson River to the Jersey shore, where a moving sign went black and then lit up:

9:47

"The time is now," Robert Manners said aloud.

The girl on the bed said, "What?"

"The time," Robert Manners said, not looking around, "is

now. 'For thus saith the LORD; We have heard a voice of trembling, of fear, and not of peace.' "

Evelyn said, "I didn't hear you."

"Jeremiah," Robert Manners said.

The girl said nothing.

"The Bible," he said.

She said quickly, "I guess you do know it by heart."

"Yes," he said. Still he had not looked around. They were silent again for a time. Then he turned around and looked at her. "So you think I ought to love my mother?"

"Of course," Evelyn said.

"What you don't understand," Robert Manners said, "is that I *do* love my mother. I *do*."

"Well, I didn't mean you didn't."

"No," he said. "No. Do you want to see how I love her?"

She looked at him. It seemed to him her eyes had become big and alive. He went over to the bed and leaned over brusquely and kissed her, forcing his tongue between her lips, trying to force his way between her teeth. His hand held the back of her head, tightly and completely.

She moved violently to one side, away from him, half falling back onto the bed.

"Bob," she said.

It came to him that the room was utterly still; that the music from outside the closed door had stopped. There was sudden terrible strength within him, a strength that negated any chance for her, even for her to consent, and his body came down upon hers. His right thumb stroked the side of her throat.

"Don't," she said. "Don't, Bob. You're heavy."

"Heavy?" he said.

"Yes."

"I can get heavier."

The thumb pushed into the soft flesh of the neck. Behind him, the door was pushed open. Robert Manners turned his head and saw a uniformed policeman standing there.

"Break it up," the cop said. "Come on, come on, up off that bed. What the hell goes on here?"

They sat up on the bed, and Robert Manners came to his feet.

"It isn't bad enough they're making all that noise with the

music," the cop said. "The neighbors complain, we got to come up here and see what's going on. The next thing we find, every bedroom in the house, something going on."

"All right, officer," Robert Manners said. The steadiness of his voice came to him as a worthy surprise. "We'll cut it out. We'll go out in the living room."

"That's the ticket," the cop said. "Kids can have good fun at a party, you don't have to act like this."

"That's right," Robert said. "Come on, Evelyn."

The cop stepped back and let them precede him down the hall. "You're good kids," he said. "You don't need cops here. Just be nice kids, is all."

Chapter Twenty-Eight

Arnold Lamin's stock had fallen. Jon Day Griffith's had gone up.

It was not a big fluctuation, but the eyes and ears of the seismographic Kyne city room could tell. Mark Loving in the feature department, Harry Kritzer in photos, knew it too.

Thus, on Monday morning when the four editors gathered in the office of Walter Kyne for a weekly session known inaccurately as a board meeting—Kyne's stenographer referred to them with artless simplicity as b.m.'s— there was no mention at all, none, of the murder case or the wire's error. There did not have to be.

What was discussed in Kyne's office each Monday morning since McCrady's death would, if it would have been categorized under one heading, have had to be described as sales. Not since McCrady had fired Webster for signing three radio stations to a unit contract had the Kyne empire had a sales manager. On the floor above the editorial offices, in the N.K. building, there was a sales department, fully manned and equipped with reams of promotional material describing the ineffable virtues of Kyne news, Kyne features, Kyne pictures, Kyne readership, Kyne advertisers, Kyne comic strips, Kyne columnists, Kyne quiz-mats and crossword puzzles, and, about once a year, Kyne himself.

But the final decisions in sales, ever since Webster, had been made by McCrady. Now they were being made by Walter Kyne, with the help each week of his four leading lieutenants.

Reading left to right as he faced them now, Kyne's eyes moved from Kritzer to Griffith to Loving to Lamin. All four, he noted, were wearing white shirts. Three of the four, Jon Day Griffith excepted, also wore cuff links. Loving's shirt was initialed in minute blue braid just above the pocket: ml.

Kyne, who was wearing a striped shirt, leaned back in his leather-upholstered chair and put his hands behind his neck. He said, "To begin with, gentlemen, all four of you blew a story last week. Did you ever hear of the *Allerup*?"

No one answered.

"The *Allerup*," Kyne said, "is the name of a Danish freighter that broke up on the rocks in the Atlantic Ocean last Wednesday, off the South African coast. They had, in addition to passengers who got out all right, a whole menagerie full of animals down in the hold. They let them swim to safety. Monkeys, giraffes, every other damned thing. Us had it. Us? We didn't have a story, a picture, a feature, nothing."

Arnold Lamin said, "I think we were worried about something else."

Now that he had mentioned the murder, however obliquely, the subject was fair game for the others. This was not, however, precisely the time to talk about it.

Harry Kritzer said, "We don't have anybody in South Africa."

"I don't believe it," Kyne said.

"The only African we got working for us," Griffith said, "is a native. He has a stovepipe hat and a spyglass and he lives in a tree."

Kyne laughed. So did Mark Loving. The others simply sat in their chairs.

"All right," Walter Kyne said. "Now Iowa. The opposition's in there murdering us with TTS."

TTS was the abbreviation for teletypesetter, a machine that not only could transmit news, as a teletype could, but actually set it up in type in the office of a subscriber newspaper. Opposition wire services already had it in use, and many papers which now got TTS were canceling out supplementary news services.

"We have seven papers in Iowa," Kyne was saying now. "We stand to lose four. We make twenty-three thousand a year from the seven Iowa papers, and the four we lose will reduce that to under ten thousand. Contract renewals are up on three and the fourth will be up in May. I'm open to suggestion."

Mark Loving said, "I assume all seven get KWF." Kyne World Features had, in one form or another, nearly nine hundred clients—more than four times as many as KPS, the news wire—in the continental United States. Some of the KWF subscribers took only comic strips. Others took columns, puzzles, and a bi-weekly page of printed news stories that were of interest but were not timely enough to merit space on the KPS wire. More than a few KWF clients took everything KWF had to offer.

"They all get KWF," Kyne said; "And they'll keep it. But they're throwing out KPS."

Harry Kritzer, the photo man, said, "What about Kynpix?"

"You only have two clients in Iowa," Kyne said.

"Two machine clients," Kritzer said. "I think we service four other points in Iowa by mail."

"Well, that wasn't an issue," Kyne said. "There is one thing. Jon here . . ." He pointed his finger at Griffith . . . "saved us three points in Indiana by making that trip last summer."

"All I did was make speeches," Griffith said.

"And you visited with client editors," Kyne said. "We flattered them that way. Instead of sending a KPS man or a salesman out to talk to them, we sent the Editor of one of the biggest newspapers in the United States—a man who had the same problems they did—a man whose business it was to put out a newspaper every day, just as it's their business to put out a newspaper every day. It brought about a lot of favorable talk."

"What do I have to do now?" Griffith asked. "Go to Iowa?"

The blue eyes of Walter Kyne settled, for some reason, on Arnold Lamin. But he was still talking to Griffith, and to the four men generally.

"No, " he said, "not now. Not while this other thing is hanging." He paused, almost imperceptibly, and wondered if the candidates seated before him were wondering what "this other thing" was. Was it the murder, or the McCrady vacancy, or both?

Nothing showed on the faces of the four editors. Walter Kyne took the letter opener from his desk and began to revolve it in his hands. "I think, Jon," he said, "that you might plan on that kind of a trip eventually, but not now. Not while everything's up in the air the way it is."

He smiled at Griffith and Griffith's mind raced. Eventually he said to himself, means what? Does it mean I don't get the McCrady job? That I'll still be with the paper? But then Kyne said not now. So where does that leave me?

"We need action of a different kind," Kyne said. "The first thing we do is, we have to save contracts."

Harry Kritzer said, "Where's the profit point?"

"On three of the four," Kyne said, "we could conceivably cut the rate back fifty per cent and still be making money. The fourth is up north, and we're paying for the AT&T line."

"If it's that hard to get to geographically why do we worry about it?" Lamin asked.

"Because they pay ninety-seven fifty a week," Kyne said. "I don't think rate-cutting would be a problem there, because while they're out of the way for us, they're out of the way for the oppositions, too. They have to pay for the service they get."

Lamin said, "You mean to say the AP state wire doesn't run up there?"

"They don't want a state wire. They want a trunk."

"They can't get a trunk on TTS," Lamin said. "All TTS is regional."

"They're buying it in a package," Kyne said. "They get the trunk that they want, and they get their state news from TTS, and they get the two services at a price that compares. When they can get that, what do they want with Kyne?"

Harry Kritzer said, "If they're getting a package from somebody else, why can't they get a package from us?"

"You sound like McCrady," Kyne said. Three sets of eyes fastened on Harry Kritzer, upon this unlooked-for accolade. "That's what McCrady would have said."

"It's what he would have done, too," Kritzer said.

"All right," Kyne said. "The only thing we can hang over their heads is the comic strips and that kind of thing. The Hollywood features and the stuff they can do without. Then you have the legal question of coercion."

"There's no coercion," Kritzer said. "Half your KPS clients bought Kynpix and KWF in a package to begin with."

"Ah," Kyne said. "But then it was voluntary on their part. Now we go to them and say, 'Look. You keep on taking KPS or we take KWF away from you.' Besides being unethical, it isn't even good business."

"McCrady would have done it." Kritzer smiled a private smile.

"McCrady would have gone about it differently," Kyne said. "McCrady would have hepped up that wire so they found themselves using it because they wanted to. Then he would have sold them a ten-year package contract and made them like it."

Arnold Lamin said, "You want me to juice up the report for

Iowa?"

"I think you'd better, Am," Kyne said. "Write Des Moines an airspecial today. Have them gimmick up as many Iowa features and exclusives as they can—say, for a period of one month. Who's your man in Des Moines?"

"My bureau chief?"

"Yes, What's his name?"

"Baldwin."

"Have him make a swing through the state next week, pay a personal call on each of these cancellation points. I'll give you the list."

"All right," Lamin said.

"Give him all the wire space you can for those Iowa specials."

Lamin nodded.

"And remember this. This murder case in New York. They're just as interested in it in Iowa as we are here. It's front page all over the country. If we're ahead on that, we may save a client we'd lose despite everything else we could do."

Lamin nodded. The others looked at him.

"It's not only beats and exclusives," Kyne said. "One minute of time can mean the difference." He held up the letter opener. "Right this minute, someplace, somewhere, one of our clients is right on deadline." He paused. "I only wish we had radio stations."

Mark Loving cleared his throat. "I brought this in for you, Walter." He took a telegram out of his pocket and put it on the desk.

Kyne read it. "By God," he said, "we do have a radio station." He chuckled and handed the yellow blank to Arnold Lamin. Lamin read it without expression, and it passed around the others and back to Loving.

It said:

MARK LOVING
KYNE NEWS FEATURES
N YK
DUE YOUR UNDERSCORING MURDERS IN WHICH
GREATEST INTEREST HERE AGREE SAMPLE KWF AND KPS

SERVICES ONE MONTH WITH EXCLUSIVE OPTION TERRITORIAL RADIO RIGHTS.
W KLEIN, WSSP ST.L.

Harry Kritzer said, "Isn't that one of the stations we used to have with the old radio wire?"

Loving nodded. "I know Willie Klein. He's got the station now and he's a nut on murders. I wrote him last week."

"Damn it, that's enterprise," Kyne said. "I should have thought of that. We all should have thought of that. Harry, what could we do to supplement a radio service like that with pictures for television?"

"We're already tied up with a television picture service," Kritzer said. "There isn't a hell of a lot more we could do."

"Wait a minute," Jon Day Griffith said. "Why couldn't we sit down and go through all the pictures and produce a special backlog production for television that they can slap on the camera the day they catch the killer?"

"You could do it as a bonus," Lamin said. "What the hell would it cost you? You've already got the pictures and the avenues of distribution."

Kritzer caught their animation. He raised his hands in illustration. "And promote it with this new radio service in mind. Make a real promotion that we can take into other radio stations and show them how we serviced one client on a single-story basis."

"If that St. Louis station is satisfied," Kyne said, "it would be the greatest sales ammunition we could have."

Arnold Lamin stood up. "I'll be damned," he said. "We're back in radio."

"And without the overhead of a radio wire," Mark Loving said.

"All right," Walter Kyne said. He too stood up. "The big problem this week was Iowa."

"I'll write to Baldwin in Des Moines right away," Lamin said. "We'll open up for added Iowa news and I'll send him around to visit the clients."

"Get the list from Miss Coleman," Kyne said to him. "Jon, you may not have to go out there at all."

"Suits me," Griffith said, and brought his long frame out of the chair like a carpenter's rule unfolding.

Walter Kyne said, "When do we start in St. Louis?"

"Soon as you can get a machine in there," Loving said. "I'll put them on the KWF list today."

Kyne reached for the water carafe on his desk and poured himself a small glass of water. "A toast, gentlemen," he said. "We're in business."

They murmured at him and started to leave.

Outside the door, Arnold Lamin turned to wait for Jon Day Griffith.

"Never undersell that blue-eyed bastard," he said. "He knows more about this business than we sometimes think."

"And less, too," Griffith said. "He doesn't even know the law of libel."

"Neither," Lamin said unhappily, "does Gerald Meedy."

"Ah, yes," Griffith said. "How is Gerald?"

Lamin told him how Gerald was.

"Well," Griffith said, "he always spoke well of you."

Chapter Twenty-Nine

Monday morning.

Robert Manners sat in the college classroom, listening to Dr. Neville Fishkin, professor of English. Dr. Fishkin's voice had a soporific quality; it circulated through the room like a well-mannered, weary hornet. Dr. Fishkin did not like Monday mornings, and he did not take particular pains to cloak the fact.

"We were talking," he said unhappily to his students, "of the ancient novel as opposed to the modern novel. Does anyone want to point out the major difference between the two?"

A stout young lady, wearing what seemed to be oversized eyeglasses, raised her hand. Dr. Fishkin said, "Miss Kent."

"In my opinion," the stout young lady named Miss Kent said in a loud voice, "the essential difference between the ancient novel and the modern novel is the analysis of motive."

Dr. Fishkin stared momentarily out of the window. There were, he noted, two pigeons stalking the ledge. It was a cold day but sunny; too nice for a Monday.

Then he got up, achingly, and went to the blackboard and wrote, in large, unconnected capital letters, "ANALYSIS OF MOTIVE."

Two pigeons . ..

Robert Manners sat in the back of the classroom, in the next-to-last row, staring out the window.

Two pigeons . . .

He thought of last night. He had resumed his delivery job at the drug store, and he had arrived in the Bronx from his weekend at home early enough last night to run half a dozen prescriptions.

The last call he had made ... it was after eleven at night . . . had been to the apartment of a man. A rich man, Manners would have judged him, from the location and the size and the furnishings of his apartment. A bachelor, Manners assumed. At least, the name card over the apartment bell downstairs said H. Kritzer. Usually, when they were married, they put only the last name on the card, without initial, but you could never be sure.

The woman in the apartment with the man named Kritzer wore a wedding ring: this Robert Manners noticed. He noticed also that whereas the man named Kritzer answered the door in his dressing robe, the woman was fully and elegantly clothed. She was standing by the window in the living room with a drink in her hand. Her hair was blonde, her lips full and red and mysterious. She wore a black dress with a deeply slashed neckline.

A bachelor, Robert Manners also assumed *H. Kritzer* to be, from the nature of the merchandise he was delivering. He had seen the druggist wrap it.

Two pigeons . . .

Robert Manners' fingers had played with the button lock on the door as he waited for the man named Kritzer to bring the money.

The terrible thoughts he had pledged never to admit again thrust themselves upon him now, even with added impact, with the rush of something that has been locked up too long. He looked at the woman standing there, and his hand opened the lock in the door. Then the man came back with the money and said good night and closed the door.

Robert Manners stood outside in the hallway and listened.

The apartment door was thick. He could hear the voices within, but could not tell completely what it was they said.

Hers: ". . . enough to tell him ... my mother's and the phone ... do I look worried? . . ."

His: ". . . can't help but wonder . . . thinks of me, is what I want to know ."

Then the man's voice became loud and near, and Robert Manners knew he had come close to the door. For a frantic moment, he thought the door might open—now, *that* would be cause enough for murder—but the door remained closed, and he heard the voice of the man named Kritzer clearly:

"I think he's already made up his mind."

The woman said something, and then the man said:

"Griffith, that's who."

Then again the woman, and again the man: "Well, if he hasn't he's going to damn quick. He doesn't like carrying this load. He's scared to death he's going to make a mistake. So if you're going to push me you better push me good. More than you've been doing. I'm telling you that."

This time, the woman's voice was clarified: "I'm doing everything I can."

"Dorothy," (the man's voice), "if we get it you can leave him."

(Her voice): "How—unless you leave the company?"

(His voice): "One year in McCrady's job and I can write my own ticket anywhere else."

(Hers): "Well, I'm tired. I'm tired and I'm upset."

The man's voice became muffled now, but the woman's—Dorothy's—was still distinct. "Yes," it said. "I do love you. Would I do this if I didn't?"

Robert Manners heard the door to the elevator, down the hall and around the turn. For a moment he was in conflict, wanting to hear more, but a strain of reason set upon him and he walked away from the door and toward the elevator, observing things as he moved.

Not to kill, this time ... simply wait half an hour, burst through the unlocked door, and see them there. They were not married . . . they would never call the police.

But a man's apartment. No. It had to be a woman alone.

I have no taste for men, said Robert Manners to himself, and he smiled and thought of the old joke ("I say, old top, 'ave you 'eard about 'odgkins? 'e's been ejected from the club. Found 'im in a stable, attacking an 'orse."

"By jove, was it a stallion or a mare?"

"A mare, of course. Nothing queer about 'odgkins'.").

You see, he said to himself, and felt curiously at peace— a strange feeling it was, one that in its very peacefulness did not bode well, did not augur of peace to come—you see, a sense of humor, a little calm thinking, and you, good fellow, can be as normal as the next chap.

Now, why did I use the word 'chap'?

He went down in the elevator and home to his dormitory room and there he stared for a long time at the locked suitcase in the corner. He did not open it, but took his Bible and went to bed, and to sleep.

Now, though, he sat in the classroom, looking out the window, and all the horror and the wonder and the joy of the feeling was back with him, stronger than it had ever been before; so strong, he wondered if anyone could help but notice.

Two pigeons . . .

I should have broken in on them, he said to himself. Caught them while they were doing it, choked him while she lay there, then taken his place. What could she have said? Left her alive, I would have. What could she have done, from the way they talked, the two of them, except put on her clothes and get away from there and hope nobody saw her?

Ah, he said to himself, why didn't I think it out? I was there! *It would have taken no planning. It would have been so easy, and yet, yet so wonderful.*

So easy, so wonderful, that it can't shape up like that again. Twice in the same place is hoping for too much. Remember yourself, Robert, you are the invisible man.

Then what?

Dr. Neville Fishkin, professor of English, said mildly, "Does the gentleman looking out the window . . . Mr. Manners... desire to expand upon the discussion?"

Robert Manners was proud of himself. Proud that he could divert his concentration so quickly, so thoroughly, proud that he could deliver an answer.

He said, and his voice was even and clear, "I'm sorry. I was looking out the window."

"Oh?" Dr. Fishkin said. "And what did you see?"

"Two pigeons," Robert Manners said.

"Ah," Dr. Fishkin said. "Two pigeons. And are you satisfied?"

"No, sir."

"Why? What were you looking for?"

"Inspiration," Robert Manners said.

Dr. Fishkin nodded. "'Be good, sweet child, and let who will be clever.' " He smiled momentarily. "The gentleman next to Mr. Manners. Mr. Krause."

And smoothly as in an automatic gearshift, Robert Manners' thoughts returned to what had been in his mind before. .

He was reasoning. Reason—the most powerful weapon known to man. Reason me that, reason me this: that if the wanting is now stronger, that if the risk is now greater, then must the act be more of anything and everything than ever before.

More? How?

First the older woman, and then the young woman and what I did after she was dead, and then the little girl and the axe and the place of the parts ...

What more?

What?

By night every crime that he dreamed could satisfy him, he had done. Still he was not satisfied. Yet what was left?

By night, he had robbed, plundered, raped, dismembered and killed.

It sounded like a description in a detective magazine. Maybe some day they would write it of him.

Meanwhile, being hunted now, knowing the indescribable sensation of being hunted, knowing the fantastic feeling of having looked up from being on the bed with the girl and seeing the policeman standing there—still, the urge was back with him, the urge he had sworn never to have again, the urge that came so terribly it could not be denied . . .

What could he do to justify it?

And the answer came to him as (he said to himself) it would to any reasonable man:

Not to change the crime, but the time—

Daylight!

Chapter Thirty

Jon Day Griffith got home early that Monday night: early for him. Ten-thirty it was, and his wife Helen was sitting in the living room, watching television with such concentration that she did not hear him come in.

They lived in a small apartment in Larchmont, only a few blocks from the yacht basin whence, some day if he should get McCrady's job, Jon Griffith would sail forth his own bright craft, to compete in the regattas, to win, and to see his name on the sports pages of the *Times* and the *Tribune.*

He thought of this on the train from Grand Central each night, observing the class of people who rode with him—a value-conscious class of people, even at the strange hour that he came home.

He was thinking of it now, coming into the living room. Helen Griffith was lying on the couch in sweater and slacks, an outfit which did not exalt her figure. She was a small woman, and at the age of thirty-eight she tended to stout. Her eyes were tired, but her face was not noticeably lined, and today she had had a new permanent.

She turned her head quickly when she saw him and said, "Oh! You frightened me. I didn't think you'd be home this early."

"I got tired," Griffith said. He took his overcoat off and put it on the armchair across from the couch and went over to kiss his wife on the forehead. He said, "Don't get up. I had supper."

She raised herself on her elbow and said, "Turn off the television and tell me all about it."

"Don't you like this program?"

She made a face. "It started out all right, but I was beginning to get tired of it. They're all the same, these mysteries."

"Well," Jon Day Griffith said. He sank heavily into the chair, sitting partially on his coat, and took out a cigarette. "There's a lot to tell."

"Start at the beginning," Helen Griffith said. "And if it will help you any, I have a feeling you're going to get the job. Then you can get your boat and maybe you won't spend so much time in that place."

"What place?"

"You know what place. The place where they have that bartender named Pedro."

"Carlo," Griffith said.

"That's the one," she said. "Do you like my new permanent?" She lifted her head. "Dramatic," Griffith said.

"Well, never mind," she said. "I want to hear every word. Don't leave out a single detail."

"Well, to begin with," Griffith said, "it's more than just the boat." Her wishful thinking about his prospects for the job excited him more than he had reason to permit. "I mean, the boat is a symbol. It's a symbol of what you do with fifty thousand dollars. You're a new person." He sat forward in his chair. "But Helen, damn it, it's more."

"I know," she said quietly.

"All that drivel about printer's ink in your veins," Griffith said. "Well, let me tell you something. You sit behind that desk of mine and look out over that overheated city room and see fifty newspapermen sitting there, and that's all it ever looks like they're doing, just sitting there, and everything is set up and automatic and quiet and nobody gets excited and then at quarter of seven the boy comes upstairs and lays that paper down in front of you and you get it with the ink still wet, and the son of a bitching thing is alive in your hands there and you say to yourself, this is a newspaper. And you sit there night after night and it comes up in your throat the same way, and you can get drunk and lie down in gutters and kick a story in the ass and swear you're going to quit and find a normal profession, and then the phone rings in your ear four o'clock in the morning and you're standing in the middle of the room, pulling on your pants and here we go again. That's why the newspaper business kills so many people, because they won't give up, they won't let go. They can't."

His wife smiled. "They don't all feel that way, the way you feel."

"I'm not so sure," Griffith said. "I think even Kyne, the poor, shivering, million dollar bastard, I think even he gets it."

"Maybe," she said. "But tell me about today."

"Okay." He sat back again. "To begin with . . . oh, let me tell you this first. Loving made a play for Mobley."

"What do you mean, he made a play for him?"

"Listen to this," Griffith said. "Believe it if you will. You know he's sleeping with Mildred."

Arnold Lamin's wife would have inquired who was sleeping with Mildred who, but Helen Griffith was intimately aware of all details relevant even remotely to her husband's candidacy.

"Anyway," Jon Griffith said, "you have the picture. There's Lamin and me, running head and head, and Kritzer doing great with these pictures on the murder. All of a sudden, Loving, with all his money, finds himself running fourth. So the first thing he does, he looks around for a man. What man is there besides Mobley?"

"Is Mobley really that good?"

"He's good," Griffith said. "There's no two ways about it, he's good. Maybe not that good, but easily the best we have downtown. But that's beside the point. Maybe Mobley gets this story and maybe he doesn't. The point is, Loving's desperate.

"So you know what he did? He pandered Mildred onto Mobley. Literally pandered her onto him. She got Mobley drunk Friday night, took him up to her flat, and all of a sudden he's so drunk he conks out cold and can't do a thing." Hoarsely and briefly, Griffith laughed.

"Did Mobley tell you that?"

"Today," Griffith said. "Do you believe him?"

"Sure I believe him."

"What about Nancy?"

"He told her too. I think she's mad at him. He saw her Saturday night, but I think they had some kind of a fight."

"Serious?"

"Who the hell knows? Mobley's seeing her tonight. He'll charm her with that off-beat folklore of his and everything'll be great."

"Well," Helen Griffith said, "I'd say Mildred didn't mind her assignment."

"*Mind* it? Mobley says she's sore as hell because he wouldn't put the blocks to her. She loves it. It's her diet."

"Isn't Loyiig good enough fon her?"

"I don't know," Griffith said. "I'll tell you something, though.

I think he loves her more than she loves him."

"Then why did he ask her to sleep with Mobley?"

"Because of this job," Griffith said. "It's poisoning every son of a bitch up there. It'll poison me before we're through. Between that and these murders, every guy in the joint has the knife waving."

"Except you," she said.

"Except me hell. If I can stick some son of a bitch and get the job, watch me go."

"You're going to get it," she said. "You deserve it."

"You know," Griffith said, "in a way, Loving deserves this job more than anybody."

She sat up on the couch. "What do you mean?"

"I mean he's bucking for it harder than anybody else. Sure, Lamin's kicking like a steer because he wants to live in Rye, and I want a sailboat, and poor Harry Kritzer is thé best photo man in the business, but with us it's just a case of doing our jobs the best way we know how." Griffith blew two concentric smoke rings. "But now Mark Loving, he has enough money, even if most of it does belong to that love-starved wife of his. Maybe he wants money so he can break away from her. What it is, God only knows, but he's trying harder than any of us. Things that are out of his province. Hell, he's a feature man. But first, he tries to muscle in on the news end through Mobley. Then—how about this?—he goes out and signs up a hell of a radio client in St. Louis."

"How did you find out?"

"He brought out the telegram during the board meeting," Griffith said bitterly. "Kyne nearly fell off his chair."

"It was a good thing for Loving?"

"It wasn't bad," Griffith said. "It was not bad."

Helen Griffith said, "But sales isn't the big thing."

"*It's* big enough," her husband said. "McCrady was a salesman. That's why they didn't need a chief of sales. With him around to oversee the department, everything was great. So naturally, Kyne's looking for somebody like him."

"But if you break this murder, then he has *it*, give it to you. He's as much as said so."

"That's just it," Griffith said. "He's as much as said so, but he hasn't said so in so many words. It does him nothing but good to have us all out breaking our ass to beat the opposition on a story this size. Then suppose he turns around and hands it to Mark Loving? What can anybody say? There's no built-in guarantee. You think Kyne's put anything in writing? Hell, he signs his checks Quisling."

Helen Griffith said doggedly, "No. The best salesmanship you can have is a good performance on a story. You went up forty thousand on the streets the other night because you had a headline nobody else had. If you ask me, that's salesmanship."

Her husband blew another smoke ring.

"And another thing," Helen said. "Didn't you save some clients in Indiana last summer when you made that trip out there? Isn't that salesmanship?"

"I suppose," her husband said. "As a matter of fact, that came up at the b.m. today."

"What did?"

"My trip to Indiana."

"How?"

"Kyne thought it might be a good idea if I made another one to Iowa."

"Now?"

"No."

"Later?"

Griffith nodded.

"Is it definite?" his wife asked.

"No."

"Then I wouldn't worry about it," she said. "What else happened at the meeting?"

"We talked about teletypesetters. The wire's getting duked out in Iowa."

"Did Kyne say anything?"

"About the job?"

"Yes." Helen Griffith swung her legs down and took a cigarette off the end-table. She tapped it against a closed book of matches. Her eyes did not leave her husband.

"I got the impression," Griffith said, "that Lamin's in the soup."

"Because of that libel story?"

Griffith nodded. "The trouble with him is, you can't tell. For all my position and title, he knows guys who know Kyne that I never even met. Just about every Kyne executive along the line is beholden to Lamin for one reason or another."

"Do you think they're really actively backing him? To the extent of talking to Kyne about it, or writing him or something?"

"I wouldn't put it past them."

"Well," Helen Griffith said, "they may tell Lamin they're putting in the good word for him, but I'll bet they're being mighty careful about it. No board of directors is going to decide the new McCrady. It's one man. Walter Kyne."

Griffith made a tent with his fingers. "Ah, there's no doubt about it. They want to be where the wind blows, except . . ." He stopped.

Helen Griffith raised her eyebrows.

"I know," Griffith said tiredly. "Except what? Except this: if they're reasonably sure Lamin's going to get the job, it would be to their advantage to be backing him going in. The more actively, the better."

"Well," his wife said, "after what you said happened in the meeting today, I don't think anybody's sure Lamin's going to get the job. Least of all Lamin."

"No," Griffith said doubtfully. "I only wish I knew how strong he is. Hell, if he's strong enough I might plug for him myself."

She smiled. "You'd never do that."

"The way I feel tonight, I'd do anything. Oh, and something else."

"What?"

"Just to complicate things."

"What is it?"

"We've established a case for me and Am Lamin and Mark Loving. Hold your horses. Here comes Harry Kritzer."

"What happened?"

"Something Kyne said. At the meeting. We were talking about Iowa ..."

"Didn't you talk about anything but Iowa?"

"That's the way those meetings go," Griffith said. "We were talking about Iowa, and Kritzer suggested holding the clients to renew their contracts by threatening to take KWF away from them, and Kyne said to him, 'You sound just like McCrady,' or words to that effect."

Helen Griffith set her cigarette down in the ash tray. "I don't like that. That's the first thing tonight I didn't like."

"You should have seen the rest of us," her husband said. "I thought Lamin was going to jump out of his chair."

"Is that all he said?"

"Well, he modified it a bit. He said McCrady would have thought that way, but then he said McCrady would have taken explosive action, or some damn thing."

"I still don't like it. Harry Kritzer."

"Maybe it was a plant," Griffith said. "That blue-eyed son of a bitch loves to see us squirm and wriggle."

"You still can't rule him out," his wife said. "He and Kyne are like that." She crossed her fingers.

"That's the beauty of it," Griffith passed his hand over his eyes. "You can't rule anybody out."

"Including you, sweetheart," she said. "You're damn right," he said.

Chapter Thirty-One

Ed Mobley and Burt Kaufman grew up together on New York's lower west side—the least ethnocentric of any of the areas of the great metropolis. Stories have been written about the docks, the lower east side, midtown, Hell's Kitchen, Washington Heights, Harlem and East Harlem, Broadway, the garment district, Central Park West, Park and Fifth Avenue; about the Bronx and Queens and all the sections of Brooklyn; even about Staten Island.

But none of any consequence has touched the lower west side, the district known as Chelsea in its northern half, and without a name to the south. It borders to the southwest on Greenwich Village, and more stories have been written about Greenwich Village than about any other area in the town, possibly excepting that magnificent fraud, Times Square.

This does not indicate that the lower west side is devoid either of color or talent. Thomas Wolfe lived in a giant old apartment in the Hotel Chelsea, on West Twenty-Third Street in between Seventh and Eighth Avenues. But he did not celebrate the district in his works.

The reason for this may lie in the fact that Chelsea is the least extreme of New York's sub-districts. Its wealth is not the wealthiest, nor its poverty the poorest, its smells not the smelliest, nor its fires the most spectacular, its docks not the biggest, nor its whores the whoringest, its drunks not the drunkest, nor even its politicians the most political.

Some day the area may be described for what it was to Edward Mobley and Burt Kaufman, who lived houses apart on West Fifteenth Street between Seventh and Eighth when they were boys. They took with them, as they grew, the same memories: the grammar school graduation ceremonies at P.S. 41 on Greenwich Avenue, where they sang the school song:

"Forty-One, dear Forty-One
To us you are so dear.

The lessons learned at Forty-One
Will help us through the years."

The vacant lot on the west side of Seventh Avenue between Twelfth and Thirteenth, where they played football after school. Engine Company 18, on West Tenth Street, and Hook and Ladder 5, on Charles Street. Loew's Sheridan at Greenwich Avenue and Seventh, and the Greenwich Theater down the street, across from where Nancy lived now. Eighth Avenue above Fourteenth Street, where the little candy stands, just big enough for a man and a stove to fit in, sold the sexiest magazines. The old Ninth Avenue el and the dock at Sixteenth Street and the Hudson River, the one you could walk out onto. The freight trains that used to run down the middle of Eleventh Avenue, the Automat on Twenty-Third Street off Seventh. St. Vincent's Hospital with its purple ambulances, and the library and the public swimming pool and playground across the street from P.S. 95 on Clarkson Street. The toughest school in New York, they called 95. Mobley and Burt Kaufman went there from 41, to the Rapid Advance class. They had an old bag of a teacher in home room. She always wore blue flower-print smocks and she smacked the hell out of anybody who got out of line. Every day at three o'clock she marched them down the stairs in a double line to the front door. Then as they were freed for the day, in pairs, they would bounce down the stairs screaming "Botcherell! Botcherell!" One day the teacher held up the line just in front of the door. "Some of you," she said, "have been yelling a dirty word outside this door when you leave the school. I don't ever want to hear it again." From that day on everybody in the class, even the three Chinese boys who got the best marks and had the best handwriting and always paid attention and never stayed home sick, yelled "Botcherell!" as they vaulted the steps to freedom. Neither Mobley nor Kaufman ever found out what it meant, if anything.

The old arts and crafts teacher at 95, a wizened man who told pirate stories with such expression that even the incorrigibles from Sullivan Street—the ones old Botcherell used to make stand in the clothes closet—listened eagerly. The guy across the street selling lemon and orange ice in 1c, 2c, 3c and

5c sizes. The two trips a year to the Polo Grounds, half the school going at one time and sitting in the upper left field stands from the foul pole out to watch Terry and Ott and Travis Jackson and Carl Hubbell. At world series time, the canvas flash-signs up over the bars, with a guy behind the canvas with a flashlight and the radio turned on, flashing the action of the ball across the green canvas diamond, and the crowds that gathered outside to watch.

The gangs on every block—sometimes two and three to a block. The signs that went up on every block during World War II, stretching across the street with half-moon holes cut in them all the way across so that the wind could get through and not blow them away: "God Bless Our Boys, 17th Street, 9th to 10th Aves."

These things Ed Mobley and Burt Kaufman experienced and, in hindsight, treasured. They remained friends, somehow a certain feat in its own right for that part of town. Mobley became a newspaperman, Kaufman a cop: now an inspector assigned exclusively to the commissioner's office. For two years he had worked on the inner "police force" of the police force, checking up on other cops. Now he stayed inside.

And he knew what there was to know.

Tonight, Monday night, he joined Mobley and Nancy at their table in the inside room at Camillo's. Mobley and Nancy had finished eating when he got there.

"Did you eat?" Mobley said. "Push over, Nance."

"I ate," Burt Kaufman said. He was black-haired and slim, and dressed quietly in gray pin-stripe. "I'll have a brandy. Listen, you two, I can get you Judge Pinelli."

Mobley said, "Who he?"

"He divorces more people than any other judge in the state," Kaufman said. "He's looking for a change of pace. He'll marry you."

Mobley and Nancy looked at each other, and Burt Kaufman said, "Oh-oh. Lover's spat?"

"She just called me hot-pants," Mobley said. "And not, I might add, in an admiring tone of voice."

"Ah," Kaufman said, "li'l Eddie went and was a bad boy."

"Li'l Eddie can be as bad as he wants," Nancy said. "He can count me out, that's all. He claims he passed out in a naked woman's apartment."

"Did she rent it naked or was she naked when he passed out?"

"I didn't pass out," Mobley said. "I got sick and puked and went home."

Nancy said, "Ask him what he was doing there in the first place."

"All right," Kaufman said. "What were you doing there in the first place?"

"I was seduced," Mobley said.

"Of course you were," Kaufman said. "Did you hear the one about the guy who was seduced by his brother's wife, and right in the middle she says, 'Kiss me,' and he says, 'Kiss you?—I shouldn't even be doing this.'?"

"I don't see," Nancy said, "where that has any bearing."

"It doesn't," Burt Kaufman said. "So all right. Tell dad all about it."

The waiter came and they ordered drinks, and Mobley recited the story of himself and Mildred. When he got through he said, "I feel like I ought to go on at the Palace. This is the third time today I've gone through this tell-all routine. Once to Griffith, then to Nancy, now you."

"Tell it a few more times," Kaufman said. "Maybe somebody will believe it."

"Yeah?" Mobley said.

"Yeah," Kaufman said. "What's the matter, you aren't reciting poetry tonight? 'How do I love thee? Let me count the ways.'"

"Shove it," Mobley said.

"Shove it yourself. You're a jerk. You stink."

"All right."

"You think if you're drunk it don't count."

"I only kissed her."

"The way I just heard it, she kissed you. The tenth time around, this is going to be a pretty lively story."

"It's not that, Burt," Nancy said. She wore a blue dress of wool that fitted her well. "It's not what he did or didn't do. He just doesn't know when to say no. He doesn't even know how. The night we got engaged, I told him I could have been any other girl and he said I was crazy. The next thing you know he's in

Mildred Donner's apartment." Her voice was low, and she did not look at Mobley as she spoke. "If he wants to marry me, why does he have to do that?"

"The hell with him," Kaufman said. "Let him talk his own way out."

"Drink your drink," Mobley said to him.

"Yeah," Kaufman said. "All right." He sipped at his brandy. "What I'm going to tell you is this, and it's strictly over this table. It has to be, for now. All right?"

"Yes," Mobley said.

"Okay," Burt Kaufman said. "The three murders. Tally and Felton and the Grabowski kid."

"Not committed by the same man," Mobley said.

Kaufman shook his head. "They were committed by the same man. Your paper had it right."

Mobley's finger played idly with the top ice cube in his highball. "Sure?"

"Positive." '

"Then what's the big secret? You just got through saying we had it in the paper."

Kaufman grinned. "Yeah, but when that was planted with that sucker you had down at headquarters, we didn't know for sure. We found out subsequently."

"How?"

"Prints. We finally found a perfect set. Matched them to Tally. Tally we'd already matched to Felton."

"Meedy's scoop," Mobley said, half to himself. "Meedy's beat."

"I got some more news for you."

"What's that?"

"Equally confidential," Kaufman said. "All right."

"You know how we linked him from Felton to Tally?"

Mobley nodded. He saw the other look at Nancy and he said, "It's all right. She knows about it."

"That strange habit he had," Kaufman said.

Mobley nodded again. "His calling card."

"Okay," Kaufman said. "Three murders and—before that—nine burglaries."

Mobley looked at him. "Nine?"

"That's what I said. Nine."

"Let me use that."

"No."

"Why not?"

"Because I say so. Ed, I guarantee you. The minute we get this guy, I let you know. It may work out so you beat the others an hour, maybe more. Meanwhile, you don't use anything."

Mobley licked his lips. "Big burglaries?"

"No. Never once any money. A little worthless jewelry, and things like underwear and handkerchiefs and scarves and perfume. A nut. To use the term, a sexual psychopath."

"Leading up to the killings?"

"Yes." Kaufman sipped at his brandy again. "We sensed the pattern. Besides what you call his calling card. Each time he stole a little more, worked a little more boldly. One time the woman was in the other room and heard a noise and came out and saw the door closing, only she was too scared to look out and see who it was."

Mobley said, "I want to ask you one thing. Was there any one article that he stole each time in common?"

"Yeh," Kaufman said, and grinned. "A handkerchief. A dirty handkerchief."

Nancy Liggett said, "My God."

"One time he could only get a clean one," Kaufman said. "It must have made him mad as hell."

"You know something," Mobley said, "this is a screwy case. The guy writes on a wall with lipstick. What kind of a crazy character would do a thing like that?"

Kaufman shrugged. "He might have picked up some ideas from a case something like this in the midwest seven or eight years ago."

"There was another one like this?"

"Don't you read your own paper? It was in that series they've been running. When you've been in the business as long as I have, there's nothing you can't link up with something else. This guy we're after, though, has some characteristics all his own."

"He must be a real whack," Mobley said.

"Sure he is," Kaufman said. "And now I'll tell you something else. So long as you are plying me with whisky and my tongue is loosened. And this also is over this table. Strictly."

Mobley and Nancy leaned forward. Kaufman, they sensed, was enjoying his role. He was also telling the truth.

"The killer," Burt Kaufman said slowly now, "is husky and young. About twenty. He has light hair. He usually wears a windbreaker, and stuffs the stuff he steals up it in front. We think he has dark eyes."

"Where did you get that?"

"Checking back," Kaufman said. "A man on the street outside the Tally place saw this guy. We got similar descriptions from people on the street—neighbors—on the second, sixth and seventh burglaries."

Mobley said, "Why, you son of a gun."

"Yeh," Kaufman said. "And every crime but one—the Felton thing—has been in the Bronx."

Mobley said, "So why don't you pull him in? What's his name?"

"We don't know his name. We don't know where to look for him. But we do have an idea when."

"You do?"

Kaufman nodded grimly. "The case against the unknown Mr. Murder is this: his crimes have become more frequent, they have become more violent, and they have become bolder in execution."

"Then he ought to hit again some time this week."

"He ought to," Kaufman said quietly.

"But you said they've become more violent and bolder," Nancy said. "He's already done everything a man can do. What's he going to do next?"

"We don't know," Kaufman said. "What the hell—maybe the next one he goes for will be a boy."

"Sure," Mobley said. "Or maybe the next one will be in cold daylight. So far he's only worked at night." . . .

"See?" Kaufman said, turning to Nancy. "Lover boy here comes up with ideas every once in a while."

"Too damn many for me," she said.

Chapter Thirty-Two

Dorothy Kyne was sitting on the couch in the living room, her legs tucked under her and a drink in her hand, when Walter Kyne came home. She said, "Darling," and smiled at him.

"I think I shall have a drink," he said. "Where's Steven?"

"He has a cold."

"I didn't know butlers got colds," Kyne said, and began to work up a drink for himself. "How's your mother's cold?"

"Better," Dorothy said. "Thank you."

"I still think you ought to move her in with us," Kyne said. "The poor old lady can't hear anything. You hadn't ought to leave her alone."

"She prefers it that way," Dorothy Kyne said. "And to tell you the truth, so do I. I wouldn't like her under foot all the time."

"So what's it like this way?" Kyne made a gesture with his glass. "Three, four times a week you go see her. I come home, nobody's here but Steven." —

"Ah," Dorothy said, "I've been here alone twice the number of nights that you have. All your cocktail parties and visiting firemen and late nights at the office. Here, sit down beside me. You look tired, darling."

"Nothing a good workout wouldn't fix," Kyne said. He sat down on the couch.

His wife put her drink into her left hand, farthest away from him. "Did you go to the gym?"

"I was not," Walter Kyne said, "referring to the gym."

"I know," she said, "but it's always nice to have Milton there give you a massage."

"How the hell do you know?"

"I take your word for it," Dorothy Kyne said.

"Besides," Kyne said, "I only go to the gym the day after big cocktail parties. There hasn't been a cocktail party since the Scripps-Howard thing last month."

"Well," Dorothy said, "isn't the publishers' meeting next week?"

"Four days of it," Kyne said. "You'll be a widow, Baby. I've taken a room at the Waldorf."

"Oh," she said.

"Can't you say a sorrier 'oh' than that?"

"I'm sorry," she said. "Oh. Is that better?"

"Decidedly," Walter Kyne said. "As a matter of fact, I decided today. Between now and then I'm going to make up my mind."

"About what?"

Kyne set his drink down on the table before the couch. "The McCrady business."

His wife watched him over the rim of her glass. "So soon?"

Kyne nodded. "It'll be the best time. All the publishers in town, and we can get all the space we need in *Editor and Publisher.* It's a natural. We'll have a little dinner for the new man, introduce him around, so forth and so on. It's just got to be that way."

Dorothy said, "What about the murder?"

Kyne shrugged. "It was a blind. I wanted to see them in action. Now I've seen them." He winked at his wife. "And don't go telling my candidates. I want to keep them on their toes."

"Who would I tell?"

"Harry," Kyne said.

Dorothy emptied her glass. "Make me another, darling," she said. "Why Harry?"

"Because you see him," Walter Kyne said. He mixed her a new drink. "He's here for dinner two, three times a month. Hell, he's coming this week, isn't he?"

"Next Monday night," Dorothy said. "A week from tonight."

"Oh, then all right," Kyne said. "By that time it will be decided."

"They must be on pins and needles," she said.

Kyne laughed shortly. "They are. You should have seen them at the meeting today. In my office. They're like a bunch of kids bucking for eagle scout."

His wife said, "Do you blame them?"

Kyne shrugged his shoulders again. "In a way, yes. I should have modified what I said, anyway. Two of them are bucking for it so you can see it. The other two are playing it closer. It's a little harder to figure them."

"What two?"

"Well," Kyne said, using his fingers to tick off the candidates, "Lamin and Loving are both whaling for the job with everything they've got. Griffith and Harry are a little different. Griffith as much as told me to go to hell in the newsroom the other night. Harry Kritzer I don't quite figure. He just goes about his business."

"Does he go about it well?"

"Damn well," Kyne said. "He's a fine newspaperman, Harry."

"In other words," his wife said, her voice carefully cool, "you haven't made up your mind."

"No," Kyne said. "But I'm about to."

"I'd help you if I could."

He turned to her. "I want you to, sweetheart. You might as well know it, if you don't already. I'm scared."

"Scared? You? Why?" '

"Scared," Kyne said, "not so much because I might not pick a good man—hell, they're all good—but because in picking one man, I might overlook someone better. Dorothy, there are too many things about the newspaper business I don't know. I don't let on, but it comes out every once in a while. The other day I stood in the newsroom raising hell because the paper wouldn't print a piece of copy, and all the time it was libel. And I didn't even know it. I had to be told right out in front of everybody." He took a generous belt of whisky. "Too many things I don't know, and what's more, I don't want to know. That's the job of the man who'll take McCrady's place, not mine."

Dorothy nodded. "Well," she said, "from what you've told me, Griffith probably is the most executive-type newspaperman you've got. Lamin is a top wire-service man. Mark Loving is the best feature man. And Harry Kritzer does the best work, day in and day out."

"That's more or less it," Kyne said. "To tell you the truth, I'd more or less ruled Harry out."

"Oh, I wouldn't do that." Dorothy Kyne shook her head slowly, to counter-balance the haste with which the words had spilled forth.

Her husband looked at her inquiringly. "Why not?"

She set her glass down and interlaced her fingers. "McCrady's job is a day in, day out job. It isn't determined by fits and starts, it doesn't depend on snap judgments. It's largely a question of maturity. Probably Arnold Lamin was better known to a lot of newspaper people than McCrady, when McCrady was alive."

Kyne laughed again. "He still is," he said. He fished into the inside pocket of his suit coat and brought forth a letter, on the stationary of the Tribune, the Kyne paper in Philadelphia.

Dorothy took it and read:

Dear Walter,
Just a note. Have been delighted with the KPS coverage of your big murder hunt, the discoveries and what not. So far superior to the other services it isn't even funny. Understand you are going to take the guy away from the wire. If he didn't deserve it, I'd howl bloody murder.
My best to you, as always. Up 18,000 on stand sales, thanks to KPS.
Sincerely,
Ellis Leeds
Executive Editor

"What's he talking about?" she said. "Lamin," Kyne said. "Leeds 'understands' we're going to take Lamin away from KPS. Taking him away from KPS means giving him McCrady's job." He took the letter from his wife. "That's the third letter of its kind I've had in a week."

"Lamin's got friends," Dorothy Kyne said.

"Well-placed friends," Walter Kyne said.

"Would you let something like that influence you?" It was a challenge, the way she said it.

Her husband regarded her mildly. "Why not? What's wrong with Lamin?"

"He libeled you on the wire."

"No he didn't. He killed it."

"But the wire is his responsibility, regardless of who killed it."

"That," Walter Kyne said agreeably, "is true."

"Well, then?" Dorothy said. "Is that the kind of man you

want running your business for you?"

"Philadelphia didn't seem to mind."

"You asked for my opinion, Walter," Dorothy said coolly. "That's what I'm trying to give you."

"Okay," he said. "Who gets the job?"

"Harry Kritzer," she said evenly, and wondered at the way her heart beat within her.

"I," Walter Kyne said, "am going to stop inviting Harry here for dinner. I think you're soft on him."

"I am," she said. "Opposed to those other three men you've got I think he's so far and away the best man there isn't even any contest. And then you come in tonight and tell me you've ruled him out."

"I didn't say it definitely," Kyne said. He was annoyed to find himself on the defensive. "I also said I could make a mistake. That's why I wanted your advice."

"Well, you've got it," Dorothy said.

"You can't get away from one thing," her husband said. "When all is said and done, Harry's a photo man."

Her eyes were alight. "And one of the others is a newspaper editor and another one is a wire service man and the other one sticks comic strips in the mail. So what?"

Once again, Kyne shrugged. "Maybe I've been paying too much attention to these murders."

"If you have been, it's nobody's fault but your own. You were the one who had the wonderful idea about throwing it out at them and letting them fight over it."

Kyne grinned. "They've sure been fighting."

"All," she said firmly, "except Harry. You said so yourself."

"Now, wait a minute. I didn't say he wasn't fighting. I only said I couldn't figure him. And I didn't know photo men could write, too."

"What does that mean?"

Walter Kyne stood up. "Did Harry write that speech for you? You didn't think that up all yourself. The next thing you'll be telling me, I'm down on him because of his name."

"That's another thing," Dorothy said, but her passion had subsided. She felt the initiative being taken away from her; wondered suddenly how much of her husband's interest so far had been suspicion.

"Look," Kyne said, standing by the table and looking down at her. "Have you got a crush on this guy? Are you secret lovers?" The way he said it, she sensed he did not know.

Dorothy felt a measure of renewed safety. "You're the one who brings him here. Did I ever tell you to invite him?"

"No," her husband said. "No, you didn't." He bit his lower lip. "It would be funny, though. That duck-legged son of a bitch Kritzer."

"What would be funny?"

"If the reason that he didn't seem to be trying for the job was that he was working on me through you."

"If we were secret lovers," Dorothy said, and felt like she had felt the night she made four spades doubled and redoubled by playing the two of trumps, "he wouldn't have to work on you. The fact itself would be all he'd need."

Kyne closed his eyes. "I think you're probably right," he said.

"Of course I'm right."

"Unless . . ." Kyne said. "Unless what?"

"Unless Harry doesn't really want the job."

"Why on earth wouldn't he want it?"

"Beats me," the publisher said. "You want to go to bed?"

"All right," she said. She smiled up at him. "Lover." Kyne laughed again.

She looked up at him. "What's funny now?"

"Where I got the idea."

"What idea?"

"Of Harry working on me through you."

"Oh?"

"Who do you think," he said to her, "is fighting for the job hardest of all?"

"Lamm," Dorothy Kyne said promptly.

"Why?"

"Those letters."

Her husband held out his hands and pulled her to a standing position. As he kissed her, his hands moved firmly downward along her back. She pulled her mouth from his and said, "Am I right?"

He shook his head. "Nope."

"Who?"

"Mark Loving."

"I suppose *he* tried to get at you through me."

"No," Kyne said, "but he used Mildred Donner to get at Ed Mobley."

"The women's page gal?"

"Yuh," Kyne said, "and our number one man on the *Sentinel.*"

"Why did he do that?"

"He wanted Mobley working for him."

"What did he do?"

"He tried to get Mildred to sleep with Mobley."

"What did Mobley say?" Dorothy found her interest mounting.

"He didn't say anything. Didn't have a chance. Mildred never went through with it. Anyway, that's where I got the idea about you and Harry. The things some of those guys will do."

Dorothy put her arms around her husband's neck.

"Where did you find this out?"

"Where do you think?"

"Don't tell me Loving told you."

"Don't be silly."

"Then who?"

"Mildred."

"Mildred!"

"I took her to lunch," Kyne said. "Believe it or not." He reached over and snapped out the light.

"Wait a minute," she said. "Let's go upstairs."

They stood there in the darkness, he thinking of Harry Kritzer, she thinking of Mildred Donner. Then he put his arm around her and they started for the stairway.

Chapter Thirty-Three

All that night, that Monday night and into Tuesday morning, a doubled Kyne staff manned the newsroom and the photo desk, waiting. A Kyne man sat in the press room at Centre Street, waiting. The last edition went in, locked up, and rolled, and still the lights burned in the city room.

Extra cops, and a dozen more policewomen, worked the streets of the Bronx, waiting.

The hunted killer had to strike again. This they knew, and they waited. Nothing happened.

Chapter Thirty-Four

Mark Loving was unable to get in touch with Mildred Donner until Tuesday morning. Then he got her on the phone. She was at her desk, alongside the financial department back on the *Sentinel* side of the newsroom. He was in his office in the N.K. building.

He said, "Where the hell have you been?"

"I was in New Jersey for the weekend."

"Where'd you go for lunch yesterday?"

"Walter took me to lunch."

"Walter?"

"Kyne," she said. "He's got a publisher's convention in town next week. He wants me to make a speech."

"How'd you go?"

"When? Where?"

"With Mobley," Loving said, and there was irritation in his voice. "I assume every operator in the building is listening in to this conversation."

"Oh," Mildred said. "It was no dice."

"Why not?"

"He won't play."

"Did you play? With him?"

"No," she said, "and right now I'm frightfully busy."

"What about lunch?"

"I can't."

Loving's voice shifted gears. "Knock that off," he said. "I'll meet you downstairs at seven tonight, in the Dell, and you be there. I want to talk to you about a lot of things. Particularly about Walter Kyne."

"Not Mobley?"

"The hell with Mobley."

"Then why did you ask me to do it?"

"You mean with him? Look, pet, I'll explain things to you that haven't been explained before. I'll tell you about a little meeting in the big man's office yesterday. It may interest you to know your man's in pretty sweet shape."

"You sound awfully sure of yourself."

"I feel sure of myself. I'll demonstrate tonight."

"I don't feel like any of your demonstrations."

"You will," Loving said. "Seven tonight."

There was a pause. Then she said, "All right."

"Oh," he said. "One more thing."

"What?"

"Besides I love you."

"I know that. What is it?"

"Where are you going to make this speech?"

"You mean next week? At the convention."

"I know. Where is it?"

"The Waldorf."

"Okay, hot legs," Mark Loving said. "'bye." He hung up the phone momentarily, then flashed the operator. He said to her, "Get me the banquet department at the Waldorf. A Mr. Petrie."

He got Petrie, whom he knew, and asked him two or three questions. Then he hung up the phone again and went to the closet in his office. It was one of those built-in closet-lavatories with a mirror and a basin. Mark Loving took down a spray mouthwash and swizzed some of it into his mouth. He looked in the mirror and patted his tie. "So," he said aloud, "Mr. Kyne is holding a banquet for the publishers. I wonder why."

Then he walked briskly out of his office, nodded to the secretaries, walked down the aisle separating the cubicle offices of the feature department, walked across the main foyer, walked into the executive section, stopped in front of the last secretary, and said, "Jane, will you tell Mr. Kyne I want to see him? It'll only take a minute."

She picked up her phone. "Mr. Kyne, Mr. Loving's here. Can you see him for just a minute?" She nodded into the phone .and smiled up at Mark Loving. "You can go in."

"Thank you," Mark Loving said, and moved briskly toward the door to the inner office. The publisher, he found, was at his desk inside, reading his Chicago paper, the *Chronicle.*

"Come in, Mark," he said. "Did you see the way the Chronicle is playing up your murder series?"

"I could show you some sales figures on that series," Loving said, "that would knock your eye out, Walter. As a matter of fact, I will. But that's not what's on my mind."

Kyne put his paper down. "Sit down, Mark."

"No, thanks. Thus will only take half a minute." Loving rested his hands, almost acquisitively, on the publisher's polished giant of a desk. "I've been meaning to say something, Walter, that I think ought to be said."

Kyne reached for a cigarette. He waved away the lighter that appeared almost chemically in Loving's hand. He waited.

"Walter," Mark Loving said, "it's no secret you're going to appoint a man to take Cy McCrady's place. It's no secret it will be one of three men." He paused imperceptibly.

Then he went on. "As one of the three, I think I ought to tell you something." Again he paused, a trifle longer this time. Still there was no response. The blue eyes watched him from the other side of the desk.

"I want the job," Loving said. "I know I can handle it. I just want you to know that no matter what happens, you'll always have my cooperation ..." a slight pause ". . . and my loyalty. I've been meaning to say it, and finally I decided to. It's just that I value our friendship. I hope you do too."

He stopped, and when still the other said nothing, he said, "That's all, Walter. Let's shake hands."

Walter Kyne reached forth his hand, and Mark Loving could not but admire the pearl cuff link. The publisher did not get up. They shook hands. Kyne said, "All right, Mark, I think there'll be some news."

Loving smiled at him genially and turned to leave.

"Let me see those figures you were talking about," Kyne called after him.

As he closed the door to the publisher's office, Loving was swearing to himself. The delicate gambit—throwing the figure three at Kyne, so Kyne could rise to the bait—had misfired.

Either Kyne had exhibited more innate wisdom than Loving read in him, or maybe in Kyne's mind, for some reason, there were only three candidates.

A moment's further deliberation caused Loving to reject the latter possibility. No, there were four. Kyne had chosen not to ask him what three he had in mind. Maybe Kyne knew he would have replied: himself, Griffith and Kritzer. Then he would have told Kyne what was wrong with the man he, Mark Loving, feared the most: If Walter Kyne only had taken the pitchout, he, Mark

Loving, could have ripped Arnold Lamin apart.

Chapter Thirty-Five

Edward Mobley took Tuesday as his day off. He was at home, and he intended to stay there, if only out of a vague suspicion that Burt Kaufman might call from headquarters. He sat in an armchair, still wearing his pajamas, with a cup of coffee at his elbow. He was reading Faulkner's story "The Bear":

".... It ain't nine o'clock yet."
"That's town time. You ain't in town now. You in the woods."
"Look at the sun then."
"Nemmine the sun too," Ash said.

"You in the woods," Mobley said to himself now, aloud. "You ain't in town now. Damn your own god-forsaken eyes."

He thought of Nancy and of last night, and of the business with Mildred, and how what could be so unimportant to him could be so important to the woman he wanted to marry.

She had told him off, Nancy had, standing in her doorway—she still had not, he remembered, equipped the door with a chain lock—and he, Edward Mobley, in the great, mighty, bumbling stupidity of a man who finds himself in love for the first time at the age of thirty-four, had said, almost plaintively, "But Nance, you love me."

"That's just it," she had said. Her eyes were bright, but she did not cry. "Get away from me, Mobley."

"Well, it makes no sense," he had said. "I told you what happened. I told you the truth. So help me."

"I know," she said.

"And you heard it from me. You didn't hear it from somebody else."

"I know."

"And I love you," he said. "I told you. I want to marry you. So what is all this?"

"Go away, Ed," she said. "Please. I just want you to leave

me alone."

Then she closed the door, and now he did not think one way or the other about the necessity for an extra lock.

He felt lost and very much alone, and stopped at the Dell on his way home for one drink and was unhappy drinking it. The bar was quiet and the lighting, the blue lighting, seemed made for his mood,, and he thought that once Walter Kyne had told him, "Ed, my life is a blue light. You know what I mean?"

"No," Mobley had said.

"Son," Walter Kyne said, "have you ever been in the engraving room?"

"Probably."

"Well, then, you think about the color of the lights. They look blue and intense and bright, so you can see everything." Kyne put a hand on Mobley's shoulder. "Nothing is hidden. The same it is with me, my life's an open book. A blue light."

This, Mobley had been inclined intrinsically to doubt. Furthermore, the reference to blue light irritated him in the way that people do become resentful at intrusions upon their privacies. For Mobley, blue light (the mention or the thought of it) projected always the remembrance of a spring night in Washington, D. C, when he was sitting in the lobby of the Statler Hotel, watching the assistant manager of the hotel sitting imperiously in his little half-booth in the center of the lobby, like a ticket-taker at a Paoli lawn fete; and waiting—Mobley, not the assistant manager—for a brunette who had legs like those on the broads in the wartime ads in Life ("Doggy legs or DOGGY legs?").

In the afternoon, it had rained, and Washington smelled clean. The brunette worked in the Department of Agriculture, which to Mobley's earthy mind suggested the word plow, a verb. Somebody in the Kyne Washington bureau had introduced him to her in the bar in the Times-Herald building, where, as in other Washington saloons, you could get whisky at a table but only beer at the bar.

That had been during his last trip to Washington, and her name was Alice, and this time he had called her up and was sitting there now, waiting; and for some reason he got up and went outside to the corner of 16th and K Streets, and began to walk south. It was something idle, to kill time, but through an arch of trees in a little park ahead of him he saw the lights and the warm-cold pillars of the White House, something that, despite half a dozen trips to Washington, he had never seen before. He kept walking, sighting the Washington Monument ahead and on the left. This, too, he had never seen before. It was very dark now, and Mobley was alone. There was no echo in his footsteps; the sound seemed to be absorbed, instead. On his left, in full view now, the Washington Monument thrust into the sky, slender and grave, almost profound, and guarded atop by a red light to warn airplanes away— something more for the protection of the monument, without doubt, than for the planes.

Then Mobley looked to his right over a long, calm, geometric mall of black water for what seemed a mile in distance, and at the end, lighted just enough to be seen, almost in the effect of a mirage, the Lincoln Memorial stood.

The building was twice the size that Mobley had imagined. The steps were twice as many. He knew as he started walking toward it that the figure of Lincoln would be twice as large. The light that bathed the building, the faint light, was blue.

He walked in sensuous darkness beside the water. Here and again, a dogwood had spilled out its first white recognition of spring. The night was clear, and the sky seemed higher than the stars. The moon was coolly yellow, in the shape of a right-hand mark of parenthesis.

When he reached the plaza, the street in front of the memorial, he found the building already had been closed for the night. Halfway up the stairs was a blockade of wooden longhorses. They were gray in color, and on each one it said, in black, DO NOT CROSS-POLICE LINE. "Girls—50—Girls," Edward Mobley said, half aloud, and gazed for a period of time at the stone figure of compassion that brooded upon him and the police barrier; then he went back across the street, and got into a bus that was empty except for a driver reading See or Peek (Mobley could not determine which). "Night," he said to the driver, and went back and sat down. After a while, the driver put away his magazine and started the bus. When he got back to the Statler, Mobley saw it was after ten o'clock. Alice, he could only assume, had been and gone.

Now, in the Dell, he had his one drink and went home.

Chapter Thirty-Six

The odds on McCrady's successor shifted overnight. The way intramural information travels in a worldwide news organization, they knew about it in the plush Rome offices of Kyne World Features, in the KPS newsroom in London; in the composing room of the paper in San Francisco, at the press clubs in Washington and Mexico City. A stringer in Vancouver, who once had known Harry Kritzer, talked it over with Kynpix's Seattle man. Tokyo had it. So did Baires—the newsman's shorthand for Buenos Aires—and staffers in Vienna and Denver made identical bets at identical times.

Griffith the favorite now, at 5 to 2.

Lamin 7 to 2.

Loving pulling up: 4 to 1.

And, still far on the outside, though backed here and there by money best described as sentimental, Honest Harry Kritzer, at 20 to 1.

Some news, it could be surmised, did no traveling at all, even via the excessively-traveled Kyne grapevine.

But those were the newest odds, influenced by the swift-heralded information: that Walter Kyne had, within the past twenty-four hours, decided to make up his mind inside of a week.

Not so strangely, the last to hear the odds were the candidates themselves. Even less strangely, Walter Kyne had not heard them at all.

There was nobody who would tell him, and nobody he would ask. It was no better than even money, to be sure, that he realized there were any odds at all.

But the odds were there, as quoted, at 11:30 a.m., EST, Tuesday morning.

At 11:35 the odds changed.

The Louisville *News*, an influential paper, independently owned but a client of Arnold Lamin's KPS, Harry Kritzer's Kynpix, and Mark Loving's KWF, announced that at the publisher's convention in New York next week it would bestow its annual news-management award—a coveted trophy awarded to an editor for his supervisory handling of an important story, a trophy never before won by anyone connected with Kyne—to Arnold Lamin.

The Kyne Press Service bureau in Louisville slapped it on the wire in the form of a bulletin.

Louisville, in the KPS network of wires—a network celebrated by a huge map of the United States in Walter Kyne's office, a map riddled by colored pins which the late Cyrus McCrady once said represented cities and large towns rather than points in the Kyne operation—Louisville, at any rate, was on the south wire, which ran from Miami up through Atlanta and terminated in Cincinnati. There, other teletypes fed the news from the south wire, such proportion of it as was of interest nationally, onto the trunk into New York.

The news at hand was of more than southern interest.

In years to come, the men of Kyne would laugh over what happened at the precise moment that Cincinnati began to relay the Louisville bulletin onto the trunk. At the time, this Tuesday forenoon, nobody laughed.

The trunk wire developed line trouble.

It looked like this:

BULLETIN
LOUISVILLE— (KPS)—THE ANNUAL NEWS-MANAGEMENT
AWARD OF THE LOUISVILLE NEWS WENT TODAY
TOARRRRRRRRRRR
     AGAIN PLS NK

"NK" represented the call-letters of the New York bureau, asking that the bulletin be repeated. Cincinnati tried again.

BUJJJJJJJJJJJJJJJJJJJJJJJJJJJJJJJJJJJJJJJJJJJJJJJJJJJJJ
JUNK HERE DT

Detroit was saying it didn't make sense.

The chief teletype operator in New York picked up his direct-line telephone to the American Telephone and Telegraph Company, from whom Kyne, like the other press associations, leased its wires. At its monitor headquarters, AT&T switched the Kyne trunk to another parallel circuit, thus putting KPS back in action while it hunted the trouble on the dead wire.

In the New York office of KPS, Arnold Lamin gazed unhappily at one of his receiver teletype sets. He had an inkling the Louisville award concerned someone at Kyne, for otherwise there would have been no reason for the Louisville bureau to handle the item as a bulletin. Lamin stuffed a wad of paper in his mouth. He did not know any of the brass on the Louisville *News*, although some of them were friends of his friends. He chewed rapidly on the piece of paper in his mouth.

Then the wire came to life again. Lamin's neck stiffened as he bent over the machine. But it was only AT&T, testing the new wire:

```
THIS NY TESTING
THE QUICK BROWN FOX JUMPED OVER THE LAZY
DOGS BACK 1234567890 TIMES
THE QUICK BROWN FOX JUMPED OVER THE LAZY
DOGS BACK 1234567890 TIMES
THE QUICK BROWN FOX JUMPED OVER THE LAZY
DOGS BACK 1234567890 TIMES
STILL JUNK HERE DT
```

"God damn Detroit!" Lamin exclaimed. The wire kept going.

```
DT SUGG TRY NEW SET
```

AT&T was suggesting that the Detroit bureau use another teletype set in its own office, on the supposition that there might be mechanical trouble in the set now in use there.

Lamin read on:

MIN PLS DT

The wire went silent again for a minute as Detroit changed the hookup plugs on its switchboard. Then:

OK TRY IT NOW DT THIS NY TESTING

THE QUICK BROWN FOX JUMPED OVER THE LAZY

DOGS BACK 1234567890 TIMES

THE QUICK BROWN FOX JUMPED OVER THE LAZY

DOGS BACK 1234567890 TIMES

THE QUICK BROWN FOX JUMPED OVER THE LAZY

DOGS BACK 1234567890 TIMES

HOW PLS NK

OK HERE NK

OK END TEST NK

CN TRY THAT BUN AGAIN NK BULLETIN

LOUISVILLE— (KPS)—THE ANNUAL NEWS-MANAGEMENT AWARD OF THE LOUISVILLE NEWS WENT TODAY TO ARNOLD LAMIN, DIRECTOR OF KYNE PRESS SERVICE.

LAMIN, WHO WILL RECEIVE THE AWARD AT THE PUBLISHERS' CONVENTION IN NEW YORK NEXT WEEK, WAS CITED FOR "THE ENTERPRISE AND ENTHUSIASM WHICH RESULTED IN EXTRAORDINARY COVERAGE OF A SERIES OF MURDERS IN NEW YORK CITY, AS WELL AS FOR OUTSTANDING MANAGEMENT OF OTHER NEWS STORIES DURING THE YEAR." (MORE)

Lamin did not wait to read more. He went over to his chief desk man, Joe Levine.

"Don't let them handle the rest as a bulletin, Joe," he said. "There's other news besides this."

Levine nodded. "That's good going, Arn."

"Hot damn," Lamin said. He walked with long strides into his office. "Nancy," he said to his secretary, "where's Ed today?"

Nancy Liggett looked up. "I don't know."

"See if you can find him," Lamin said. "I want to thank him for some help he gave me."

The phone rang. It was Ellis Leeds, chief of the Kyne paper in Philadelphia.

"You old son of a bitch," Leeds said.

"Hello, El," Lamin said. "Who rigged this one? It's a beauty."

"I don't know who rigged it," Leeds said. "If it was rigged at all. But you know who's got an old pal out in Louisville?"

"No. Who?"

"Harry Kritzer," Leeds said. He began to laugh. "Wouldn't it be funny if he'd called their attention to his work on this thing and they looked at your wire instead?"

"Oh, Christ," Lamin said. The idea intrigued him, although he was unwilling to believe it. "It didn't happen that way."

"Why the hell do you care how it happened?"

"I don't," Lamin said. They said good-by and hung up, and the KPS chief turned to his secretary. "Did you find Mobley?"

"No," Nancy said.

Lamin studied her. "Well," he said, "no hurry." It was 11:35.

At Kyne points all over the United States—soon to be all over the world—the odds flashed anew.

Arnold Lamin was no worse than even money now—probably odds-on.

Chapter Thirty-Seven

Lamin was not in his office when Gerald Meedy walked over there to congratulate him. One of the eight clocks on the pillars in the newsroom, the one facing Meedy, said it was two minutes after twelve o'clock noon.

Meedy opened the door to Lamin's glass-enclosed office and said to Nancy Liggett, "Mr. Lamin around?"

"He's in with Mr. Kyne," she said. "He may be a while."

"It wasn't anything important," Meedy said. He stood there, looking at her. "Is Mobley in today?"

"I don't believe so," Nancy said.

Meedy licked his lips. He was wearing a clean shirt, and he had shaved that morning. Now he said, "Could I ask you something?"

She smiled an automatic smile.

"Could you go to lunch with me?"

Nancy looked at him, puzzled. She said, "Any special reason?"

He licked his lips again. "Yes."

"Well?" she said.

"There's something," he said, "I want to tell you." He paused. "Important."

She looked at him. "I only have an hour for lunch."

"That'll be enough time."

She could not say no at this point. "I planned to go at twelve-thirty."

"I'll meet you at Camillo's."

"Isn't that rather expensive?"

"I can afford it," Meedy said.

He was waiting for her at the bar when she got there. She saw that he had a drink in front of him, but that he had barely touched it. He was studying the paintings on the walls with what obviously was manufactured interest.

"Hello, Nancy," he said. "What are you drinking?"

"I don't know," she said. "Maybe a Manhattan. Hello, Geòrgie."

Geòrgie the bartender smiled hello at her and started to work up a Manhattan. Nancy said to Meedy, "Why don't we take our drinks to the table? Then we can order."

"All right," Meedy said. "Do you want to go inside?"

She had been in the inside room at Camillo's too many times with Edward Mobley. She said, "No, let's eat out here."

"All right," Meedy said, and took her arm. Meedy had never been to Camillo's before. He did not realize you paid on the spot for drinks you had at the bar before sitting down.

They sat along the wall in back and Nancy decided the occasion was not particularly suited to small talk. She said, "All right, Gerald. What's the big secret?"

Meedy concentrated on the menu. He did not look at her. "No special secret," he said. "Just something I thought you ought to know."

"You thought?" She accented the pronoun.

"I'm interested in you," he said, still not looking at her. "I have been for a long time. Sue me."

She folded her hands on the table and looked at him. "What was it you wanted to tell me?"

"It's something you ought to know," Meedy repeated. What had gone so well in rehearsal before his mirror came hard now. He decided to go ahead with it quickly. "About Mobley."

"What about him?" Her voice told Meedy nothing.

Meedy went on with the script. "I would suppose," he said, "that the most important thing about a husband ought to be his faithfulness. Not the question of whether or not he's faithful, but his *willingness* to be faithful."

She did not say what she was supposed to say. She did not say anything. Gerald Meedy licked his lips and went ahead. The original script had been altered somewhat, in his favor, he assumed, from something he had been told in a taxicab last night. The person who had told him was Mildred Donner.

"Look, Nancy," Meedy said now. "I'll say this right out. The reason I'm telling you is I think I'm in love with you."

He was not prepared to see her look quite so surprised. In a way, it angered him. He plunged onward.

"Your boy friend, the lovely, faithful Mr. Mobley, spent the night with Mildred Donner Friday.”

He was ready for almost any reaction but the one he got. Nancy Liggett began to laugh.

Meedy said angrily, “It's the truth.”

Her laughter was infuriatingly genuine.

“All right,” Meedy said. “What's funny?”

She put her hands to her face and shook her head. He looked at her figure, the part of her body above the table, and wondered dully how he could possibly have said anything damaging to himself. His physical longing augmented his discomfiture. He squirmed unhappily in his chair.

A waiter came over and said, “Did you want to order, sir?”

“Later,” Meedy said. “Come on, Nancy, what's funny?”

She took her hands away from her face. “I am.”

Gerald Meedy said, “What?”

She nodded her head up and down. “Me.”

“I don't get it,” Meedy said.

“You wouldn't,” she said.

“How can you love a guy like that?” he demanded. Her face became gravely lovely. “I don't know. It's a good question.”

“He doesn't love you.”

She reached out and patted his hand. “You're a nice guy, Gerald. In your way.”

He debated whether he should draw his hand away and decided against it. “If he did it before, he'll do it again.”

Nancy nodded solemnly. “Tell me something, Gerald. Look at me.”

He looked at her defiantly.

“Gerald,” she said, “did you ever spend the night with Mildred?”

His anger had the best of him. “Yes,” he said. “As a matter of fact, I did. So long as you bring it up, it was last night.”

Again she laughed, and the sound of it maddened him even further.

“I wish to hell you'd tell me what you're laughing about.”

“Why, Gerald,” Nancy said, and stopped laughing. “You say you love me and he doesn't, but you say the two of you each spent a night at Mildred's. Something's wrong.”

“He's engaged to you,” Meedy said. “I'm not.

“I know,” Nancy said. “Now let me tell you a secret, if you'll promise not to tell."

He did not like the look in her eyes. There was a brand of merriment there, newly implanted, and he did not know how to deal with it.

"Promise," Nancy said again.

He spread his palms. "So all right. I promise."

"The way you promised Mildred not to tell about Ed?"

"I didn't promise Mildred anything."

"All right," she said.

"Well?"

"Oh," Nancy said. "The secret. It's this: I like my men experienced."

He looked at her without comprehension.

"Gerald," Nancy said, "do you still want to buy my lunch?"

"Go ahead," he said, sulkily. "Order."

"We can talk about Arnold Lamin if you like."

"I don't want to talk," Meedy said.

Chapter Thirty-Eight

Jon Day Griffith had Ed Mobley on the phone. It was 12:45 p.m.

"We're done, Ed," Griffith said. He had just told Mobley about Lamin's award. "It'll take a miracle."

"Nancy isn't talking to me," Mobley said. "I got my own worries."

"Well, it was a good fight," Griffith said.

"Maybe something'll happen yet," Mobley said.

"It better happen quick."

"All right," Mobley said. "I'll be home all day."

Chapter Thirty-Nine

Tuesday afternoon.

The clock on the bank building at the corner, a block down from the first buildings of the University, said 1:04 p.m.

Robert Manners walked under the clock and along the avenue, in from the corner. There was a radio repair shop, and then a children's shoe store, and then the A & P supermarket.

Now, the voice inside him said, *anyone, anywhere, now.*

"They shall roar together like lions: they shall yell as lions' whelps…. I will bring them down like lambs to the slaughter."

He watched the women in the supermarket. They would be going home with their packages. But they would be going home to waiting children, or mothers, or family.

Find one alone!

An apartment house stood on the next corner down. Robert Manners walked toward it.

The single ones live in the small apartments. Think of the small apartments. The one where the Tally woman lived—small apartments there.

Stay away from that house!—the voice said. They're watching it. Are you crazy?

Not that crazy—this he replied to himself.

He put his hands in the wide pockets of his black windbreaker and walked on, watching the women on the street.

The one where that man was—the one who had the woman Sunday night—a small apartment. Eight blocks from here. The apartments beneath that one, the apartments above it are the same size.

In one of them, you will find a woman—alone.

Keep your hands warm.

"Thou art my battle axe and weapons of war: for with thee will I break in pieces the nations, and with thee will I destroy kingdoms."

He was walking quickly now.

"Come against her from the utmost border, open her storehouses: cast her up as heaps, and destroy her utterly: let nothing of her be left."

Robert Manners walked into the building where Harry Kritzer lived. He found Kritzer's name—6M—H. Kritzer— over the mail boxes.

He looked at the other M's.

One of them said—*2M—Geraldine Locke.*

He walked toward the self-service elevator.

A clock on a little table in the foyer said it was 1:26.

Numbers in a little window on the wall panel next to the elevator told him it was coming down. It took a long time.

Then the doors rolled back noiselessly and two little girls—about, he would judge, eight years old—came out. They had roller skates on. Robert Manners smiled at them.

What, he asked himself, *are they doing home from school?*

He went upstairs in the elevator. The ride from the first to the second floors was the slowest elevator ride he had ever known.

He got out, walked down the long, elegantly-carpeted hall, around the turn. He stopped in front of the green doorway. There was a brass knocker on the door, directly over the letter M.

Robert Manners took two deep breaths. Then he rapped loudly with the knocker.

There was silence when he was through.

Why isn't she home?

He knocked again, loudly and long.

No one answered the door.

She has to be home!

He knocked viciously this time.

The door to the apartment across the hall, behind him, opened.

"What do you want?"

He spun and saw a woman standing there—a small, bird-like woman, a woman in her forties, a woman who wore a gray dress.

He looked at her enough to realize, in one sudden sweep, how closely she resembled his own mother. In the same instant, however, his eyes told him also that the apartment behind her, as she stood in her doorway, was a counterpart of the M apartments.

Damn fool, his mind told him. *All the other times, all the terrible times you were never satisfied, she was here, waiting for you to come.*

And you did come!

He propelled his right hand, across the hallway and against her face. The solid weight of his body, behind the hand, hurled her backwards, into the apartment. His left hand swept the door slamming shut behind him.

She fell backwards onto the floor and, free of him, she screamed. It was both throaty and high, a searing sound.

He fell on her. She twisted her face free and screamed again.

His hand, heavy at the throat of her dress, found the lace handkerchief. A shaft of sunlight, slatted by the Venetian blinds of her window, played on the hair that was so much his mother's hair.

He felt the old urge of defilement, and he raised his body from hers. His hand held her mouth tightly. The other hand clutched her handkerchief.

"Don't scream, mother," he said. "I've got what I came for."

He started to move his hand from her mouth to his belt buckle, and her body contorted violently and she screamed again.

Get out of here! Get out! Get away!

He leaped up, the handkerchief balled in his fist, and he flung open the door.

The woman came to her knees and screamed.

He found the stairwell halfway down the haft to the elevator. His hand both balancing and propelling on the iron banister, he vaulted the half-flight to the landing, turned and jumped the other half-flight to the first floor. He burst through the door into the downstairs foyer, bucked the double set of heavy glass outer doors with his shoulder.

From around the corner he could hear the screams of the woman. She had thrown open her window.

A man in an apron had come to the door of a butcher shop across the street. He waved his arm at Robert Manners and shouted, "Hey! Stop! You! Hey!" He started across the street, and a taxicab went by, shutting him momentarily from Robert Manners' view.

In that instant, Robert Manners turned and started to run, up the street away from the corner. He heard the butcher shouting behind him, coming after him. He turned the next corner, running into a long block of six-story apartment houses. A woman with a dog was coming toward him. He veered off the sidewalk and into the street.

The butcher had turned the corner behind him. A hundred feet ahead, two oil-truck men were fitting the nozzle of the hose from their truck into a socket in the sidewalk in front of an apartment house. One of them stood up and watched Robert Manners as he ran. As Manners passed him, the oil-truck man seemed to realize the meaning of the shouting from the man in the apron down the street.

The oil-truck man reached out at Robert Manners as he passed the back of the truck. Manners spun his shoulder away and ran on.

The subway kiosk was at the next corner. He swept down the steps, vaulted the waist-high turnstile, raced onto the platform.

The ticket agent yelled something behind him and came out from his booth. People waiting for the next train looked up as Robert Manners dashed between them, heading for the front end of the platform.

It was a local stop. The tremendous clatter of an oncoming train opened up an avenue of sound, obliterated the shouting behind him. The clatter became a roar and a northbound express train rocketed by, lighting up the darkness of the center tracks.

In that moment, Robert Manners jumped to the local track beside the platform and, moving like some jungle animal from tie to tie between the rails, bolted into the blackness.

A great green eye stared at him from the signal box guarding a long right-hand turning in the tracks. One single electric bulb burned yellowly on the wall to his right every forty feet.

He was into the curve now, the lights of the station blotted out behind him. Far ahead in the winking darkness he saw the lights of the next station.

Quarter of a mile, he told himself.

The noise of two trains now. He spun uncertainly for a

moment in time. One was coming at him from behind—but no oncoming brightness threatened the track he stood on. Instead, a southbound express plunged past him on the track to his left, pillars away. It was with him and gone, and he saw a northbound local going by on the track farthest away.

He, turned and ran again. Up ahead, a blue light shone on the wall. His breath came harshly now, tight and high in his throat, and his mind tried to measure the remaining distance to the next station. Head up, he stumbled, fell heavily on his shoulder against the outside rail. The knuckles of his hand, the one that held the handkerchief, showed sudden blood from the fall. He pulled himself up, running again.

What amount of time had gone by, he did not know. Still he ran, the breath coming hard to his throat now in the damp, black cold of the underground. To his left the third rail, rimmed on top by wooden runners, was a ribbon of gray in the dark. The current that ran through the third rail could kill a man. Its voltage was something, Manners knew, like the voltage that ran through the electric chair, where murderers died.

The ties were unevenly placed. Running from one to the next, he felt his left foot give, felt it turn beneath him. Again he fell, wildly this time with the pain shooting through his ankle. He fell to his left. His elbow struck the outside rail, and his hand, thrown out, came to rest on the insulated strip above the third rail.

He pushed himself up. There was silence over the breadth of the four tracks now. No trains were coming, from either direction. He got halfway to his feet, and the pain tore at him, and he went to his knees on the dirty ties, directly beneath one of the widely-spaced electric bulbs along the tunnel wall. In the light from the bulb, he could read the headline on a torn, discarded newspaper lying between the tracks:

No trains were coming. He rested there on his knees, wondering what he would do if a train came on his track. He would step carefully, in between the local and express tracks, in between the pillars, to let the train go by—if he could stand up.

And then he knew suddenly why there would be no train coming on his track, no southbound local. They would hold up the train at the station where he had jumped from the platform to the tracks. Hold it up so they could hunt him.

Then he saw it. In the lights of the station up ahead, the figure of a man, letting himself down from the platform to the tracks. More than one man. Two. Four.

Something flashed up in front of his eyes, and instinctively he ducked his head.

I never saw a flashlight that big.

The light and the men behind it were moving toward him now. He looked behind him. From back of the curve, the probing beam of another light finger-painted the pillars in the blackness, moving upon him.

The blue light on the wall was fifty feet ahead of him. Head and shoulders low, he moved painfully, quickly the remaining distance. Underneath the blue light, a sign, gray with age and dirt, proclaimed: *Emergency Exit.*

The concrete wall on his right was cut away. Set into the cutaway, a winding flight of iron stairs, lit by one grimy light bulb, carried him up what seemed the inside of an iron well.

Coming to the top now, hearing voices behind him, he knew he was inside a manhole. His hand found the manhole cover above him—and he was amazed at the ease with which it came away, almost as if someone had jerked it free.

He came out head and shoulders, hard by the curbing of a street corner, and the two cops and the two detectives, waiting for him there, brought him out the rest of the way.

Chapter Forty

The clock on the pillar nearest Jon Day Griffith, in the Kyne newsroom, said 4:43 p.m.

A story for the following morning's *Sentinel* had just crossed his desk—the story of Arnold Lamin's award from the Louisville News.

The story would be buried in the *Sentinel*—buried as much as Griffith could bury any story he was ordered by Walter Kyne to run on page one.

He let his phone ring a couple of times while he swore to himself. Then he picked up the receiver and said, "Well?"

The voice on the other end was Edward Mobley's. "They've got him, Jon."

Griffith did not ask who it was they had. Out of the maddened turmoil within him, springing from a cloudy compound of despair, frustration and defeat, out of the dream he had worked for, a dream that had shattered like a smoking flashbulb, he asked only one question:

"Are we ahead?"

"We're all alone," Mobley said.

Griffith's eyes swung to the clock.

4:44.

The *Sentinel's* final deadline for the one-star edition was 6:25. The paper would hit the stands at 7:30. "How long?"

"I don't know," Mobley said. "Maybe an hour."

"No more?"

"They chased him down a subway. He was in some dame's apartment. The precinct handled it to start with."

"Where is he now?"

"Downtown. Burt Kaufman just phoned me."

"Where are you?"

"Home."

Edward Mobley admired Jon Day Griffith, admired him for the economy and the pointedness of his questioning. The questions kept coming.

"Did he confess?"

"Enough," Mobley said. "They've got him spilling his guts."

"But he started to talk in the station house?"

"Apparently."

"What are you going to do now?"

"Go downtown. Kaufman will fill me in."

"You got enough to go with now?"

"Yes," Mobley said. "What are you going to do?"

"Extra," Jon Day Griffith said.

"What about the wire?"

"They can read about it in the *Sentinel*. Hold on. Give it to Burt." Griffith started to call across to Burt Healey at his desk. Then, instead, he waved his arm until he had Healey's eye.

Healey jammed his cigar into his mouth and came through the little swinging gate to where Griffith sat.

"Take this," Griffith said. "Take it on my typewriter. Here."

He stood up, then walked through the gate and over to the desk of Sam Knight, the *Sentinel's* chief make-up man. As Knight glanced up, Griffith leaned down and put his hands on the desk.

"I want the top of the front page, down to the fold. I want the rest remade inside of ten minutes. Don't say anything about this."

Knight stared at him.

"You'll know why," Griffith said, "in exactly two minutes."

He picked up the phone at Knight's hand. "Circulation."

Looking to his right as he waited for the call to go through, he saw Burt Healey at the big desk inside the wooden rail. Healey had the receiver of his phone between his ear and his shoulder, so that his hands were free to use the typewriter. The position left his head cocked absurdly to one side.

"Hello," Griffith said now into the phone. "Benny? Well, give me Benny." He waited. "Benny? Jon Day. How many trucks you got downstairs? How soon can you get ten more? No, all right. I want to spread midtown, Grand Central, Penn Station, the bus terminal, by five-thirty. All right, then, the hell with the bus terminal. No. I want to run twenty thousand. No, I didn't talk to the press room. I'll take five trucks. Get more as soon as you can. There'll be, a replate anyway. Probably a quick one."

When he hung up the phone, Burt Healey was standing next to him. He thrust forth a copy of what he had taken from

Mobley:

A 20-year-old college student has confessed the murder dismemberment of eight-year-old Laura Grabowski, the rape-slaying of Judith Felton, and the strangling of Lena Tally.

Police captured the youth, Robert Manners, after a chase through a Bronx subway tunnel today. He was fleeing following what police said was a fourth murder attempt on a Bronx woman.

Griffith said, "That's it?"

"That's it," Healey said.

Griffith took a pencil off the desk and, in large, bold handwriting, wrote two words in front of the first paragraph:

"Police say...."

He turned to Knight. "Is that page open?"

"All right," Knight said.

Holding the sheet of copy in his hand, Griffith stepped over to the horseshoe shaped desk where the headline writers worked, Healey at his heels. The five men in shirtsleeves around the edge of the desk were bent over sheets of copy but the thin man with the green eyeshade who sat inside the horseshoe was looking at him expectantly. Griffith handed Healey's bulletin across the table to the thin man.

"Eight columns, fourteen point bold," Griffith said. Two of the men in shirtsleeves looked up quickly.

"Keep your face shut about this," Griffith said, addressing them as well as the man with the green eyeshade. "Nobody gets up from this desk."

The thin man inside the horseshoe laid the bulletin on the desk in front of him and as he read it, reached, with a hand that was not entirely steady, into the pocket of the vest he wore. He took out a cigarette, placed it between his lips. He did not light it. He reached for a pencil, scribbled the type size at the top of the page and checked two paragraph marks, picked a brass cylinder out of the basket at his elbow, stuffed the bulletin into it and dropped it into the pneumatic tube which was connected with the composing room downstairs. Then he took a pile of blank copy paper and began to scrawl words across the top sheet in big bold letters. Dissatisfied, he crumpled the paper into a ball, dropped it behind him, and started again.

Griffith stepped back to Knight's desk.

"What shape's the paper in?" . "Snafued," Knight said.

"Financial hasn't gone down. Sports is only half up. City's still open."

"Ads in?"

"All in," Knight said.

Healey came over from the horseshoe-shaped desk. In his hand was the hastily blocked headline the man with the eyeshade had written:

**YOUTH CONFESSES
TRIPLE SLAYINGS
NABBED AFTER ATTACK**

"That's all right," Griffith said. "That's good. I'll take this down with me. Phone the press room and tell them we're going to go."

As Healey reached for the phone, Griffith looked across the wide newsroom and saw Arnold Lamin in his glass-enclosed office. Lamin was on the telephone. He had his feet up on the desk, and he was gesturing with his hand as he talked.

Sam Knight was getting up from his chair. Griffith turned to him.

"Sam, take this downstairs with you and get it set. You know what we want." He handed Knight the headline. "I think I'm going to stay up here."

Griffith stood, tall and alive, waiting for Healey to get off the phone. Then he said, "Burt, this was a precinct thing. It must have been on the ticker."

Together, they went over to the police ticker. With a wave of relief, Griffith saw that it had gone untouched for a long period of time, even though the copy boy was supposed to tear off the police news and distribute it at least once an hour. On a pillar back of the police ticker, a squawk box tuned in to police-call frequencies had been tuned down, by someone, until it was barely audible. This was not unusual—especially not now, with Kyne men staffing headquarters at Centre Street—but it was a blessing nonetheless.

Griffith looked across at Arnold Lamin's office and grinned. He found he was sweating as he started to run the paper that had come off the ticker through his hands, searching for the item he wanted.

He found it, buried between a false alarm and a heart attack:

ZZZZZ SLIP 184
282 PCT ROBERT MANNERS, M W 20, ARRESTED OUTSIDE EMERGENCY SUBWAY EXIT FRONT OF 32126 E. 147 ST. ATTEMPTED ASSAULT.
ZZZZZZ

On an impulse, Griffith began to read the succeeding items. There was no further reference to a Robert Manners. Then the ticker started to clatter again, and Griffith read the new item now coming over:

ZZZZ SLIP 198
12 PCT REPAIR CREW TO 24TH ST & NINTH AVE. ONE-WAY SIGN ON LAMPPOST REVERSED.
ZZZZZZZ

"That'd make a cute little box," Griffith said. "Let's write it."

Healey read the new alarm and smiled. "Well," he said, "we've got to do something to keep busy for the next half hour."

Griffith looked at the clock. It was five minutes before five o'clock.

A thought came to his mind. He walked, long and loose, back to his own desk and picked up his telephone. "I want to talk to Walter Kyne."

He waited, and as he waited his eye roamed the *Sentinel* side of the newsroom. By now, financial and sports both knew that the deadline had been moved up. It would be a patchwork paper, probably thirty-two pages instead of the customary forty, that hit the streets half an hour from now with the word EXTRA fudged blackly across the top. But Mobley would call, and they would still be in front with the story, and as soon as possible they would go again with another edition, this time a full run of 200,000. No, Griffith said to himself, 250,000.

Now he found himself talking to Walter Kyne's secretary.

"Mr. Kyne," she said, "has left for the day."

"Do you know where he went?"

"I'm sorry, Mr. Griffith. He didn't say."

Griffith hung up the phone. Burt Healey came over to the little wooden gate and said, "Jon, what about pictures?"

"We don't need pictures," Griffith said. "And Kritzer doesn't have to know about this. Not yet."

"Okay," Healey said. He took another cigar from the breast pocket of his shirt. "There are times when I thank God for Ed Mobley."

"He should get the Pulitzer prize for this," Griffith said.

"You may get something, too," Healey said. They both smiled.

"By the way," Griffith said, "in the confusion, what happened to that little story about Lamin?"

"It's still on page one," Healey said.

"That's nice," Jon Griffith said. Healey turned to go back to his desk, and again Griffith's eye ranged over the men who were working for him. They were a good team. They could rise to a challenge like this and still make the *Sentinel* look like a newspaper, and they could do it coolly and without chatter.

His hand rested tentatively on the telephone. Then he picked up the receiver again. "Get me Walter Kyne at his home."

He hung it up. Within a few seconds, it buzzed, and he lifted the receiver and said, "Hello? Walter?"

"This is Mrs. Kyne," the voice at the other end said.

"Oh," Griffith said. "Dorothy. Jon Day Griffith. How are you?"

"Just fine, Jon," she said. "I haven't heard your voice in the longest time."

"I'm looking for Walter," he said. "Do you know where he is?"

"He may have gone to the gym," she said. "I wasn't expecting him home until later."

"I see," Griffith said. "Well, can you give him a message for me as soon as he gets in?"

"Well," she said, "I won't be here during the early evening.

I have to go to my mother's. Matter of fact, I was just on my way out. Wait; I tell you, I can leave it with the butler. What was the message, Jon?"

Somewhere in Jon Day Griffith's mind, the drawer to a filing cabinet rolled soundlessly open. "Just ask him," he said aloud now, "to call me at the office as soon as he comes in. Can you do that?"

"I certainly can," she said.

"Thanks a million," Griffith said. "Nice to talk to you, Dorothy."

"Good to talk to you," she said. "Good-by." Griffith hung up the phone; slowly, this time.

"I have to go to my mother's."

It came to him as a man might come upon the page he wanted, thumbing through a picture magazine. The night they worked late, with the little girl's body newly discovered, and picking up the phone to get Harry Kritzer and being cut in on a call Kritzer was making.

The woman on the other end had been Dorothy Kyne.

"I've been at mother's since ten o'clock," she had said.

"I can't stay here indefinitely," she had said.

What would Harry Kritzer have to do with Dorothy Kyne's mother?

Griffith put his elbows on his desk and rested his mouth against his folded hands.

The enormity of what he was thinking startled even himself.

He picked up the phone. "Get me Harry Kritzer."

"I'm sorry," the operator said. "Mr. Kritzer has left for the day."

"Okay," Griffith said. "Never mind."

Where did Kritzer live? Somewhere in the Bronx.

Griffith raised his head. "Copy boy!"

A boy came over.

"Get me a copy of the Bronx telephone book."

The boy went away. He came back with the book and Griffith took it from him, placed the book in his lap, and looked up Harry Kritzer's telephone number.

When he found it, he picked up his phone again. "Give me an outside line."

He dialed the number himself. On the third ring Harry

Kritzer answered.

Swiftly, Griffith's fingers depressed the bar that held the receiver on his telephone, disconnecting the call.

He stood up and walked to the window back of his desk, looking silently out at the skyline in the early December darkness. The clock on the pillar over his right shoulder said 5:16 p.m.

Burt Healey came over to the swinging gate behind him and said, "They've started to roll, Jon."

Griffith turned. "When will we have them on the street?"

Healey shrugged and took the cigar out of his mouth. "Grand Central, maybe twenty-five minutes, half an hour."

Griffith nodded. "Burt," he said, "tell me something."

"What's that?"

"If you became suddenly very sure of something," Jon Day Griffith said, "and there was one other thing you could do in another direction to make you even more sure, but that something else was—well, say it was unethical—what would you do?"

Healey looked at him. "It would depend on how much I wanted whatever it was I wanted."

Griffith grinned. "You're a moralistic son of a bitch."

"Anybody who's moralistic around here," Healey said, "is crazy."

Griffith watched him walk away. Looking over Healey's shoulder toward the battery of desks in the center of the room, he saw Gerald Meedy sitting there, reading a newspaper.

Griffith looked at the clock. 5:18. Then he came through the little gate guarding his office space and walked over to Meedy's desk. "You doing anything, Gerald?"

Meedy looked up. There was a smudge of carbon paper on one of his fatty cheeks. "What do you want?"

"I want you to do something for me."

"What?"

Griffith rubbed his hands together. "The cops caught some burglar in a subway tunnel up in the Bronx earlier this afternoon. Some amateur photographer who lives in Harry Kritzer's building got a good picture and he knows who Harry is. He developed the shots and I understand he gave them to Harry. Harry's home now. Run up there and bring the picture down."

"You got motorcycle messengers for that," Meedy said.

Griffith smiled a patient smile. "There's a good little story goes with it. Go up to Harry's and then maybe you can talk to this guy and get yourself a story."

Meedy did not move.

"With a by line," Griffith said.

Meedy stirred and got up.

"And call me when you leave Kritzer's place," Griffith said.

"All right," Meedy said.

"Without fail," Jon Day Griffith said.

The clock said 5:21.

Meedy won't cross you, Griffith said to himself. He might, if Lamin still had him, but Lamin hates him for that libel thing. No, he won't cross you. He can't.

He walked back to the telegraph desk of the *Sentinel*, where Archie Ginsberg sat.

"Archie," he said, "what would you say if I told you I wanted to place a bet?"

Ginsberg looked up. "On what?"

"On me," Jon Day Griffith said.

Chapter Forty-One

The phone rang in Arnold Lamin's office, and the operator told him Philadelphia was calling Mr. Arnold Lamin personally. It was 5:25.

"Arn?" It was Ellis Leeds. "What's your problem?" Lamin said. "What's going on up there?"

"Nothing special. Why?"

"I mean about the murders."

"What about the murders?"

"Listen," Leeds said. "There were three New York cops down here, tracking down a lead. Half an hour ago, they got called off."

"You sure?"

"Sure I'm sure."

"Well," Lamin said, "maybe they checked whatever it was they were supposed to check and came on home."

"They didn't come on home. I just finished telling you they got called off by New York."

"Well," Lamin said, "there isn't a damn thing going on."

"You sure?"

"If something happens," Arnold Lamin said, "we'll have it."

The door to his office opened as he was hanging up the telephone and Mark Loving came in. "I'm looking for Mildred," he said. "Where the hell is she?"

"I think I'm the one person in the Kyne organization who wouldn't know," Lamin said.

"Well, the hell with it," Loving said. "I wanted to congratulate you, anyway. Just heard about the award."

"Thanks," Lamin said.

"I take a little credit for it," Loving said smoothly. He would not have talked this way, except that Nancy Liggett, Lamin's secretary, had left for the day, and the two of them were alone in the glass-walled office. "I was talking to Walt Fisher out in Louisville last night." His tone of voice dared Lamin to prove him a liar. "He said they were considering you and three other possibles, and that they were going to make up their minds this morning. I told him if he didn't give it to you I'd take five comic strips away from him.”

“That was nice of you, Mark.”

“I didn't have to do it.”

“I'm wondering why you did.”

Loving shrugged and smiled, and the dimple in his chin became enlarged. “I thought it would be a good thing for the Kyne organization.”

“And you told Walter Kyne all about it.”

The smile did not leave Loving's face. “No. Why should I?”

Lamin put a small piece of copy paper in his mouth and began to chew on it. “I don't know,” he said, at length. “I'm getting to be the perfect Kyne example. I don't trust anybody.”

“It has its advantages,” Loving said. “I just wanted you to know where I stood. You're going to be a big man, and the day somebody shoots Walter Kyne, you'll be even bigger.”

“Oh?” Lamin said.

“You're the new McCrady,” Loving said, “and the next Walter Kyne. You're over the top.”

“I wouldn't say that.”

“Okay,” Mark Loving said. “I'll take your word for it. But if you happen to get it, remember what I said.”

He made a gesture of half salute and went out.

The son of a bitch, Arnold Lamin said to himself. If he can't be a winner himself, he's going to back the winner.

And, he added, he's all actor anyway. He hasn't quit any more than I have.

Lamin's thoughts returned momentarily to the call he had just received from Leeds in Philadelphia. Impulsively, he stood up, looking out through the glass partition so he could see the *Sentinel* side of the room.

Nothing seemed amiss. Jon Day Griffith was at his desk, penciling copy.

It was 5:35.

A copy boy came from the back of the room, carrying a bundle of newspapers. He distributed several to the *Sentinel* desks, handed one to Jon Day Griffith. Lamin saw Griffith look at the paper, then point with his finger toward the KPS side of the room, and the copy boy headed his way.

Lamin met him at the door to his office and took the paper

from him. He stared at the front page:

EXTRA
* * *
**YOUTH CONFESSES
TRIPLE SLAYINGS**
* * *
NABBED AFTER ATTACK
New York Sentinel
Police say a 20-year-old college student has confessed the murder-dismemberment of eight-year-old Laura Grabowski, the rape-slaying of Judith Felton, and the strangling—

It was to his eternal credit as a newsman that Arnold Lamin reacted instinctively.

"Joe!" he yelled at his chief desk man. "Get this on the wire!"

Chapter Forty-Two

It did not occur to Gerald Meedy to take a taxicab. Instead, he boarded the Lexington Avenue line of the IRT subway. It was the height of the evening rush hour, and Meedy found himself carried into the car and deposited, arms wedged at his sides, with his nose unhappily close to a thin old gentleman whose sentiments towards onions and soap led Meedy to suspect he used one to the exclusion of the other. In an effort to avoid the fumes, Meedy raised his head sharply, and found himself staring, at a car-card advertisement.

DO YOU OFFEND?

"Ah," Gerald Meedy said, half aloud, and read on. The enlightenment he derived had to do with a brand of mints, on sale at candy counters everywhere. It was something that Meedy thought about. If you were married, your wife would tell you if your breath was bad. When you were not married, you ran the risk of offending. Meedy looked back at the thin old man who reeked, and decided he was married.

There was no relief at Eighty-Sixth Street; only a little at One Hundred and Twenty-Fifth. At the rush hour, people boarded Bronx trains to go to the Bronx, and they would not get off till they got there.

Meedy's stop was one of the first Bronx stations. He clawed his way out of the car and headed briskly for the street above, pausing only to purchase a package of mints at the subway newsstand.

Then he walked the three short blocks to Harry Kritzer's address, regarded only in passing the empty police car drawn up outside the building, and went in to examine the cards over the mail boxes. One said *6M—H. Kritzer*, and Meedy went inside and took the self-service elevator to the sixth floor.

He found Harry Kritzer's apartment around the corner from the long hall that led from the elevator. He knocked three times, loudly, and Kritzer opened the door. He was in shirtsleeves, without a tie, and his face seemed to Gerald Meedy a trifle more flushed than usual.

"Hello, Harry," Meedy said.

Kritzer stared at him. "What the hell do you want? What did you come here for?"

Meedy walked unbade into the living room. "Nice place you got here."

"For Christ's sake," Kritzer said. He was still holding the doorknob. "What do you want? Will you please tell me what you want?"

Meedy's brow nettled, and he turned to face the photo editor. "Just the picture," he said. "And some of the details."

"What picture? What details?"

Meedy spread his hands. "What Griffith was talking about."

"What Griffith was talking about?"

"Didn't you talk to him?"

"About what?" Kritzer said—he said it, Meedy thought, almost frantically.

"About a picture and a story. He said you had something for me."

Kritzer slammed the door shut and walked rapidly toward the center of the room. "I don't know what this is," he said tautly, "but I have nothing for you, I have not talked to Griffith, and I want you to do me a favor and get the hell out of here."

"Oh," Gerald Meedy said slowly. He took a large, dirty handkerchief from his rear pants pocket and blew his nose. Then he examined the result, wadded the handkerchief, and returned it to its resting place. "You didn't talk to Griffith? About a suspect or the police or something, or a picture?"

"I keep telling you," Harry Kritzer said. "No."

"Why, the son of a bitch," Meedy said. "He said he was going to give me a by fine. Where's your phone?"

"You're not using my phone," Kritzer said. "You're getting the hell out of here."

"What's the rush?" Meedy said.

"I'm sick," Kritzer said. "I have to be alone." He strode back toward the door to the apartment. "Come on. Out of here. Now." He opened the door.

Dorothy Kyne walked in. "Why, darling," she said, "I was just about to use my key. Did you . . ." She stopped.

Standing in the center of the room, Gerald Meedy looked at her. She was beautiful, as she had been the one other time he had seen her, in the office. Tonight she wore a full-length mink coat and very high heels. Her face was arched in surprise, but not in recognition.

Gerald Meedy said, "Mrs. Kyne." His tone was one almost of wonderment.

Harry Kritzer moved first. He went to the glass-topped table next to one of the chairs in the living room and poured himself a straight shot of whisky.

Dorothy Kyne closed the door behind her. She said, "Who's this?"

"Gerald Meedy," Kritzer said, and socked down an-other ounce. "Griffith sent him up here."

"He's from the office?" Kritzer nodded as he drank.

"Well," Dorothy Kyne said, and sat down on the edge of the nearest chair. "Well, well, well."

"Griffith," Kritzer repeated again. "Now, how the hell did he find out?"

"Griffith," Dorothy said. "I talked to him on the telephone earlier, but he was only looking for Walter. I didn't tell him...."

"You sure you didn't?" Kritzer asked. His voice was high. 'You sure you didn't ask him up for cocktails, just to meet the folks? What the hell goes on here, anyway?" He looked savagely at Meedy. "Smart boy, aren't you? Smart. Real smart. Was it really Griffith that sent you? Your old friend Arnold Lamin, maybe? Or did you come on your own? I ought to kick your teeth in, Meedy. It wouldn't do a damn bit of good, but on the other hand, it might relax me."

"Now, wait a minute," Gerald Meedy said. "Wait a minute. Hold your horses. The more I see of this the less I like it."

"You're a nice boy, Gerald," Dorothy Kyne said. She smiled winningly at him. "We don't like it either. Do we, Harry?"

"We love it," Kritzer said, but he looked at her, following her lead almost prayerfully.

"Let's have a drink, Gerald," Dorothy Kyne said. "And then let's talk."

Gerald Meedy looked from one to the other. "I'll have a drink," he said. "I'll have a drink, but we're not going to talk. You think I came here on my own, you're a liar. You think Lamin sent me, you're another liar." He laughed dramatically. "While he could use me, I was great for Lamin. We were buddy-buddy. Everything was la-de-da, perfect. Now, oh, no. Lamin's going to be a big man now, he's got no use for little Gerald Meedy. And Griffith." He laughed again and accepted the Herculean shot of bourbon Kritzer had nervously poured for him. He quaffed deeply of the contents of the glass, then coughed and sputtered so that he had to put the glass down. He pulled out his dirty handkerchief, wiped it across his mouth, put it back, and picked up his glass again. "They're all the same. They all laugh at me and think I'm a hustler and a rat, and they're the lousiest rats walking around. No." His voice rose and he looked at Harry Kritzer. "You never did anything for me, but you never kicked me in the tail, either. At least you're a decent human being, Harry. Everybody kicks me. I took Lamin's secretary to Camillo's for lunch today—bought her a lunch at *Camillo's*—and she kicked me. Kicked me like I was an alley rat." He belted his whisky again. "You know why? Because I told her I loved her." The dramatic laugh once more. "Human emotions don't count in our business. Machines. Cameras. Comic strips. Teletypes. We're all walking teletypes!"

Kritzer and Dorothy looked at each other.

"We're listening, Gerry," the photo editor said. "Have another drink."

"I think I will, Harry," Meedy said. "I just think I will. It's nice of you to say that." He, who so seldom touched whisky, found its effect now most rewarding. "You were scared when you saw me walk in here, Harry. No, don't say it. I know you were scared. You wanted to get rid of me. Well, I want to tell you something." He accepted a fresh drink, more lethal than the first. "If I had been you and I was expecting such a beautiful lady, like Mrs. Kyne here ... you are beautiful, Mrs. Kyne, I want you to know I think you're beautiful."

"Thank you, Gerald," she said. "I wish we'd met before this."

"So do I," Meedy said. He saluted her with his glass, slopped a bit of bourbon over the edge, then drank fully. He wiped his lips with the back of his hand. "So do I. Yeah, so do I. Now—what was I saying?"

"That Griffith and Lamin are rats," Harry Kritzer said, attentively.

"You're right," Meedy said to him. "You—are—so—right. Let me sit down."

Kritzer patted the couch. "Gerald," he said, "I'm in your debt. We both are, Dorothy and myself. No matter how innocent this visit of hers might be, we all know, Mrs. Kyne and you and I, what it would look like in the wrong hands." He leaned over. "It's in your hands."

Gerald Meedy, having sat down, stood up again. He swayed slightly. "I," he said, "shall be as silent as the grave. No." He put up his hand. "Don't say anything. Don't say anything more. The least thing a man can have in this world . . . and a woman, too ... is a good friend. A friend he can trust." He nodded profoundly. "Well, you can trust me. Twenty years from now, I'll laugh at all of them. They need me now. Oh, yes, they need me. They'd cry if they knew how much they needed me. But they don't have me. I'm my own man."

Dorothy Kyne took a handkerchief from her purse and dabbed prettily at her eyes.

Meedy finished his drink. "No tears," he said. "No tears. Now, I'm going to go. Where I'm going to go, I don't know. I—have—not—got—the—slightest—idea. But I'm going." He waved his arm. "Out into the night."

"Stay with us, Gerald," Dorothy Kyne said. "Have another drink."

"No," Meedy said. "I might have just one small drink, just for the road, but I know when three's a crowd. Two's company, you know. Oh, yes. I got to do one thing. I have to phone that low, thieving, miserable, wife-beating son of a bitch Griffith. Harry, where's a phone?"

Kritzer paused momentarily. Then he said, "In here." Meedy followed him, unsteadily, and waited while Kritzer dialed the office.

Gerald Meedy took the receiver and said, "Mr. Griffith I want—to—talk—to—Mister—Griffith. This's Meedy." He waited. "Jon? This's Meedy, I'm at Harry's. I got the picture. I got the story. I'm coming in with it. Save me a by line, you skinny bastard." He slammed down the receiver, and his face became lit in a smile. "Okay, Harry?"

"Okay," Kritzer said, doubtfully. "But don't get drunk and tell him any more."

"I'll tell him," Meedy said carefully, "that I found you here without anybody else and without any picture and without any story and it—must—all—have—been—a—misunderstanding."

"That's right," Kritzer said in a gentle voice. "That's just it, Gerry."

"Now I'm going to go." Meedy's voice was suddenly loud. "I'm going to go downtown and tell—him—off."

Kritzer reflected on the wisdom of encouraging Meedy to stay. He decided against it. "All right, Gerry," he said, and clapped him on the back. "Remember, we're counting on you." He guided him out toward the door to the apartment.

"Mrs. Kyne," Meedy said, and smiled down at the publisher's wife. On an impulse, he reached into his pocket and drew out the package he had bought in the subway.

"Mint?"

"No," she said. "Thank you just the same, Gerald."

"You?" he said to Kritzer.

"Maybe one for later," Harry Kritzer said, and took one. "Thanks a million for everything, Gerry."

"Don't worry about a thing," Gerald Meedy said, and marched out the door.

Kritzer and Dorothy looked at each other.

"Griffith must know," she said.

Harry Kritzer shook his head thoughtfully. "No. He doesn't know. If he did, he'd never have sent Meedy."

Chapter Forty-Three

The electric clock on the wall in Mildred Donner's little kitchen said ten minutes to six. Mildred was not in the kitchen. She was in her bedroom, seated at her vanity table, wearing a slip.

She smiled to herself in her mirror and her mirror smiled back, but it was more than an exchange of pleasantries. There was an errant line here, a wisp of eyebrow there, a tired furrow in the neck, all of which commanded immediate attention.

When the doorbell rang, she was not so ready as she would have liked, but she realized she was ready enough. She got up, put on the same wrap she had worn for Edward Mobley, and went smoothly to the door.

"Hello, darling," she said. "I've been waiting for you."

"I made it as fast as I could," Walter Kyne said, and came in the door.

Chapter Forty-Four

"Carlo," Mark Loving said, "what the hell time is it?"

Carlo, the bartender in the Dell, said, "It's a little after seven, Mr. Loving. Does your glass want refilling?"

"My glass and me both," Loving said. "Where the hell is that blond broad?"

"Who was that?" Carlo said. "Were you expecting some one?"

"I was," Loving said. He had folded his overcoat on the bar and was dressed impeccably in gray suit and splendidly-knotted crimson tie. "Mademoiselle Donner, women's writer of the mighty Kyne publishing empire. Seen her?"

"Not today," Carlo said. "Hot damn," Loving said.

"There's someone coming now, sir," Carlo said. "I can hear them on the stairs."

Loving looked toward the stairway. "It sounds like a party of twelve."

Gerald Meedy came heavily down the final steps and turned into the blue-lit barroom.

Mark Loving said, "For God's sake."

Meedy weaved toward him. "Every—place—I—go," he said in a high, whining voice, "there's—one—of—you—bastards."

"Sit down, Gerald," Loving said. "Have a drink."

"Oh, no," Meedy said, but he sat down. "You—don't—want—me. Not—after—what—I—did—last—night."

"What are you drinking?" Loving said. "What did you do last night?"

"I don't know what I'm drinking," Meedy said. "Bourbon. You want to know what I did last night?" He shook a pudgy finger in Loving's face. "All right, I'll tell you what I did last night. I made your woman, that's what I did. Now what d'y' want to do about it?"

Mark Loving smiled his salesman's smile. "Welcome to the club," he said easily. "How do you like Mildred?"

Gerald Meedy considered the question at length. "All right," he said at last. "She's all right. My compliments."

"Your health," Loving said. "Perhaps some day, Gerald, we'll both grow up and quit this sleeping around. It's bad for office morale."

Meedy's eyes grew big. "Bad!" he exclaimed. "Bad! I could tell you things, about who sleeps with who, things that'd curl your hair. Curl your hair, Mr. Loving, curl your hair!"

Loving studied him in the half-light of the bar. "You might not be able to tell me as much as you think," he said. "I know a lot of things about people."

Meedy smiled, almost in pride. "You don't know this. Boy, what you'd give to know this!"

"Who does know it?"

Meedy licked his lips. "The two people involved . . ." He put out his hand . . . "of course. And—me."

"Drink up, Gerald," Mark Loving said. "You're talking, of course, on the executive level."

"They don't make levels any higher," Gerald Meedy said.

Mark Loving marshaled the forces within his brain as they seldom had been marshaled before. "Facts," he said now, "are facts. I'd be sure of mine, Gerald, if I were you."

"Sure!" Meedy said loudly. "Don't you think I'm sure? Where do you think I've just come from? My own eyes are sure. I trust my own eyes, even if I don't trust anybody else."

"I'll bite," Loving said. "Where did you just come from?"

Meedy fixed him with an owlish look. "Oh, no," he said. "You don't pump me. No, sir. I've got one friend in that joint upstairs. One friend. You think I'm going to betray him, you've got another think. An—other—think."

"You mean among the executives," Loving said smoothly.

"Cor—rect," Gerald Meedy said. "Let's talk about Mildred."

"Certainly," Loving said. "Have another drink, Gerald."

"I will," Meedy said. "Just a short one."

Loving signaled the bartender. In what he felt was a sure understanding of inferior intellects, he told himself that Gerald Meedy was telling the truth; also, that no matter how drunk Meedy became, his newly-exhibited dedication would not bring the information voluntarily from his lips.

Loving had just come from upstairs; had been in the city room where both sides, KPS and the *Sentinel,* now were working feverishly on the biggest story of the year. Meedy had not been there: he could not have been there, for he had been someplace getting drunk. Griffith and Lamin both were there; he, Mark Loving, had seen them.

That left Walter Kyne and Harry Kritzer.

Kyne had no use for Meedy, not since Meedy's libelous story; not so much, Loving knew, because Meedy had kicked it but because it had bared Kyne's ignorance of the law.

Harry Kritzer.

So what? Loving explored the possibilities. Kritzer was a bachelor. What scandal could he be involved in?

Mark Loving stared straight ahead, unseeing. Things he had noticed, a party once at Kyne's house, came startlingly into focus. Yet there was no way to be sure, except one.

Loving set down his glass. "Gerald," he said softly, "do you want to talk about Mildred?"

"Sure," Meedy said. "Le's talk."

"All right," Mark Loving said. "But first, let me put your mind to rest about one thing. There's no point in carrying secrets to the grave if they aren't secrets."

Meedy said, "Wha?"

"Just between us, Gerald," Loving said, "I've known about Harry Kritzer for a long time. A long, long time." Meedy's eyes told him nothing. "What about him?"

"You know what about him."

"All right. Suppose I do. I'm—not—telling—you."

"I told you it was all right, Gerald," Loving said. "You don't have to tell me anything. I know."

Meedy turned his head away. "You didn't hear it from me."

"Of course I didn't," Loving said. He paused. "She's beautiful, isn't she?"

Meedy looked at his glass of whisky and nodded, half to himself. "Walter Kyne's wife," he said now, "is the most be—a—utiful woman I—have—ever—seen."

Chapter Forty-Five

They located <u>Mildred Donn</u>er at her home, shipped her down to headquarters to <u>interview the parents of</u> Robert <u>Manners</u>. They were <u>unable to locate Walter K</u>yne, but a little after seven o'clock the publisher walked swiftly into the newsroom. He seemed to know the basic facts of the story already. He went quickly into conference with Arnold Lamin, then came out of Lamin's glass-walled office and walked across the newsroom to Jon Day Griffith's enclosure.

"Why didn't you give this to KPS?"

Griffith smiled up at him. "I did."

"Only after you extra'd."

Griffith nodded. "If I'd given it to them when I got it, the oppositions would have found out about it. Somewhere a client would have read the wire and given it to AP."

"Yes," Kyne said, "but our wire would have had it first."

"Our wire still had it first," Griffith said cheerfully. "And your New York paper was on the street with it."

Kyne thought about it. "I think you're right," he said at last. "That was good thinking, Jon. But Arn's mad as a wet hen about it."

"He's got no reason to be," Griffith said mildly.

"All right," the publisher said. "What shape are we in now?"

"We were selling the extra at ten to six," Griffith said. "The one-star is on the run now. I decided to go with just a short run on the extra. Just a few thousand."

"Why?"

McCrady, Griffith was thinking, would never have asked why. Aloud, he said, "We were far enough ahead on the story to get out another edition behind the extra and still be in front. I mean, the regular one-star, hitting the street at seven-thirty. I went with an incomplete paper to get that extra out. I didn't have trucks to deliver them. My trucks were in the garage. I pulled five trucks. Okay. Now we have all the trucks we need, we have a full paper at the regular one-star time, we've already hit with the extra and we're still ahead."

"How many do you usually run off on the one-star?"

"Two hundred thousand," Griffith said. "That's city and suburbs. We run an extra forty thousand for the mails and trains."

"Did you arrange for fast handling?"

"On what?"

Kyne gestured impatiently. "On the papers that go out of town."

"Hell, no, I didn't," Griffith said. "I don't worry about out-of-town sales. Hell, that's a subscription audience. They have to take the *Sentinel* whether they want it or not, and even if we shoot it out of a cannon they'll hear it over the radio or see their own local papers first."

"Well," Kyne said, "the least you could have done was run more than two hundred thousand of the one-star for the city."

"I know it," Griffith said.

"Why didn't you?"

"Who said I didn't?"

"How many did you print."

"Three hundred and fifty thousand," Griffith said. "Wait a minute. Here she blows."

A copy boy entered the swinging half-door with Griffith's copy of the one-star *Sentinel*, the edition that regularly hit the streets at seven-thirty, but which tonight actually was the evening's second edition, having followed the extra.

"Leave two of those," Griffith said to the boy. He spread out his copy of the *Sentinel*. The headline had been altered slightly, after Griffith's desk had talked it over.

**YOUTH CONFESSES
"I KILLED THEM"**
New York Sentinel
NABBED AFTER ATTACK

Below the headline, still covering eight columns but with the by line of Edward Mobley now in bold, black capitals, ran the lead. It had been rewritten, and after the first six lines it dropped into the first two right-hand columns, while the space to the left was devoted to equal-sized cuts of the Tally woman, Judith Felton, and little Laura Grabowski. Above the three pictures, in italics, ran the lead: "Something made me . . .!"

"Kyne studied the display. "Where's a picture of the killer?"

"We'll have one in the next edition."

"Why not this one?"

"Look, Walter," Griffith said, "if we'd sent a photographer down there, the whole thing would have busted up. That's assuming they'd let him up there to take pictures while they were still questioning the Manners kid."

"When did the others get it?"

"Exactly at six o'clock," Griffith said. "Arnold had it on the wire at five-thirty-seven. We checked our wire room. At five-forty-one, AP's Chicago bureau sent a query on it to their New York office. At ten to six, INS got a rocket from Boston. One minute later, AP had a bulletin that they were holding this kid, but they couldn't confirm the confession. Right on the nose at six INS had a bulletin on the confession. AP had the same thing just about a minute later."

"What about the local papers here?"

Griffith shrugged. "They'll have it with a paragraph or two in their seven-thirty editions. But there's only two mornings that come out with their first editions at seven-thirty the way we do. Another comes out at eight and the other one at ten-thirty."

"Won't they extra too?"

"Why should they? They're not the ones who had it. We are."

"How's the wire doing?"

"Ask Lamin," Griffith said.

"Are you giving them everything you've got?"

"Soon as it comes in," Griffith said. Then he added: "Now."

Kyne looked at him sharply. "I would say, Jon, that you have thought of just about everything. I want you to know this is magnificent."

"You can thank Mobley," Griffith said.

"I intend to," Walter Kyne said. "But you rate something too. As I say, you thought of everything, with the possible exception of one thing."

Griffith raised his eyebrows. "What's that?"

"When you have a story locked up like you had this one,"

Kyne said, reciting from memory a statement once delivered by the late Cyrus McCrady, "you do one thing ahead of anything else. You copyright it."

Jon Day Griffith began to laugh.

"What's so funny?" Kyne said to him.

"Walter," Jon Day Griffith said, "sometimes you're right out of 'The Front Page'. Where do you think we're keeping this Manners kid? In my roll-top desk?"

"What difference does that make?"

"He's public property," Griffith said. "Christ, anybody with a little ingenuity could have spotted the arrest on the police ticker. It isn't a question of time, it's a question of availability. The only thing you want to copyright is something nobody else can get."

Kyne nodded seriously. "Then all we were was ahead."

"By something like two hours on the biggest story of the year," Griffith said. "But you want egg in your beer, Walter, we may just be able to give you some."

"How?"

"By midnight," Griffith said, "Mobley expects to have an exclusive copy of the confession." He leaned back in his chair. "And that, my friend, we will copyright."

Kyne smiled a terrible smile of success, waved his hand, and moved off, headed back toward the KPS side of the room. Griffith watched him go, and the exultation welled anew within him. So Meedy wouldn't talk about Kritzer and Kyne's wife, he told himself—so what? You've got this baby. *You've* got it!

Walter Kyne, too, was thinking of the McCrady question as he walked toward Arnold Lamin's office. Stacked one against the other, Griffith and Lamin had outdone each other to the point where to choose between them would be to invite injustice. Griffith clearly had won the race. But Lamin had won this day an award whose import could not be denied. You had to think as a publisher. How much easier would it be to cite both Griffith and Lamin and then select either Loving or Kritzer for the job.

And if it had to be between Loving and Kritzer, it would be, Kyne told himself in terms of his own personal preference, Harry Kritzer, his old friend.

Then, however, would it be a case of selection on merit?

Walter Kyne did not know. What he did know was that he

had bent his men so far; that he could not bend them any more; and that his own ignorance, so damningly exposed at every turn in his conversation of the past few minutes with Jon Griffith, dictated that, beyond the reason of expediency, he, Walter Kyne, make up his mind at once.

He stood near Arnold Lamin's office, reading the copy as it came over the receiver teletype. Then he walked over to Lamin's door and leaned in.

Lamin had a sandwich on his desk, but he was chewing paper and studying sheaves of copy before him.

Kyne said, "How you doing?"

"We're beating the hell out of the opposition," Lamin said. "We had a twenty-three minute beat on the confession."

"Have you got men out?"

"Every damn place in the town," Lamin said. "We've had guys in this guy's dormitory room, out at his house, interviewing his classmates, his college sweetheart. That just came in by phone. The sweetheart angle. We're handling it now."

"What about downtown?"

"Griffith's got downtown blanketed. He's giving us everything he gets."

"You're not sore?"

"About what?"

"About his holding up the break."

Lamin put his elbows out, fists clenched, and stretched. "Well," he said, "as I told you a few minutes ago, Walter, if it had been the other way around I would have given it to him as soon as I got it. I have on all the other breaks on the story so far." He was telling Kyne, not with complete truth, that every other break on the story so far ad been developed by KPS. "For instance, that business of linking the killer to all three murders. You see how that stood up?"

"Well," Kyne said, "Griffith had his reasons."

"I'm sure of that," Lamin said. "I appreciate his problems. Believe me."

"Well, all right," Kyne said. "I got the impression you were put out."

"Everything's fine," Lamin said. "KPS is so far out in front it isn't even funny."

"By the way," Kyne said, "there's the chance Griffith will get an exclusive text of the confession. Watch for it.”

Lamin looked up. “Thanks for telling me,” he said. “I will.”

“He's going to copyright it,” Kyne said.

“I'd suggest a joint copyright on the wire,” Lamin said mildly. “By KPS and the *Sentinel.* It'll look better out along the line.”

“You may be right,” Kyne said. “I'll be in my office if you need me.”

“Do you want me to clear copy with you? Or will you be coming back out?”

“Neither,” Walter Kyne said. “I haven't told anybody this but you, Arn, but I'm going into my office to have a drink and make up my mind, and I think you know what about. I need an executive director, and I'm not good enough.”

Lamin's leathery face broke into a smile. “Well,” he said, “put in a good word for Arnold Lamin.”

Kyne nodded at him, and smiled, and closed the door.

Chapter Forty-Six

They let the photographers at Robert Manners. The woman whose apartment he had invaded (strange, no one at Kyne had yet awakened to the fact that Harry Kritzer lived in the same building, for whatever the fact was worth), and the butcher and the oil-truck men who chased him, the station agent who came out from his change booth when Manners vaulted the turnstiles, the cops who dragged him up out of the sidewalk entrance of the emergency exit, his classmates, his foster parents, his burglary victims, his thin girl friend, the druggist who employed him part time—all of these, and more, were photographed again and again.

They did not let the newspapermen at Robert Manners —not yet. Only the photographers, and they came back from upstairs with stories of a sullen, silent youth who talked, who had answered only one question—a question thrown at him by a photographer named Andy:

"Why did you do it?"

It was not a particularly choice question to ask. But what the photographers talked about was the youth's reply.

"Ask her."

The photographers had assumed, from that, that Manners was telling them to ask the woman he had attacked today. Robert Manners could have told them otherwise. This woman was not his mother. She only looked like her.

The newsmen milled about and jabbered into the press-room phones at Centre Street. One or two of them thought to congratulate Ed Mobley on his beat, for purposes, besides congratulation, of finding out where he got it. But Mobley was not downstairs with them. He was upstairs in the office of Burt Kaufman. They both had their feet up on Kaufman's desk as they waited for Manners to be brought upstairs for further questioning.

"Take a breather," Kaufman was saying now. "Let's talk about you and your doll."

"Nuts," Mobley said. "I'm in trouble with that dame, and

ever since I realized I was in trouble with her I've been so much in love with her it makes me ache."

"Well, Nancy loves you too," Kaufman said, "if it's any consolation. She's loved you for a hell of a long sight longer than you've loved her."

Mobley nodded dismally. He had his suit coat off, and his shirt was no longer clean. His shoes needed a shine.

"Furthermore," Kaufman said, "she's treated you right."

Mobley shook his head. "That thing with Mildred the other night. What does it mean? Hell, she sleeps with someone different every night."

"That makes it worse with Nancy," Kaufman said.

"But I didn't do anything," Mobley said.

"You would have."

Mobley thought for a moment. "Well, I'll tell you this. I would have then, but I wouldn't now."

"Well, tell her that," Burt Kaufman said. "It's as simple as that."

"Yeah," Mobley said, "everything's simple."

"You'd be surprised," Kaufman said, "how true that is. What were you doing when I phoned you today?"

"I was home in my bathrobe."

"And you got the biggest story of the year."

"Simple," Mobley agreed. "Burt, it doesn't work that way. They'll be rewriting Richard Harding Davis until Michaelmas if they find out how Edward Mobley, five-star reporter, cracked the case."

"What are you going to do?" Kaufman said. "You can always buy me a drink."

"Hell, I can do more than that," Mobley said. "I can fix you up with Mildred."

"I'm not saying no," Kaufman said. "What the hell, it might square you with Nancy."

"Sure," Motley said.

"Come on," Kaufman said, "you can talk her out of it. Turn it on like you always used to. Remember that broad Janice we both ran with on Eighteenth Street?"

"She taught you the facts of life."

"Back of the saxophones in her father's hock shop on Eighth Avenue. What the hell was her father's name?"

"Uncle Somebody-or-other," Mobley said.

"We did all right in those days," Kaufman said.

"We did pretty good today."

"Yeah. And by the way, who knows how you got this story?"

"Griffith and Nancy. Nobody else."

"All right," Kaufman said. "Keep it that way, an' you love me."

"The poet in you," Mobley said.

"Recite me some lines of poetry," Kaufman said, almost dreamily. "Reach me one of your cigarettes and recite me some relaxing lines."

"'Th' expense of spirit in a waste of shame / Is lust in action;'" Mobley said. "'And till action, lust / Is perjured, murderous, bloody, full of blame, / Savage, extreme, rude, cruel, not to trust;'..."

"Stop it," Burt Kaufman said. "That doesn't relax me at all. Who said it?"

"Shakespeare," Mobley said tiredly.

"It figured," Kaufman said.

Chapter Forty-Seven

At ten minutes to ten, that Tuesday night, Mark Loving, director of Kyne World Features, walked into the office of Walter Kyne. The door was open. Kyne was at his desk. He was looking at two of the other New York papers, but Loving acquired the immediate impression that he was not putting much effort into it.

Kyne looked up. "Come in, Mark. Have a drink."

"I will," Loving said. "All three. You look tired, Walter. You look like the last couple of weeks came and spun you around in a circle." He sat down in a leather-upholstered chair over to the side of Kyne's desk, facing the publisher.

Walter Kyne had whisky and glasses in some recess within his desk. "Chase it with water," he said. "That way we don't have to get up for soda."

"Mix mine about half and half," Loving said. "Don't worry about any ice." He looked at his fingernails. "You know something? I'm worried about Mildred."

Kyne poured with a steady hand. "Mildred?"

"Mildred Donner," Loving said. "She's gone off her whack. We're going to have to do something. Talk to her, or something." He waited for Walter Kyne to say "We?", but Kyne said nothing. Instead, he handed Loving his drink, grasped his own, and said, "Cheers."

"Salud," Loving said. "This is good whisky."

Kyne leaned back. He wore a perfect-fit brown suit, and his tie was neatly in place—so neatly that Loving wondered whether he had tied it more recently than this morning.

"What," Walter Kyne said now, "is the matter with Mildred?"

"She's sleeping around," Mark Loving said. He sipped at his drink. "And the kind of trash. My God, Friday night Mobley, last night Meedy, tonight who knows?"

"She didn't sleep with Mobley," Kyne said.

Loving's reaction was compounded of admiration and surprise, but he managed to cloak them both. "Oh," he said. "You know?"

"I know," Walter Kyne said.

"And you know about me and Mildred?"

"For some time," Kyne said.

"Well," Loving said, "I just don't understand what's got into her. Up to last weekend, there was none of this. Then—wham."

"Oh," Walter Kyne said, "I rather imagine she'll work it out. I suppose an unmarried woman is prone to a spell or two like that."

"Yes," Loving said. "But Meedy!"

"I must ask Meedy," Kyne said, "if she's fun in bed."

"Why don't you ask me?"

Their hair was down; they were involved in the kind of conversation which, to occur during business hours between an executive and his superior executive, must have every advantage—those of time, place, atmosphere, liquor, newly-won success—or not occur at all. Yet each was holding something back from the other, and each knew it.

"No, the hell with it," Kyne said now. "I'd rather hear it from Meedy."

"It's not that he's just a leg man with dirty fingernails," Mark Loving said, "I don't mind the difference in our positions. It's a funny thing, Walter: If my wife is having an affair with a man and you find out about it, maybe I don't mind so much. But if someone like Meedy were to know about it, it would be entirely different."

Kyne pursed his lips and thought. "Because," he said at last, "you know I could keep it to myself, but you wouldn't trust Meedy."

Loving nodded emphatically. "Exactly. Exactly it. You've named it."

"On the other hand," Kyne said, idly, "it's more or less an academic point. I know nothing about your wife."

"No." Loving did not move in his chair. His voice did not change. His eyes watched the publisher's face. "But I know something about yours."

Walter Kyne reached for his drink. "Kritzer?"

Deep within him, Mark Loving felt a surge of alarm. Kyne was not supposed to have said that.

Outwardly, Loving smiled. Then he played the last card in his hand.

"Meedy knows it too."

Walter Kyne put his drink down on the desk.

"We're going to have to take care of him, Walter," Mark Loving said. "We're going to have to do something for him."

"We?" Walter Kyne said.

"You and I, Walter. You and I. We wouldn't want this information to get around."

Walter Kyne nodded. He nodded his head slowly, many times. Then he looked up. "You and I," he said. "Buddies."

"Pals," Mark Loving said.

"I would have to have a little time," Walter Kyne said, "to think."

"You take all the time you want."

"You're very nice," Kyne said. "Here, let me have your glass. You're a conniving son of a bitch, but in your way you're very nice."

"You sound bitter," Loving said. "Don't be bitter."

"No," Kyne said. "Don't be bitter. Do you have everything you came for?"

Loving lifted his glass and examined the contents carefully. "Everything," he said, smiling, "except what we started to talk about."

"What was that?"

"Mildred."

"You love her?"

"Surprisingly enough, damn it, yes. I do."

"I might be prevailed upon to give her back to you."

"You?"

"Yeah," the publisher said.

"Oh, baby," Mark Loving said. "Wheels within wheels."

"Within more wheels," Walter Kyne said. It occurred to him that all at once he was deriving a certain degree of enjoyment, if not satisfaction, from this conversation. The look on Loving's face told him now that Mark Loving was not the only man in the room with a trump card in his hand. What had been a last effort at face-saving on Walter Kyne's part had succeeded, vividly, because Loving—this Kyne suddenly realized—really wanted Mildred. Kyne smiled now, and said aloud, "It was your fault, Mark. Really, it was. You played it awful dumb."

"You and Mildred," Loving said, and Kyne was not sure

whether Loving meant it as part of the conversation, or whether he was merely thinking out loud.

"Your fault," Kyne said again. He wagged his finger. "You set her loose."

"Oh?"

"Yes. Oh." The smile remained. Walter Kyne was enjoying his role. "She's a warm-hearted girl, Mildred. She likes men."

"Apparently," Loving said.

"But..." The publisher paused. "She was playing according to your rules. So what did you do? You more or less order her to go to bed with Mobley. That's a trigger, my boy. A green light. She's off. Only it doesn't happen with Mobley, and that makes it even worse. Now look at you—you're all upset."

"I wouldn't say that."

"No," Kyne said. He looked thoughtful. "You might say you got what you came for tonight. On the other hand, maybe I got what I came for too." He drank from his glass. Suddenly he felt more relaxed than he had in weeks. Mark Loving hadn't taken Kyne's wife, but Kyne had, in a sense, taken Loving's mistress. He was one up there. Loving was aware of certain information about Kyne's wife, true; and he had shared it, and now he would get what he wanted. Kyne wasn't a stuffy man, but there were certain things that a man just did not want spread around. They could upset his business and ruin his pride.

Loving was a conniver—in fact, a blackmailer—but he had relieved Walter Kyne of a great burden. Loving had done what Walter Kyne couldn't do with the dilemma of selecting a new executive director: solved it.

"Drink up," Kyne said now, "and have another. Tomorrow we may both be down on Orchard Street with a pushcart and an umbrella."

Loving drank. "Stirrup cup," he said.

"Yeah, boost yourself up into the saddle," Kyne said. "What the hell."

"It's a funny business," Mark Loving said.

Chapter Forty-Eight

At ten minutes past three in the morning, Nancy Liggett awoke. In her dream, there had been a buzzing, repeated and incessant, one that had fitted itself to the action of the dream. Now, sitting up in bed, she knew it was the ringing of her doorbell.

She reached for her robe, turned on the light beside the bed, and, with the light behind her, went out into the hallway to the door.

"Who is it?" she asked.

"Me," the voice outside the door said. "Ed." Nancy opened the door. "Oh," she said. "Look at you."

"Can I come in?" Mobley said. "I had to talk to you, Nance."

She switched on the light in the hall and opened the door wide, and he came in. Then she closed the door, and they stood there and looked at each other.

"Well," she said softly, "now you've seen me at my worst."

"Likewise," Mobley said, "and vice versa." His hands mutely called her attention to himself.

"Poor darling," she said. "What can I get for you? Coffee?"

She started to turn, and Mobley caught her arm. "First," he said, "we can be married three days from now. Will we, Nance? Can we?"

There was no trace of sleep in her eyes; they were bright and alive as they looked into his. "You know we can," she said. "You always knew."

"Ah, mother of us all," Mobley said, and his voice had the unlikely ring that heaped happiness upon weariness. "Yes, I want coffee and you and more coffee and more you and then more you and then maybe just a touch, a wee touch, more coffee."

Nancy shook her head, as if she were communing momentarily with herself. "For someone who's as tired as you look, you have boundless energies, Mr. Mobley."

Mobley grinned. "Do you know that story?"

"Come out in the kitchen with me," she said. "What story?"

"About the British soldier," Mobley said, following her. "'My compliments to the duke,' it ends. You know." Nancy giggled. Mobley put his arms around her from behind and nuzzled the back of her neck.

"Now, stop," she said. "Tell me about tonight."

"Nothing to tell," he said. "We murdered 'em. Kaufman put me so far ahead it was comical. That's all. What's this?"

"You know perfectly well what this is," she said, "and take your hand away. I'll burn myself."

"Put butter on it," Mobley said. "On what? The burn?"

"Suit yourself," Mobley said. "Every woman ought to have a fetish." He took his hand away. "Speaking of fetishes, you ought to see this kid they brought in on these murders. Alla-ga-zam, baby, he's all right. He had a woman's handkerchief in his hand when they caught him. Then they found a trunk in his dormitory room full of women's handkerchiefs and panties and every other damn thing."

Nancy straightened up. "Well, that's what Burt Kaufman was saying the other night in Camillo's."

"I know," Mobley said. "I know. But you come face to face with it, you still can't believe it."

Nancy stirred instant coffee into the two cups beside the burner on the stove. "I can believe it."

"I can't," Mobley said. "I can't believe anything. I can't believe you're going to marry me. 'What was I . . . That I should get sic exaltation, I wha deserv'd most just damnation, For broken laws...'?"

"Ah," Nancy said. "Hold your hats, boys. Three-thirty in the morning, and here comes the poet laureate of the Kyne organization."

"Here comes something else, too," Mobley said. He was walking behind her as she carried the coffee into the living room.

Nancy jumped slightly, steadying the cups of coffee in her hand with a rare display of balancing. "Bastard," she said.

"That's what I like to hear," Mobley said. "Get tough with me. Call me names."

"I think you have a fetish or two of your own," Nancy said.

"Agreed," Mobley said. "Would you care for details?"

"No," she said. "Sit down and drink your coffee."

He took off his coat and tie and sat on the couch, and she

came and sat down beside him.

"Nance," he said, after a while, "what would you say if I quit?"

"Quit your job?"

Mobley nodded. "Have you got a razor? I need a shave."

"Well, you don't need one now," she said. "Why do you want to quit?"

"Because I'm fed up," Mobley said. "I want peace and regular hours and no hundred and twelve dirty bastards running around cutting one another's throats."

"It didn't involve you," she said.

"The hell it didn't." He set his cup of coffee down in the saucer. "The hell it didn't."

"Well, it's over now," she said. "Why don't we talk about that in the morning?"

"I don't know," he said.

"If you want to quit, quit," Nancy said.

"The trouble with it is," Mobley said, "it's not all over now. Tomorrow there'll be something else. Something different. Every minute in that joint is a crisis."

A lock of hair had fallen upon his forehead. To Nancy, as she watched him, he looked at once both old and very young.

"You must be tired," she said.

"I'm not tired. I'm tired tired but not sleepy tired, but I'm the kind of tired tired where I might be sleepy tired any minute." The thought of it made Mobley yawn. "And sleep," he added, "for a week."

"Then when are you going to marry me?"

Mobley yawned again. "We'll get married in bed. I always wondered why they never did that. The reverend comes with the book, they play here comes the bride, your father gives you away, some son of a bitch throws minute rice, and then instead of us going away, they go away."

"I think it would be uncomfortable," Nancy said.

"Lots of things in life are uncomfortable," Edward Mobley said. "Did you ever stop to think of the poor bastard who sits in the middle between the two big guys up front in a moving van?" He waved his hand. "It's part of the rigid art form. They never change places. Then when they start moving the furniture, the little guy always carries the piano and the refrigerator and the two big guys carry the lamps and pillows."

Nancy smiled and put her hand to his cheek. "What has that got to do with anything?"

"Nothing," he said. "You're beautiful."

"No poetry?"

"No poetry."

"I like it just as well without it," she said.

"Well," Mobley said, "I have nothing against poets generally. It's just that it's difficult at four o'clock in the morning."

Nancy's fingers were soft upon his face and the outline of his jaw. "What's difficult?"

"Let me drink my coffee," Mobley said.

"Well," she said, "look at the reluctant dragon."

Mobley leaned forward and placed his cup and saucer on the little table in front of the couch. "I guess," he said, "it would ruin me."

Her hand went back to his face. "I wouldn't want to ruin you."

He shook his head. "No. Not what I'm talking about. I mean the other night with Mildred and now tonight." He gave vent to a pale smile. "I shall acquire a reputation. False-alarm Mobley."

"It was different then," she said.

"It sure was," Mobley said. "A curative evening, if I may say so. Sweet, I love but you."

"That's nice," Nancy said, and she twisted her body so that she was in his arms and her mouth was against his.

At length, he drew his head back. "Maybe," he said wearily, "I'm not so tired as I think."

"You sound tired."

"Yeah?"

The buttons on her robe were big and velvety as he undid them.

"I was reading a book," she said. Her eyes lovingly followed his hands. "It said it isn't good for you to fall asleep directly afterwards."

"I," Mobley said, "have all I can do to keep from falling asleep beforehand. Look at that beautiful white nightgown."

"I'm glad you like it."

"And it's a shorty. Half-length. My."

"Mmm-hmm," she said.

"And you can see through it."

Nancy looked down. "Well," she said, "damned if you can't."

"One would almost say," Mobley said, "that you were expecting me."

"Or someone else."

"Yeah?" His hand moved up her leg. "Who?"

"Oh, I don't know," Nancy said. His touch caused her suddenly to shiver. "Maybe Gerald Meedy." She reached a groping hand to her right and snapped off the light. "He took me to lunch today."

"And?"

"And told me about you and Mildred."

"Ah," Mobley said.

"He said Mildred told him you slept with her."

"How did she come to tell him that?"

"He said he slept with her himself. Last night."

"That," Mobley said, "I believe … Do you like that?"

"Yes," she said, and then she brought her own hands upon his waist. "Now you."

Chapter Forty-Nine

Through the night the teletypes chattered and the big presses downstairs in the O.K. building gunned out an inferno of sound. The counting machine on each press ran to 700,000 and stopped. Drivers backed their circulation trucks expertly, swiftly, into the waiting stalls just off the street and carted 2,100,000 copies of the New York *Sentinel* to newsstands and airports and railroad stations and hotels. Late suburban trains hauled an extra load of *Sentinel*s in their baggage cars. Now, at three-thirty in the morning, the final morning edition, the three star, was on its way.

EXCLUSIVE!
Confession Text page 2
"I KILLED THEM"
YOUTH CONFESSES
New York Sentinel
NABBED AFTER ATTACK

There had been a strange, not unfunny moment, in the city room, almost on the dot of midnight, when Walter Kyne came in and walked over to Jon Day Griffith. Kyne had been drinking, yet it did not tell upon his impeccable dress, nor on his erect, classic Roman carriage; only, Griffith noticed, in his blue eyes.

"Jon," Kyne said, "I've got a special headline for you." He set down a piece of Kyne stationery, upon which he had written, in bold, blue penstrokes:

"See?" Kyne said. "Stick that on top of everything." Griffith looked up wearily. "No."

"Why not?"

"Because it's a defensive line. We don't have to proclaim a thing. It's all over page one as it is. What do you think that word 'exclusive' means?"

Kyne looked hurt. "I worked for an hour on this."

Griffith scanned it. A trace of a smile found the corners of his mouth. "It counts," he said. "Within half a unit."

"Well?" Walter Kyne said.

"No," Griffith said. It seemed to him that the publisher's shoulders sagged. The editor of the *Sentinel* was moved to pity. "I'm sorry," he said. "I didn't know you were working on this."

"I had to do something."

Now Griffith, sitting at his desk, looking up at the publisher and listening to him, knew that Kyne was drunk.

"I had to do something," Walter Kyne repeated, almost plaintively. "Do you know why?"

"No," Griffith said. "Why?"

Kyne studied him. "Because," he said at last, "because I made up my mind."

Griffith picked up a rumpled pack of cigarettes from his desk and sent a bony index finger fishing within.

"I decided," Walter Kyne said, "to give you and Ed Mobley a bonus. Fifteen hundred dollars each."

Griffith found the cigarette. His hand was warm and wet.

"Well?" Kyne said challengingly. "Is it fair?"

Jon Day Griffith felt a weight of hopelessness upon him. "It's fair," he said. "And I've still got work, Walter."

"Okay," Walter Kyne said. He turned away; then he looked back again. "Sometimes a man can't help things, Jon. He goes the way he's gaited. He protects what he thinks he should protect, and the hell with it. I wish to Christ I was happy tonight."

"You damn well ought to be."

"I know it," Kyne said.

Jon Day Griffith found himself remembering what Cyrus McCrady once had said about Walter Kyne. "All I know," McCrady had said, "is that his father was a great publisher. Something of the old man should have simmered down to Walter, but I'm damned if I can spot it."

If McCrady were alive tonight, Griffith could have told him

what it was. It was this: that even now, with Walter Kyne standing there, drunk and defensive, even now Jon Day Griffith could not bring himself to ask him the one simple question that would let him sleep tonight.

Who won, Walter?

Chapter Fifty

To the old but obviously expensive brownstone house, the house he owned just off Fifth Avenue on East Eighty-Fourth Street, Mark Loving came home, shortly before midnight. He let himself in the front door, walked up the wide night of stairs to the second floor, where the kitchen and dining-room and living room were. There, momentarily, he paused; then he walked another flight of stairs to the third floor, where the two giant bedrooms were: one for himself, one for his wife.

Again, at the third-floor landing he paused. He took off his overcoat, folded it over the railing along the stairwell. Then he walked glidingly toward his wife's bedroom, opened the door, snapped on the ceiling light, so that she came awake, lying in bed and blinking up at the light.

Mark Loving did not like his wife's looks. Anne Loving was tall—almost as tall as he—and big-boned, with a face whose features, in themselves neat and cute, as in the button nose and the rosebud mouth, were too small for the rest of her. She worried a good deal about her figure and her diet, but the worry was carried out on a basis of general principle rather than in specific hope of kindling her husband's interest anew. He had done with her long ago, and it was nothing but deep-seated weakness on her part which would not let her admit it.

"Baby," Loving said from the doorway now, "I'm in."

She blinked again and came more awake, sitting up in bed so that a shoulder strap on her nightgown fell down along her arm, exposing skin that was pale and fleshy.

"Did you hear me?" Mark Loving said. "I said I've got it. I am the new executive director for the Kyne publishing empire."

Anne Loving said, "I didn't expect you, Mark. What time is it?"

"The hell with what time it is." He walked over and stood by her bed, looking down at her. "You look like something the cat forgot to drag in."

"Don't talk that way," she said. She was awake now. "You always talk cruelly to me. Do you really have the job?"

"Isn't that what I said?"

"How do you know? Did Kyne tell you?"

"Not exactly."

"Then how do you know? How can you be sure?"

"I'm sure," Loving said. "So sure, I have a little change in our arrangement, all blocked out in my mind. Do you want to hear about it?"

"Sit down," she said.

Loving sat down on the edge of the bed and took her, hand in his. It was a docile, unprotesting hand. It offered no action, no mystery, no opposition, no battle.

"Sweetheart," Mark Loving said—he was choosing his words with care—"I can not say that I feel for you any longer as I once might have felt. Do you understand that?"

She blinked her eyes. "Is that a roundabout way of saying something?"

"What do you mean, roundabout?"

"Do you want to sleep in here tonight, with me? I know it's been a long while."

As always, the unexpected reaction was the one that irritated Mark Loving the most. "Darling," he said, "you don't seem to understand. I'm in a new position now. A position where I can go away from you. Do you understand that?"

She smiled bravely at him. "You always talk that way. You taunt me all the time."

Loving looked at her. Then, abruptly, he reached for the telephone on her bedtable. "See if this sounds like somebody taunting somebody," he said, and he dialed Mildred Donner's number.

He was surprised over the speed with which she answered.

"Baby," he said into the telephone—he watched his wife as he spoke—"I'm coming down there tonight. It may be for good, too. What do you think of that?" He paused, and his brows contracted, as if in heavy concentration. "Meedy? There? Now? All right, look, that was great last night. I know you were upset about the weekend. But let me tell you something, this is the ball game. I've got this, do you see, I've got the job. It's going to be the way we always said. I don't care about—what?" He licked his lips. "Oh. So he told you, too. No." He paused again, and his eyes left his wife, concentrated now upon the conversation at hand. "No, on the contrary, Mildred. I can't say I understand what you see in him ... Of *course* I see what he sees in you, damn it... Okay, so I'm glad you feel that way about him. I'm glad he's happy with you. Yes. I want him to be happy. It's important that he keep his m— that he's happy. And I want you to be happy, too. I'm glad for both of you."

He hung up the phone, and for a while he stared at the flower-patterned wallpaper in his wife's bedroom. At length, and with effort, he looked back at his wife.

"Well?" she said.

"Well," Mark Loving said, "you were right, sweetheart. I'm nasty too much of the time, and I go around saying things I don't mean at all."

Anne Loving felt a surge of excitement. She stretched her arms up to receive him.

"Now, wait a minute," Loving said. "Don't rush things. First I'm going to get a drink, then I'm going to get into my pajamas, and then I'll be in to see you."

"All right, lover," she said. "I love you."

Loving nodded absently. He was still thinking of Meedy and Mildred, and now Mildred had become more attractive to him than ever before. He never should have put her up to that business with Mobley. "I love you too," he said, and stood up and walked out of the room without looking back at her.

Chapter Fifty-One

At ten minutes of one in the morning, Walter Kyne came home. His wife was in the drawing room waiting for him, still fully dressed, wearing the low-cut black dress she knew he liked.

He walked in and looked at her. Then he took off his coat and scarf and threw them on the couch. He took off his suit coat and tie and threw them on top of the other clothing. He went to the side-table and began to mix himself a drink.

"Whore," he said.

"Now, Walter," she said, "you're drunk."

"And due to get drunker," he said. "Do you know what we're going to do tonight, my pet? Have you any idea?"

"Walter," Dorothy Kyne said. She was sitting on the couch, sitting erect and beautiful. "What did Meedy tell you?"

"Nothing," Walter Kyne said. "Not a thing."

"Meedy's a liar," Dorothy said.

"Knock it off," the publisher said. "It wasn't Meedy." He brought his drink to his lips and then took it down again, planting himself in front of her and regarding her almost buoyantly, she thought, with his head cocked to one side. "It was somebody besides Meedy. Meedy told this somebody. This somebody sat in my office and said, 'I know something about your wife,' and I said, 'I know it too. Harry Kritzer.'"

"But you didn't know."

"No," Kyne said. "I didn't."

"The somebody could have been bluffing."

Walter Kyne nodded. "He could have. But it wasn't worth the chance I had to take."

"What chance?"

"The chance that maybe he was right. Because the least thing I can do, my love, is save face. The least thing I can do is act like I knew it all along. It isn't even self-respect. It's just being able to come up with an answer so you don't sit there like a fish with its mouth open." Kyne gestured with his glass, almost in salute. "So I came up with an answer. I came up with the right answer."

"Maybe," Dorothy said—she said it without visible hope—"it isn't true."

Come on," Walter Kyne said. "I told you knock it off. Anyway—as I said—do you know what we're going to do tonight?"

His wife put her face in her hands. "It isn't," she said brokenly, "that I don't love you."

"That's perfectly all right," Kyne said. "Will you please let me tell you what's going to happen tonight?"

His wife began to cry. "It's long," she said, "and it's complicated."

"Listen to me!" Walter Kyne made it a drunken command, and at the sound of it she looked up at him. "Here is what we're going to do. We are going upstairs to bed, you and I, and we are going to pretend that I am Harry Kritzer." He was watching her as he talked.

"Don't," Dorothy said. "I came home to you. I'm here."

"I know it. You couldn't think of anything else."

"It wasn't that."

"You understand," Kyne said unsteadily, "I began to suspect some time ago. And then the other night, when you gave me this routine about how Harry ought to get the job. All right. That's what drove me to go to ..." He stopped.

"Finish it," she said.

"No," he said. "No. Put it this way. You've come home to me. And I've come home to you."

He snapped off the light. "For," he added, "the time being, anyway."

"Walter," she said.

"I've got to take it out on somebody," he said. "Come on upstairs."

Chapter Fifty-Two

Arnold Lamin came to work at eleven o'clock in the morning the next day—Wednesday. He nodded smilingly at Nancy, who looked, it seemed to him, a little tired. He hung his coat on the rack at the rear of his office, and when he stepped to his desk Nancy got up and came over and said, "This is from Mr. Kyne. He wanted you to get it personally." She handed him a house-mail envelope. It was sealed.

A thrill, in combination hope and uncertainty, ran down Lamin's back, and he tore off a generous corner of scratch paper and stuffed it in his mouth.

Aloud, he said, "When did this come in?"

"Just a few minutes ago."

"All right," he said, and opened the envelope.

He took out and unfolded what seemed to be a story that covered several pages of typewriter paper. On top, clipped to the other pages, was an interoffice memo:

To: Arnold Lamin
From: Walter Kyne
Copies To: Griffith, Loving, Kritzer
AL:
I have had the secretary do the attached in story form for the wire. Please move it out today, as noted, for advance release in newspapers of next Sunday. FYI, the same story is being sent to **Editor-and-Publisher** *for inclusion in their issue of next week. WK.*

Lamin sat carefully back in his chair. Then he flipped the memo back, abruptly, and began to read the story. He read it from beginning to end.

NewYork—(KPS)—Marcus F. Loving was named today to succeed the late Cyrus McCrady as executive director of the Kyne Newspapers and allied organizations.

The appointment, announced today by Walter Kyne, publisher, carries with it supervision of Kyne Press Service, Kynpix, and Kyne World Features both domestically and abroad.

Mr. Loving, a veteran of eleven years in the Kyne organization, has been director of Kyne World Features for the past six years. The latter post, Mr. Kyne announced, will now be filled by Edward Bambler, who up to now has been midwestern manager of KWF.

Mr. Bambler, upon accepting the KWF post, announced the appointment today of Gerald Meedy, longtime news and feature writer in the New York headquarters of the Kyne organization, as his special assistant.

Mr. Loving declared he accepted the post of executive director "in a spirit of humility and hope."

He said:

"The horizons of the publishing world are ever-broadening ones, and we here at Kyne are conscious of the daily increasing responsibilities we bear in these troubled times. With this in mind, I have, at Mr. Kyne's suggestion, issued, as my initial action in my new position, two directives. "They are:

"1. Formal citations to Edward Mobley, reporter for the New York Sentinel and Kyne Press Service; Arnold Lamin, director of Kyne Press Service; and J. D. Griffith, managing director of the New York Sentinel for their enterprise in producing a world-wide beat for Kyne on New York's triple slayer, who was captured last Tuesday.

"2. The establishment of a new consolidation in Kyne outposts throughout the world by means of a special ambassador who will leave immediately upon a two-year tour of friendly nations all over the globe."

The man selected to make this tour, whose purpose it will be not only to knit further together the far-flung Kyne organization but also to bring the gospel of a free press to peoples of all nationalities, is, Mr. Loving added, unusually qualified for such an assignment.

"Our ambassador," Mr. Loving said, "will be Harry J. Kritzer, veteran chief of Kynpix, whose extended absence will, we feel, be balanced only by the important good we are certain he will accomplish while abroad. Mr. Kritzer's itinerary will include every continent on the face of the earth, beginning with Africa."

Mr. Kyne and Mr. Loving chose today's auspicious occasion to review jointly the unprecedented series of firsts and exclusives recorded by the organization on the "triple-slayer" story which gripped not only New York but the entire world. Listed were the following:

First to link the murders of Lena Tally and Judith Felton to the same killer.

First to link the murder-dismemberment of eight-year-old Laura Grabowski to the other two slayings.

First with the news of the Killer's arrest and confession.

First with the full text of the killer's confession.

"There was not much else we could be ahead on," Mr. Kyne said, "but nonetheless we also scored beats on a number of other developments indigenous to the main story."

An important part of the Kyne coverage of the triple murders was the work of Kynpix, which supplied consistently superior pictorial coverage not only for newspapers but, in collaboration, for television. Equally forceful, publisher Kyne pointed out, was the outstanding job of feature coverage turned in by Kyne World Features under Mr. Loving's direction.

Mr. Loving's experience, leading up to his selection as successor to the late Mr. McCrady, has been wide and varied, touching on every facet of the publishing industry.

A native of Bethlehem, Pa., he started his newspaper career as a copy boy, and at the age of twenty-four was managing editor of a small Pennsylvania daily. A restless spirit took him into the fields of radio, advertising, and sales merchandising, from which field he came to the Kyne family, joining the sales staff of KWF. Further advancement was rapid, culminating today in his appointment to one of the most important positions in the entire publishing field.

Mr. Kyne announced that a special banquet honoring Mr. Loving will be held next week during the Publisher? Convention in New York. Another banquet the same week will honor KPS chief Lamin, who last Tuesday was named winner of the coveted Louisville News news-management award.

Arnold Lamin placed another piece of paper in his mouth without bothering to remove the first. He was surprised to note that the thing that struck him the most was the appointment of Ed Bambler in Chicago as successor to Loving in the KWF job. Having seen that it was Loving who got McCrady's job, and that Kritzer was going to Africa, Lamin—by now an expert at reading between lines—could not bring himself to be amazed at Gerald Meedy's appointment, even though he knew none of the details. Possibly Loving deserved his new position, and possibly Kritzer deserved to go to Africa, but Meedy did not deserve to be special assistant even to the Staten Island dogcatcher. Meedy was getting this as a reward. What for?

Was Meedy working for Loving all along? Lamin considered the possibility; then he dropped it. Meedy was in disfavor with Kyne. What good could he do Loving?

There were only two other possibilities. One was that Bambler, the new successor to Loving, had insisted on having Meedy as his assistant. This was ridiculous enough to bring the suggestion of a smile to Lamin's embittered mouth.

The other possibility was that Meedy opened a door someplace and saw the skeleton jumping on the inside. In due time, Lamin would learn the details—possibly from Loving himself—but meanwhile the picture he got, for a man who knew nothing of the story going in, was remarkably accurate. It even embraced that African traveler, Harry Kritzer.

The only thing that did not fit was Bambler. It was a slick thing—as slick, Lamin reflected, as the way Walter Kyne had addressed the interoffice memo that accompanied this story to him, Arnold Lamin, with carbon copies to "Griffith, Loving, Kritzer"—in that nonchalant order.

He blamed himself, in a way, did Arnold Lamin. He had been defeated by the unforeseen, just as the unforeseen, in the form of the Louisville award, had nearly elected him. Thus it had canceled out, leaving him still, in his own mind and the minds of many others, the best-qualified candidate for the job. If he had only foreseen. . . .

And that, he realized, was what made the Bambler appointment strike him as forcefully as it did. Bambler, whom Lamin knew fairly well, now seemed to symbolize the unforeseen.

But Lamin had to know. He picked up his telephone and said, "Get me Ed Bambler in Chicago," and waited. In two minutes or so, Bambler came on and Lamin said, "Congratulations, Ed. I suppose you heard."

"Hello, Arn," Bambler said. "Loving called me half an hour ago. It beats me."

"Well, it shouldn't," Lamin said. "You were the logical second in command to Mark in KWF."

"Yeah," Bambler said, "but who had any idea Mark was going to get the McCrady job?"

"Well," Lamin said, "it's a good thing for you anyway. I see you've already made your first appointment."

"Yeah?" Bambler said. "Who?"

"Gerald Meedy," Lamin said. "According to the story we're putting out, you announced he was going to be your special assistant."

"I did?" Bambler fell silent for a moment. Then he said, "Let me ask you something."

"Ask away."

"Who's Meedy?"

Lamin began to laugh.

"What," Bambler said at the other end of the conversation, "is so funny?"

Lamin shook his head, still laughing. "I can't tell you, Ed. It's only funny here."

Chapter Fifty-Three

No one was in the dell at that time of early Wednesday afternoon—no one except Carlo, the bartender, and two customers, who were Harry Kritzer and Jon Day Griffith.

"We shall drink," Griffith was saying. "We shall drink to Harry Kritzer, visitor to deepest Africa."

Kritzer nodded and picking up his glass. "King of the apes," he said. "Skoal."

"Save me a porthole on that tung-oil freighter you're going on," Griffith said. "I might go with you."

"Nobody's going with me," Kritzer said. "I loved her, Jon. That's the fact of it. I loved her. I would have blackmailed him myself if I hadn't." He smiled wryly. "After all, I knew it ahead of almost anybody. But no. I loved her."

"You're using the past tense," Griffith said.

Kritzer nodded again. "You're right. I felt sure she was going to leave him last night, when it came out. No, she didn't leave him. She went crawling back to the blue-eyed son of a bitch the minute they blew the whistle."

"It was part of the swindle," Griffith said.

"Maybe you can understand, then," Harry Kritzer said, "why I'm not sore. About your sending Meedy out to my place."

"I'm not going to apologize for that," Griffith said. "If it had worked, I wouldn't have had the right to apologize."

Harry Kritzer said softly, "It worked."

Griffith gestured with his hand. "But not for me. So I still don't have the right to apologize. No apology will turn a slimy bastard like me into something else. I just want you to know you're one hell of a man. I've thought that before, but never more so than now."

Kritzer smiled tightly. "My motives were dishonest, and they still are. I tried to work on him through her. Now the only reason I'm not sore about yesterday is because of the way she acted afterwards. To coin a phrase, it opened my eyes. You might even say I was grateful to you."

"Before you get grateful, let's change the subject." Griffith signaled the bartender for a refill. "I'd like to see Lamin along about now."

"Arn's all right," Kritzer said. "He's a good newspaperman."

"We're all good newspapermen," Griffith said. "Even Loving."

Harry Kritzer laughed shortly. "That's what Kyne's butler told me one night, right after McCrady died. He said he was very happy for Mr. Kyne . . ." Kritzer's voice mimicked that of Steven, the butler . . . "that there were so many capable gentlemen to choose from."

"This capable gentleman," Griffith said, "is of a mind to get stinking drunk."

"Likewise this capable gentleman," the photo chief said. "As a prelude to safari."

"Did you beef when you found out about it? The Africa routine?"

"I laughed," Harry Kritzer said. "You want to know the truth, I laughed. I thought about the old story of the sultan and the rare fruit. You remember that one?"

Griffith shook his head. "So?"

"So I thought of you and Lamin and the way you knocked each other's brains out around the clock, and now Loving gets it, and there was this story of the sultan who sent two couriers out to bring him a rare new kind of fruit, and they come back and the first guy has the biggest grape in history. But the sultan doesn't like grapes, so he tells the guards seize this guy and shove it, see? And the guy starts laughing like hell, so the sultan says what are you laughing at, and the guy points to the other courier and he says, 'He's got a pineapple.'"

Griffith smiled. "So you're going to Africa and I've got a pineapple."

"To tell you the truth," Kritzer said, "I don't mind going away. It'll be good for me. There's nothing to tie me down here. I'm straightened out about Dorothy. I'm in good shape physically. What the hell have I got to complain about?"

The editor of the *Sentinel* thought for a moment. "I guess not much," he said at last. "Tell you the truth, I feel sorriest for my wife, and for Betty Lamin. They both had their hearts set on things."

"Listen," the photo man said, "you go home and tell your wife she's lucky you went as well as you did on the murder story. If you hadn't scored the way you did, and Loving got the job, he would have fired you tomorrow. He loves nobody, that boy."

"Including you," Griffith said.

"Including me," Kritzer nodded. "But I'm safe. I'm safe for the same reason that Gerald Meedy is assistant to the new director of Kyne World Features."

"Good old Gerald," Griffith said, and raised his glass on high. "A toast to Gerald!"

"A toast to Gerald!" Kritzer agreed. "He can not keep his mouth shut. To Gerald."

Griffith set down his glass. "Come to think of it, he kept his mouth shut with me. He didn't tell me a thing."

The shorter man said, "I wouldn't be surprised but what he didn't tell Loving either."

"But Loving knew he knew."

"Yeah, but I'll bet he wormed it out of him."

"Why don't you ask Gerald?"

Harry Kritzer said something about Gerald that made Carlo straighten up behind the bar. Jon Day Griffith said, "You offended Carlo."

"I'm sorry, Carlo," Kritzer said.

"Don't mention it twice," Carlo said. "Will you gentlemen have one with me?"

"No," Harry Kritzer said. "You have one with us."

"Well," Carlo said, "in that case I'll buy the next one."

"If that ain't fair and square," Kritzer said, "I'll..." He looked toward the far end of the dimly-lit room, where the telephone in the booth had started ringing.

Carlo went to answer it. He came back out of the booth and said, "Mr. Griffith, sir, it's for you. The office."

"Ah, Jesus," Griffith said.

"My desk doesn't know I'm here," Kritzer said. "How come you told yours?"

"I only told Healey. He'd only call me if it was important." Griffith went back to the phone booth.

The conversation lasted only a brief time. Then Griffith emerged from the booth and came back and sat down. He drank from the fresh glass that Carlo set before him.

"What's the matter?" Kritzer asked. "Emergency?"

Griffin nodded in mid-swallow and continued to drink.

"What are you going to do?"

The *Sentinel* chief set his glass down on the bar. "There's nothing I can do."

"Why? What happened?"

"This just isn't my day," Jon Day Griffith said. "That was Healey on the phone. Ed Mobley just quit."

Chapter Fifty-Four

A venerable Justice of the Peace in Asheville, North Carolina, droned the words that made Edward Mobley and Nancy Liggett man and wife. They checked into a hotel at three o'clock of Thursday morning. At eleven o'clock Thursday morning they boarded a Piedmont Air Lines plane for Louisville. At Louisville they changed to an Eastern Air Lines plane for Chicago. At Chicago they checked into the Palmer House, and Nancy phoned her family in Rock Island, Illinois.

"Darling," she said, setting down the telephone at last. "They're surprised."

"Why?"

"They don't know why we had to get married in North Carolina."

"Because they do it fast there."

"But they said there's no wait in Illinois either."

"Yes," Mobley said, "but I don't know a man in Illinois who can give me a blood test as fast as Dr. Kenney."

"I never knew you knew anybody in Asheville," Nancy said, "let alone your Dr. Kenney."

"I know a lot of people," Mobley said.

"A lot of strange people," she said.

"I'm in practice," he said. "When do we meet your family?"

"That wasn't nice," Nancy said. "You'd better be polite to my father. He can give you a job."

"Yes," Mobley said. "I understand he operates a male whorehouse downriver."

"Do they have those things?"

"What?"

"I don't want to say it," Nancy said. "It's still daylight."

Edward Mobley told himself he loved her for saying that. Aloud, he said, "Male whorehouses? Hell, yes. I used to know a ballplayer who worked in one."

"That's terrible."

"He only did it in the off season," Mobley said. "And never mind about my getting a job. I can walk into any newspaper office in the United States and get a job.”

“But it wouldn't be any different,” she said. “You might as well have kept on working where you were.”

“I know it,” he said.

“You can go to that college that wanted you to teach English,” Nancy said. He nodded.

“I've been drinking of that.”

“You'll never make any money.”

“I might write a book,” Mobley said. “There are all kinds of honest work to be had. I'm not worried.”

“Anyway,” she said, “I can get a job.”

“You stay home and have babies,” he directed. “I have our future all mapped out.”

“I can see our children,” Nancy said. “They'll be quoting Chaucer before they get teeth.”

“They could quote worse,” Mobley said. “And their father will be an honest man. I feel so damn pure I could sing.”

Nancy went over to him. He was standing, looking out of the window, still wearing the trousers of his chocolate-brown traveling suit but bare from the waist up.

“He-man,” she said, and placed his arms about her. “Worried about going straight.”

“It's one of the best things you can worry about.”

“Weren't there any honest men working for Kyne?”

“Damn few,” Mobley said. “Certainly nobody that mattered.”

“Were you one of them?”

“Maybe in a way.” He kissed her hair. “But I was getting polluted.”

“Jobs are all the same,” she said.

“You know a hell of a lot all of a sudden,” he said.

“I knew enough to marry you.”

“I'll ring for the bellhop,” Mobley said; “He can wrap some toilet paper around a comb and play 'Hearts and Flowers'.”

“You think about it,” Nancy said. “You must have broken Jon's heart, quitting like that.”

“You told me to quit.”

“I said do it if you wanted to.”

“I didn't want to?”

“I don't know,” she said. Her fingers touched the whorls of dark hair upon his chest. “I just want you to be happy, and you have to be sure."

"You married me just to moralize," Mobley said darkly. "The next thing you'll be telling me is that Walter Kyne is the Apostle Paul."

"They all want you," she said. "You don't have to be dishonest."

"No," he said. "You don't have to be dishonest. Lamin figures to get the job. I'm sitting on my ass in my apartment doing nothing and the best friend I have in the world, a guy who doesn't any more care who gets the job than he cares about Kelsey, but just a guy who likes me because we grew up together and did things that were good to do at the time ..."

"Burt Kaufman?"

He nodded. "So start over. Lamin figures to get the job. Kaufman calls ace reporter Mobley with the scoop of the decade. Mobley calls Griffith. Griffith plays it extra smart and sics Meedy on Kritzer. Meedy tells Loving. Loving tells Kyne. Kyne gives the job to Loving and goes home and beats the bejesus out of his wife. Now Loving goes running to Mildred, only from what you tell me Mildred's shacked up with Meedy and Meedy doesn't have a broad of his own so he likes Mildred so Loving can't have her because if he takes her back Meedy will tell the big secret they gave him the new job to keep him from telling. Kritzer's in Africa. Some son of a bitch from this town who can probably throw a stickier knife than anybody in New York inherits Loving's job. I'm going to win the Pulitzer prize and I didn't even buy Burt Kaufman a drink.

"No," he said, and took a deep breath. "You don't have to be dishonest."

"We'll talk about it some more," she said.

"I hate everybody at Kyne."

"Think of me," she said. "I quit too."

"I was thinking of you," he said. "When do we leave for Moline?"

"Rock Island," she said.

"Well?" he said. "When?"

"Tomorrow morning."

"And what were we going to do the rest of today?"

"Sleep," Nancy said. "Remember?"

"I remember," he said. "Just let me lock the door first, so

Robert Manners doesn't show up delivering any headache pills." He walked toward the door. "You'd better take your things off. You want to look nice."

"Don't talk about Robert Manners," she said. "You give me the creeps."

"He could read to us from his Bible," Mobley said. "I hear he's memorized it."

"Is he Catholic?"

"No."

"Well, it doesn't make any difference," Nancy said. "I might like to meet somebody who can quote more than you can."

Chapter Fifty-Five

THE LAMENTATIONS OF JEREMIAH...
"How doth the city sit solitary, that was full of people! how is she become as a widow! she that was great among the nations, and princess among the provinces, how is she become tributary!"

They led the father and the mother of Robert Manners to see their son in The Tombs.

"Twenty minutes," the detective said. "And I stay here."

It was a bare room, and a side door opened and two guards came in with Robert Manners between them.

"They stay here too," the detective said.

The mother was crying. She went over and put her arms around her son, her head against his chest. He stood there stiffly, not looking at her, not holding her.

"My boy," the mother said. "My only boy."

The large man who was his father made no move to go to his son. He stood there, his hands clenching and unclenching.

"The only boy," the father said. "Him we had to adopt."

"The Lord was as an enemy . . .

"All thine enemies have opened their mouth against thee: they hiss and gnash the teeth: they say, We have swallowed her up: certainly this is the day that we looked for; we have found, we have seen it."

Robert Manners spoke. He said, "I want to go back."

"You have fifteen more minutes," the detective in the room said. "You may not see them again for a while."

"I want to go back," Robert Manners said again. "I've seen them. Now I want to go back."

Still his mother clung to him. "Robert," she wept. "My boy that I love."

Robert Manners' voice was low and completely controlled. "I don't want to be in this room any more."

His father spoke now. "Let him go. Take him back." He stared at his son. "All my life I worked, and now you and the

house is gone and the neighbors cross the street when I come
and I have to see your mother cry and all night she reads out
loud from her Bible. I say you ought to go now and we're going
to go now that's what I say."

He stepped forward and put his hands on his wife's
shoulders. She came away from her son like the skin peeling off
a bad burn. Her body shook. "God have mercy," she said. "God
have mercy."

The detective in the room said, "Okay. Here we go. Take him
back."

The guards on either side took Robert Manners by each
arm. He did not look back.

When he had gone, the mother put her hand to her face and
said, "I forgot. I didn't see him long enough, and I forgot."

"What was that?" the detective asked. "The lawyer," the
mother said. "I wanted to tell him about the lawyer."

"Ain't no lawyer going to help him," the father said. "Come
on."

"Mrs. Manners," the detective said, "his legal rights are
being protected. If you have a lawyer for him, he'll have all
privileges."

"Ain't no lawyer going to help him," the father said again.

In his cell again, Robert Manners found the Bible they had
given him at his request, and he began at Lamentations 3.

*"I am the man that hath seen affliction by the rod of his
wrath.*

*"He hath led me, and brought me into darkness, but not into
light.*

*"Surely against me is he turned; he turneth his hand against
me all the day."*

Lying there upon his cot, Robert Manners found himself
reflecting that perhaps capture had been one of his purposes,
too. It would give him, he knew, a great deal of time for thought.
It would give him no opportunity for action. And, though he
viewed his crimes neither with remorse nor underestimation, the
fact remained that always the thinking had been more enjoyable
than the doing.

It was not the way it should have been, but it was the way
it was. Perhaps his plans had never been completed
enough—perhaps the need for action (and the realization of the

need was in itself a form of thought) had always interceded too quickly.

That was the way it was, and it was too bad.

He turned back to his book.

"Thou hast covered thyself with a cloud, that our prayer should not pass through.

"All our enemies have opened their mouths against us.

"Fear and a snare is come upon us, desolation and destruction."

The door to the cell opened and a little man with glasses and a bald head came in. The guard closed the door behind him and stood outside.

"Hello, Robert," the little man said.

Robert Manners did not say anything. The little man sat on the edge of the cot and looked down at him.

"I'm Dr. Steckel, Robert. I want to talk to you. Do you want to tell me why you didn't want to see your parents?"

Robert Manners turned on his back, his hands clasped behind his head, and looked at his visitor.

"What's that book you have there?"

"Bible," Robert Manners said.

"Some special part?"

"Jeremiah."

The bald man nodded.

"You know Jeremiah?" Robert Manners asked him.

"Very well."

"Not," Manners said, "as well as my mother."

Chapter Fifty-Six

Edward Bambler, newly appointed as successor to Mark Loving as director of Kyne World Features, arrived in Grand Central Station aboard the Commodore Vanderbilt from Chicago at eight-thirty Friday morning. Bambler was a thin man in his late thirties, and his appointment had come as a genuine surprise, at least to him.

He suspected, with true instinct bred of the company he worked for, that it had come as a surprise to others, too, and it was a situation he was not fully prepared to meet. He knew, for one thing, that Edward Mobley, the finest reporter in the Kyne chain, had resigned, and without knowing the facts behind it, it occurred to him that Mobley might have quit in protest of Loving's appointment to the McCrady job. If that were true, and if Mobley had good friends in the city room, as Bambler assumed he did, then some of their anger over the situation which caused Mobley to leave might spill over and be directed at him, Bambler.

On the other hand, Edward Bambler told himself, it would not take much to represent himself as an innocent party, which, in truth, he was. Such a situation might even rebound in his favor.

He set down his bag in front of a vestibuled food counter alongside one of the station ramps and ordered coffee and a sugar doughnut. He would, he realized, be expected to change his scale of living to meet the elevation of his new position. Nor would it be wise for him to show up at the office this early in the morning.

First he would check into a hotel, and then shave and change to a clean shirt and tie, and have his shoes shined. Later in the morning—perhaps at eleven-thirty or so—he would telephone the office. Whom would he phone? The only executive he knew was Arnold Lamin. Even as Loving's midwest lieutenant with KWF, he had met the new executive director only three or four times, and then only to say hello.

Well, he would phone Lamin. It did no harm to plot these

things in advance. When you worked for Kyne, a certain amount of plotting was necessary. It was even welcome. Something connected with plotting had gone into the decision that made Mark Loving the new McCrady, the same something that had forced upon Edward Bambler a special assistant, named Gerald Meedy, whom he did not even know.

He would have to meet Meedy, too, and he would have to get someone to fill him in on the facts, so that he would not go in with his guard down.

Would he, he wondered, be expected to call Walter Kyne by his first name?

It was a dismal reflection for Edward Bambler, that he knew so few of the answers. But he was not, this morning, an unhappy person. The horizons stretched before him, gray though was the December morn, and he was not unaware that the new executive director of the Kyne publishing empire was a man whose previous post was that of chief of Kyne World Features. Now Edward Bambler was chief of Kyne World Features, and he appreciated the precedent that had been set. He drank his coffee and paid the girl behind the counter and went away without eating the sugar doughnut; at the first newsstand he came to, he bought a *Sentinel* and turned, immediately and professionally, to the comic page.

CPSIA information can be obtained
at www.ICGtesting.com
Printed in the USA
BVHW030722070422
633580BV00001B/10

9 781627 551151